THE PASSING STAR

Jean Stubbs

THE PASSING STAR

Published by Sapere Books.

20 Windermere Drive, Leeds, England, LS17 7UZ,
United Kingdom

saperebooks.com

Copyright © The Estate of Jean Stubbs, 1970
The Estate of Jean Stubbs has asserted her right to be
identified as the author of this work.
All rights reserved.

No part of this publication may be reproduced, stored in any retrieval system, or transmitted, in any form, or by any means, electronic, mechanical, photocopying, recording, or otherwise, without the prior written permission of the publishers.
This book is a work of fiction. Names, characters, businesses, organisations, places and events, other than those clearly in the public domain, are either the product of the author's imagination, or are used fictitiously.
Any resemblances to actual persons, living or dead, events or locales are purely coincidental.

ISBN: 978-1-80055-361-3

ACKNOWLEDGEMENTS

Although this book is based on fact it is not a biography. I suppose you could call it 'a documentary novel'.

The biographer, though liable to prejudice like the rest of us, offers precise information about a certain person. The novelist creates the illusion that this person is living on every page. Consequently, I have taken liberties which no biographers would permit themselves. Where contradictions existed I chose one piece of information that best suited my purpose and the book. All the extracts from Duse's letters are actual translations, most of the conversations are imagined. Two or three scenes are based on chapters from D'Annunzio's *Il Fuoco*, some are blown up from scanty reports, others faithfully digested and reproduced. Where I have been wholly truthful is in my attempt to understand and recreate Eleonora Duse through the medium of writing.

I should like to thank Molly Francis for introducing me to Eleonora Duse; Mr Gordon Richards of the Wimbledon Park Branch of Merton Library for supplying me with so many reference books for such a long time; the British Museum for further research facilities; my uncle, Rowland Darby, for 'cette rosse' and research suggestions; Wyatt Rawson for translating numerous Italian passages; and my children for sharing the house with myself and this great Italian tragedienne while I put her on to these pages. My gratitude is also due to the legion of biographers and experts, too numerous to name, whose books I have researched in order to produce this novel.

OVERTURE

What is there to say? I am a vagabond, a nomad. I was even born travelling.
Eleonora Duse

ONE

The child's sombre eyes viewed three worlds. First, the family world of the Compagnia Duse which never changed: a little group of relatives, living, travelling, eating, sleeping, quarrelling and working together. Then the outside world which altered continually as they toured Lombardy and Venetia. Thirdly, the most curious world of all, where everyone pretended to be somebody else and the other people paid to watch them.

Three worlds lay within her, too. There was Eleonora: often hungry, often cold, one hand stretched out to Papa and the other to Mamma, teased by the uncles, petted by the aunts. Then the *figlia di commediante*, the player's child who shrank to the back of each temporary school class and ran home to temporary lodgings pursued by cries of mockery and derision. Last and best was her inner world, colouring and transcending all other worlds and selves; able to torment or exalt her, and seeming more real than that which was called reality.

Small and thin and pale and plain, with her father's sad black eyes and her mother's weight of black hair, she watched and listened and speculated. She lay awake while her parents played their games of pretence on the theatre boards; trembling in the dark, since candles were an expensive luxury. And peeped fearfully above the blanket to spy demons forming in the shadows. Then, crossing herself as her mother had taught her, she scampered from the bed and snatched her coat, to take refuge on the roof.

Far above and beyond her shone the stars. And squatting above the town, queen of the chimney pots, she wondered what they were and how long they had been there. She imagined herself passing from the childish form of Nella Duse to become some exalted being who bore her name, and merging into an exalted company which carried her out of herself completely.

Starting, with a suddenness that hurt her, at the slam of a door or the voices of the company returning at last to sleep, she froze like some small animal caught in a predatory gaze, then shivered awake in a confusion of cold and ecstasy, scrambled nimbly through the window and crawled into bed. She crouched, bereft, knees to chin in the manner of the unborn, until her mother crept under the blanket on one side and her father on the other. And warmed by contact and security, she became simply her parents' child once again — and dreamed of polenta.

Polenta. How hungry she was, growing a little, gnawed by an appetite that never arrived at the right time. The Compagnia Duse ate their main meal in the evening, when the show was over and the takings in their pockets. But she felt hunger most in the morning, while they slept on exhausted after their evening performance. As she grew older she saved a crust of bread, a piece of fruit, a finger of cheese, under her pillow or in her pocket. And she nibbled it when she woke. Polenta. Once at Piacenza, she and Libero Pilotto stole a great bowlful from the kitchen, hid themselves and ate, giggling and afraid, scooping their fingers round the empty dish.

In the summer she trod the dusty roads behind the wagon loaded with paper scenery, sitting beside the driver and swinging her legs when she felt tired. She saw the workers in the vineyards gathering bunches of grapes and dropping them into woven baskets. One man, straightening his back, grinned at the solemn child hanging behind the troupe with a bunch of wilted flowers in her hand. She had threaded two or three blossoms in her hair, and lingered, a draggled coquette, eyeing the grapes without hope. He reached for a bunch and gave them to her, and her face was suddenly radiant. She grinned back, showing excellent white teeth, bobbed a curtsey in the dust and accepted them with a queenly gesture of thanks. He laughed with the others, shook his head, and watched her skip down the road — a bulge in either cheek.

'Did you thank the Signor?' asked Angelica, worried. 'Did you curtsey nicely?'

She nodded, tore off a miniature bunch of grapes and handed them to her mother. Angelica took them.

'Always remember to behave like a lady,' she said, popping one moist black globe into her mouth. 'They mustn't think we are nobodies.'

'I am not nobody,' said the child, and was angry.

But in the summer one could be content with bread and sunshine.

'Is our company the best in the world?'

Laughter. The question was not meant to be funny and her temper cracked into life. Mamma ran forward to restrain the flailing arms and stamping feet, 'My precious, my little Nella. We are — listen to me now, listen — we are not a rich company.'

The child knew that, and was contemptuous of the answer. She had asked whether they were the *best*, not the richest, for Angelica often said it was not what one possessed that mattered but what one *was* — so, were they the best?

A silence fell, during which she sensed old hurts and disappointments pressing upon them.

'We are not the best,' said Alessandro, at length, 'but your grandfather was Luigi Duse, the finest exponent of the *commedia dell'arte* in his day. One day, perhaps… only, with this and that and the other thing… well, one must have luck in the profession. Talent is not enough. Hard work is not enough, even. One must have a pinch of luck, just enough to rub between finger and thumb.'

Smallpox lay in wait at Chioggia, cutting their audiences, preventing them from recruiting the odd street child to stand round-eyed as Cosette while the company ranted Victor Hugo's lines at the locals.

'Well, never mind,' said Alessandro, 'our little Nella will do just as well. Better, perhaps.'

Angelica bent her head over her mending, and gave up any hope she might have nourished for the child's future.

'She is all of four years old,' said Alessandro, embarrassed and helpless. 'A bright little thing.'

Angelica inclined her head and drew the child to her to explain what must be done. Eleonora crossed from reality to fantasy in bewilderment, clinging to her aunt's hand, peering at the mass of strange faces. Fantasy in turn became fearsome reality as she found herself the focal point of some adult trouble. A slap from her aunt, to make her cry, sent her running offstage to her mother's arms; who caught and held her, whispering that she must not mind, that she was supposed to cry in order to amuse the people.

'It's all in fun, my baby,' she whispered. 'We must entertain them.'

'They laugh when I cry?' asked the child, horrified.

She refused to go back, climbing on to a trunk still sniffling and drying her eyes on her sleeve. Occasionally she whispered, between hiccups, 'They laugh when I cry.'

At Vicenza, her mother's home town, they visited friends as other people do. She could pretend then that they lived there always, that each night she lay in the same bed and each day brought the same view to the windows. She and her mother visited the photographer's studio. Angelica's hair was set in flat curls round her broad forehead and looped behind in a long chignon. She wore her best dress: a pale crinoline with slashed bodice and sleeves, and a border like bars of music without notes. Every stave was marked, top and bottom, with a smart gilt button. But whereas in Angelica's gown dark lay on light, Eleonora's dress was light on dark, in a child's version of the same design. She frowned when the photographer told her to smile. Smiles were not made to order in a difficult world, they must be won. So she looked steadily from the dais and frowned slightly. But Angelica was proud, one arm resting artistically on her daughter's shoulder, the other holding her daughter's hand.

Dolls had come and gone, but not like this one. The child paled with pleasure when it was given, but ran away without thanks because she had no words. She smoothed the waxen cheeks and hands, examined the cambric petticoats edged with lace, fingered the velvet gown and the watered silk ribbons on the bonnet. The doll smelled of camphor balls and dried violets. She rocked it to her chest and closed her eyes, and pretended that she and the doll lived for ever in a white room that never changed, in a town from which they never moved. On the morning of departure she could neither eat nor speak, keeping the doll inside her coat against the rain; but at the last moment she ran back and placed it carefully on the bed. She kissed its waxen face and stroked the coarse ringlets, settled its bonnet and dress to advantage and left it.

Why? they all asked. She did not answer, brows drawn, mouth heavy. The doll, being part of her, must have a home. One of them must have a home. As the town grew small behind them she wrapped her empty arms about her, and wept for her loss.

They had walked through the night in order to fulfil some engagement, and arrived too early to broach the inn's dubious hospitality. Angelica bent over the bowl of the fountain and washed her hands and face delicately, dabbed herself dry, and motioned Eleonora to do the same. Then she rested on the stone bench and rummaged in her bundle for bread.

The square was not entirely empty. On the opposite side another child sat alone. Their eyes met, and Eleonora detached herself from the company, seeing someone even less fortunate than herself. Side by side they sat, handfast, until the sun rose.

Her name was Déjanira, but where she came from, to whom she belonged, and where she was going, they could not find out. When they walked into the inn Déjanira followed them. For the short length of their stay she became Eleonora's shadow, sharing her food in the day and her bed at night. And as the trunks were packed, and they prepared to move on, Eleonora asked her mother if the child might stay with them. A compression of Angelica's lips, a shake of head. The refusal was no more than either of them had expected, and Déjanira stood back as they loaded the wagon.

'She was my *friend*,' said Eleonora, as they harnessed the horses, but no one heard her.

She turned her head again and again to wave, as they rumbled out of the square. On the stone bench by the fountain Déjanira sat and watched them go, hands in lap, with the hopeless fortitude of the destitute.

Houses and landscapes changed. Town followed small town. Here an obscure theatre might be empty for a week. There a fair absorbed them between sweetmeats and shies. Elsewhere they became part of a local festival. Eleonora could mouth words by heart long before she comprehended their meaning. She knew the weariness of winter streets at nightfall, and the savour of other people's good dinners. And through the daily hardship there ran the perpetual theme of unrest: pack the trunks and move on.

Yet there were moments of astonishing beauty: copper pans shining on the white walls of an inn, the living fire in the grate, the table resplendent with food and wine, the romance of trains steaming in increasing numbers across Lombardy, the smoking red flare and acrid stench of naphtha lights in a dark amphitheatre. And Alessandro, her father, wove dreams to comfort and delight her in those moments when she wrapped her arms around her body, as though to comfort it, and her shoulders shook with sobs.

'Listen to me, Nenella. You will not always be the same. When you were christened at Vigevano we placed you in a glass casket, mounted with gilt, from the property box. Then your uncles and I bore you high upon our shoulders, dressed in our best clothes. Who could have known we were strolling players — so fine, so manly, with such clothes and such bearing? Who could have guessed that the gilt was not real gold, and the casket only a stage prop?

'As we walked slowly and reverently to the church of San Ambrogio we passed a group of Austrian soldiers.' Here he paused and spat, for though Venetia was still in their hands a new Kingdom of Italy had been proclaimed at Turin, and Garibaldi's name had spread through the country with the rapidity of his ragged volunteers. Total freedom was not yet an Italian birthright, but it would be, and so he spat in contempt of the soldiers.

'Walking so proudly,' he continued, 'bearing this wonderful casket aloft, with Nenella inside, they thought we carried the relics of a saint. They saluted us! They saluted *you*, Nella. Surely, I said to your mamma at the time, this is an omen. A great omen.'

She lay against his shoulder and allowed him to dry her tears. Now and again she hiccoughed in remembrance of the slight, real or imagined, that had devastated her.

'The company was not always like this,' said Alessandro. 'Your grandfather was once the toast of Venice, the darling of Padua. For ten years they wept when he wept, and laughed when he laughed. He held them in the palm of his hand, and they made themselves small for him. Ah! He was unsurpassable, that one! But you are his granddaughter. You understand me, Nella?'

She nodded, and hiccupped.

'When you are a little taller and fatter,' said Alessandro hopefully, 'they will see that the genius of Luigi Duse has descended upon Eleonora Duse. And you will hold them in the palm of your little hand.'

His prophecy remained unfulfilled. She was not a prepossessing little girl. Her voice had a soft, shrill quality which rendered her inaudible beyond the front rows; and she mouthed her lines to the perpetual accompaniment of a hissing 'Speak up!' from the wings. A child with no childhood, she cleaned out the dressing rooms and swept the floors, remembering to the end of her days one little theatre in Albissola, where the dust lay so thick that it made her cough. She strained to pitch her voice so that all could hear. She rattled the words off glibly and emphasised them with clockwork gestures. She postured and strutted, a professional little marionette in a troupe of obscure players. Her mouth compressed in trouble, was heavy in anger. Her eyes seemed too large and anguished for such a childish face. Ill-dressed, ill-fed, trapped in a mesh of adult failure, she was plain at best and ugly at worst. She knew it, and sometimes her aunts would confirm that knowledge.

Cramped by necessity, her dream world grew richer and stranger, bearing on its wings both beauty and peril. The beauty came in flashes. Watching an aunt languish in love upon the stage she would hear the voice of love itself, then tumble back again from exaltation to shoddy substitute. Often, circumstances being her enemy, she was gripped for hours and occasionally days by an inexplicable demon of sorrow. Bread stuck in her throat, wine tasted rough and sour, the road stretched endlessly into nowhere, and she was afraid. Huddling away from all comfort, she struggled in a paralysing fog of depression. At these times even her clothes appeared to be possessed by trouble and hung wretched and shapeless on her body. Since the company had problems enough they found it easier to let her alone, but Alessandro observed her with pride and sympathy.

'Aha!' he always said. 'She has the *smara*, poor thing. She is a true Venetian.' His round face begged assent, though the child had been born, as they all knew, in Lombardy.

'What is the *smara*?' she asked, lifting her head from her arms to frown at him.

'Tell me how you feel, and I'll tell you!'

'Oh...' She pondered, rubbing her mouth to and fro on her hand, 'As though a grey mist held me in so that I could see nothing. As though everything has always been sad, and is sad now, and always will be sad. As though nothing was good, and nothing was certain. As though there were bad voices in my head, and bad things waiting for me in the dark — and nothing was of any use, any more.'

'Oh, oh, oh,' he crooned, rocking her upon his shoulder, 'that is the *smara*, my child. That is the *smara*! And here is the cure for it!'

From his buttonhole he drew a white rose, one of last night's properties, already fading. With a bow and flourish he handed it to her.

Sullenly she stared at, but would not take it.

'See,' Alessandro coaxed, holding it before her sombre gaze, 'there are now two roses — one in each eye.'

Then she accepted the flower. Her fingers stroked the petals, graceful and languid, lingering over them as though the rose were a talisman against all evil.

TWO

As Eleonora approached adolescence her mother's health deteriorated. The delicacy of constitution had become chronic invalidism, and Angelica's black hair lost its lustre, her eyes their shine. The proud carriage of her head and shoulders was ruined by bouts of coughing. No one dared name the illness since it could be neither minimised nor cured. Tacitly, she and the company accepted the fact that she could no longer be a fully working member. Her conscientious, uninspired performances became intermittent, and to justify her keep she busied herself with the costumes. And now she clung to her daughter harder, endeavouring to impart the small graces and good manners learned in that respectable Vicenzian household of her youth.

Needing her mother more as she grew older, the girl accepted that her mother was sick, but not that the sickness was mortal. They had always been quiet people, in contrast to the volubility and excitement on which the rest of the company thrived. So they sat in silence, while Eleonora learned her lines and Angelica plied her faulty needle, exchanging smiles and glances in which love mingled with concern. Alessandro endeavoured to soothe them both by suggesting that the girl might well try her hand at the part of Juliet, since the aunt whose prerogative this was had aged past conviction.

To prepare the way for this leap, which would arouse passions of theatrical size and volume, Enrico allowed Eleonora to play minor roles in some of their popular melodramas. Jealously watched by the aunts, copying what she had seen them do, she learned how to die by poison, how to stab and be stabbed. Rolled her eyes, clutched her throat, drew her lips in a snarl across her teeth, fell without making noise, writhed in a death agony.

'She has fire!' cried Alessandro, delighted. 'She is a true Venetian.'

Enrico conceded that she was no worse than the other women, and younger. But once, when a middle-aged uncle wooed her on stage, his shabby image was superimposed in her mind's eye by a lover of heartbreaking beauty, and she stretched out her arms in adoration.

'Good,' said Enrico, surprised.

A certain rough talent emerged. She was nothing to look at, a plain little scarecrow with one dress and a sulky face, but she was competent enough for the Compagnia Duse and arrogant enough in her secret self to be ambitious. Also, now and again, knowledge beyond her immediate experience took over and caught her by surprise. She did not care to mention this, because her tinder temper and gloomy silences had earned her many a slap on the arm. She did not want to be charged with lunacy as well. Only, when she had swallowed the highly coloured water that represented poison, the liquid burned her throat. She clasped her neck with terror and conviction.

'That was good,' cried Enrico. 'Next time — let it reach your stomach, too.'

His talent was sufficient to spark off her own. She begged his favours, on stage, with awkward beauty and sincerity.

'Very good!' cried Enrico. 'Try to love your uncle *all* the time!'

Their laughter tore through her, and she became wooden enough to please even the aunts for the rest of that scene.

More often, nothing happened at all and she mouthed and gestured in a void, sightless and earless. But just as there was no promotion, except by a process of age and necessity, there was no demotion either. So Eleonora annexed one small part after another, since no one else was young enough to play them, and acted well or badly without fear of losing work.

Angelica should have been in bed, but she knew her duty, and drooped heroically in the wings each night in order to see her daughter safely home. On a bench at the local inn, after the evening performance, they sat a little apart from the others, who ate and drank and joked and talked of the next town. Silent and exhausted, all dark eyes in a thin face, Eleonora saw and did not see the crockery shining in the firelight, the flames starting in the grate. Smelled and did not smell the odours of meat and wine and garlic. The crossing from reality to fantasy was growing longer and deeper, and she found the journey back more difficult.

Head bowed on arms, she pondered over the tears that had run down her face in the third act: not her tears, but the tears of the girl she played. The masks were assuming life. Her eyes widened and she shook with cold. But when food was placed before them she sickened immediately, pushing away her plate.

'You will feel better presently,' said Angelica, comprehending — as her husband did not — the emotional cost of a half-grown girl playing adult roles. 'Eat, my baby. Eat, *dolcezza*. Eat for Mamma.'

'In a little while,' the girl whispered. 'Wait a little.'

'Your papa is pleased with you,' Angelica offered, pushing the plate nearer to tempt the child. 'He says you are a true granddaughter of Luigi, Nella. Perhaps you will be a great actress some day, like Adelaide Ristori, and then how proud we shall all be.'

The plate was thrust back, with a hint of temper. Angelica removed it to a safe place, knowing that the girl was capable of hurling it to the floor if driven.

'Ristori began just as you have done,' she went on, in her soft voice that Eleonora had inherited and found such a professional drawback. 'And now look at her! Travelling all over the world, married to a real Marchese. Think of that, Nella. Fine clothes, nurses for the babies, applause from thousands, crossing the world in big ships.'

'Not in *this* company!' said Eleonora bitterly, coming to life.

Angelica lowered her eyes, but accepted the comment as she accepted all else, with understanding and humility.

'Perhaps not in this company,' she admitted, 'but there are others. And you are young.'

The girl sat up, rubbing her eyes, drinking her water.

'If I ever have money,' she said, 'I'll be warm. Clothes are very nice, but warmth is better. The cold makes me stupid,' she complained. 'I can't move, can't think, can't speak properly in the cold.'

Angelica had finished eating, and folded her hands patiently in her lap. Still the girl rubbed her eyes and drank her water. But the landlord hovered with his reckoning, and the company rose and straggled through the door into the wintry street. Alessandro whispered a few words in his wife's ear.

'Come, my love,' said Angelica, touching her daughter's shoulder, motioning towards the door.

The girl rose like a sleepwalker. Then, remembering how hunger would gnaw her in the morning when there was nothing substantial to eat, she seized a chunk of bread from the basket and left.

The morning, though chilly, was fresh. June sunlight gleamed on a field of flax and warmed the marble statues on the banks of the Brenta. Between the blue flowers, under a blue sky, she walked from one *mutilée* to another, keeping them company, offering silent sympathy, eating her piece of bread: restored. Mouse-like and observant, she stood for several minutes before one broken relic of nobility pitying the loss of marble arms. Once, Eleonora could see, they had curved upwards — *so*, with a graceful crook of the elbow — and held that basket of fruit high on the head. Now only two lovely hands clasped their burden, and between them and the shoulders lay nothing but air.

There is a poetry in poverty. She bolted the last bit of bread, arranged herself in the attitude of the fruit-bearer and supplied the missing link of arms. Tonight, she thought, when she had that long wait during Enrico's soliloquy, she could stand like the statue. After all, she was supposed to be a slave girl, and slaves carried baskets of fruit. And as no basket of fruit was available from the property box then the audience must imagine one. The audience, not yet forgiven for laughing at the tears of a four-year-old child, was still the enemy: capricious, demanding, predatory. Let the savages *imagine* a basket of fruit.

As she came offstage that night one aunt swung her round sharply.

'What the devil are you doing, gawking there with your arms over your head?' she demanded of the mutinous face. And as no answer was offered, 'They were looking at you instead of listening to Enrico. Now stop your tricks, do you hear me? Stop your nonsense!'

They could not kill her, she supposed. So as Enrico began his speech the following night, she again raised an imagined heaviness of fruit. His words receded. The faces blurred. Elated, she felt rough wickerwork against her fingers, sensed a glowing crown of oranges fresh from the trees. In her state of grace she was not quick enough to avoid a ringing slap on the cheek as she walked off, but did not deflect by one jot from her purpose. Thereafter they let her pose as she pleased, masked her when they could and at last grew tired of grumbling.

Angelica went to hospital now as soon as they arrived in any town, taking the mending with her, which she did extremely badly. The hospitals, with their load of pain and sickness and death, their callousness towards the poor and insignificant, horrified the girl. Angelica, patient and dignified, submitted to everything, and thanked them, saving her ration of soup for her daughter.

'Eat up, my baby. Eat for Mamma.'

She swallowed the cold thick soup out of love, and often brought it up afterwards in privacy.

A peasant girl was admitted with a fever, and they sheared her like a trembling sheep. Bundled her into bed, raving and weeping, holding her rough blonde crop in both rough hands. The hair lay on a table, and Eleonora put out a finger tentatively to touch the shining mass. Coming to sweep it away they found her, hands over mouth, crying pitiably that it was alive and beautiful.

'These players,' said the nurse, 'make a theatre out of nothing!'

At the lodging house the girl brushed and brushed her own black hair until the rhythmic strokes soothed her. Suppose, suppose *her* hair had been golden, and they had cut it off?

Raving and weeping, she cried aloud in the grip of her tormentors and was jolted out of hell by her father banging on the door. Their frightened eyes met in the glass, and for a few moments they stared at each other, bemused.

'What's the matter?' whispered Alessandro, afraid to hear.

She lifted one thin hand and touched the luxury of her hair.

'It's still there,' she said pitifully. 'I thought they'd cut it off!' And she began, still pitifully, to laugh.

Snub nose in air, moustache bristling, Alessandro roared with laughter. He put his hands on his hips and his belly shook. He whirled her round and round until her long hair lashed them together in shining strands. They were quiet together, loving and safe with each other, happy.

'A true Venetian!' he cried in delight. 'An incarnation of Venice itself, Nella. Ardent in flesh and spirit. Passionate, glorious, full of pain, full of joy, full of laughter. Venice, the loveliest city in the world, a marble ship sailing on the green waters of the Adriatic. I can see those red sails under an evening sky. *Al ritorno. Per te.* The dream of sailors, writing sentiments of the heart to those who await their return. Ah, one day you will hold a Venetian audience in the palm of your hand.'

She laid her face against his waistcoat, thinking.

'But I don't hold them,' she said. 'They're much too big, much too noisy. They don't listen — and sometimes they laugh in the wrong places.'

He knew the theatre, and was a fair assessor of talent, though having little himself.

'An audience can be a monster,' he admitted, 'but a monster who begs to be tamed. Once tamed, you possess it, and it possesses you. Then both of you must go on possessing each other until one of you grows tired.'

She thought of the gypsies on the road: the men beating their wives, the wives always coming back, bearing their burdens with fortitude, cooking for husbands who misused them.

'Like an unhappy marriage?' she asked.

'No, no, Nella. Like a glorious and terrible love affair. Like Beauty and the Beast.'

Seeing his daughter's face change, and being uncertain which character she was about to assume, he slapped her behind very jovially and returned her to the daily round.

THREE

On a May evening in 1873 the Compagnia Duse walked wearily through the Palio Gate of Verona. In their midst, sickened with anxiety, trudged Eleonora, the part of Juliet written out in an exercise book and clutched to her flat chest. The aunt, after scenes of hysteria and shrieks of betrayal, had relinquished the part. Threats and reproaches accompanied Enrico's choice. Eleonora, said the aunt, was sullen and unmindful of her elders. She was unpredictable, her performances uneven. She altered her lines, tried out new ideas, disconcerted those who learned their words and went through the same positions and gestures in the same way night after night after night.

'But she is young. She is the same age as Juliet,' cried Alessandro. 'She can, perhaps, be made up to look quite pretty. A little paint, a ribbon or two. A smile in the right place.'

At rehearsal Eleonora was unconvincing and her voice faded.

'She will be terrible!' the aunts warned, pleasurably.

'No, no,' said Enrico and Alessandro, soothing, doubting, hoping. 'She is holding herself in readiness, that is all.'

'Sandro,' coaxed the aunt who had played Juliet for fifteen years, though no chicken to begin with, 'this is a part which calls for passion, my dear. What passion — apart from downright bad temper — does this child possess? She is not properly developed. Look at that bosom!' Inflating her own. 'Look at that heavy mouth, that scowl! How can such a child become a palpitating, desirous, sensual woman?'

But he was obstinate, like his daughter.

Angelica refused to go into hospital at once. She said, 'Afterwards,' and Alessandro understood. Both were hoping that the child might triumph a little, since she was all they would possess of immortality.

So Eleonora, passing beneath the Palio Arch, suspended between Juliet and herself, saw the young corpse on a white bier, strewn with white roses. The vision remained tantalisingly out of reach: an image of beauty that is already doomed and does not know it. The death of youth and love caught her imagination. Through her tears the iron grating wobbled. And the voices of the company, already speculating on lodgings and supper, became one voice — that of the Nurse calling Juliet.

'What, ladybird! God forbid! Where's this girl? What, Juliet?'

Noiselessly, barely moving her lips, Eleonora repeated over and over again the opening lines, whose tone still eluded her.

'How now! Who calls?'

And then in reply, *'Madam, I am here. What is your will?'*

Her entrances, she knew and had been told, were poor and ineffectual. So should she be vivacious and playful, soft and submissive, or young and careless? Could she, should she, bear with her in that first appearance the faintest aura of coming tragedy? Or would it be more moving if she were totally unaware, totally hopeful, totally innocent? Or was there something else still, not yet grasped, not yet understood, which would open up the whole part to her?

Overcome by fatigue and responsibility she sobbed aloud. Eyes closed, head uplifted to an implacable deity, the exercise book clutched like a prayer.

'Sweet Mary, Mother of God!' cried the aunt, out of patience.

'Poor thing, poor thing,' said her father in pity. 'It is the *smara*!'

Half in sunshine, half in shadow, the old amphitheatre at Verona was a bowl of intimidating proportions, built for the exploits of gladiators rather than the première of a fourteen-year-old girl whose voice was not of the loudest. Nevertheless, the acoustics were excellent; and the monster, clad in shirt sleeves and kerchiefs, glittering with a galaxy of eyes, sat good-naturedly enough in its stone seats. Ready to applaud if it were amused, to doze off if it were not.

Shivering in her white dress, though the late afternoon was warm, Eleonora stared at the sky and willed her daily self to be lost in blue. A lark sang, and she watched its flight, becoming light of heart.

'I bade her come,' said the Nurse. *'What, lamb! What, ladybird?'*

Eleonora, holding her breath, drew out a bunch of white roses from beneath a cover.

'Where did you get those from?' hissed her aunt.

'God forbid! Where's this girl?'

'From the flower market under the Fountain of the Madonna, this morning — and you just leave me alone!' Eleonora hissed back, furious.

'What, Juliet?'

She took a deep breath and walked on, her face buried in the flowers. Their scent bemused her, giving the answer she had sought for her entrance. Lifting her head quite naturally, dreamy and obedient, she cried, 'How now? Who calls?' And turning to Lady Capulet with a pretty obeisance, said, 'Madam, I am here. What is your will?'

Her light voice carried well on the quiet air, and the monster murmured a little, pleasurably moved by the sight of such a child.

There was no need for their charity. They were there, that May afternoon in Verona, not to judge but to witness.

At Romeo's feet, trembling, she dropped a single white rose. And he, transported beyond the stage directions, picked it up and put it to his lips. Netted and entwined, he followed the progress of the flowers, as bemused as she. Petals fell upon his upturned face from the balcony. Thorns pricked his hands upon the marriage bed. The scarecrow had gone, and in its place was Juliet. Her words came from a girl in love for the first time: painfully halting, rapidly flowing, stammered, moving into lyrical cadences. The lark sang, and she looked upwards, seeing the sky illuminated like a pearl.

Between acts, the company let her be, silenced by something beyond their immediate experience.

A Veronese sunset turned the stone to flame as the children consummated their bond. And when she cried out in terror, 'It is not *day*!' the audience groaned softly.

Night came. In the silence before the final act the torches were lit, stinking of pitch. But everyone was past caring how the torches stank; they were waiting for death. Bells sounded across the city. Bats swooped and cried thinly. The first stars appeared.

Pale face, pale flowers, pale dress, gleamed on the bier. The audience let Romeo die without so much as a spatter of applause. It was her death they awaited, breath held. They rose with her from a deadly sleep, to confront chaos; were strewn with the last of the roses on the last of her love; and died with her, beautifully.

Applause whipped and whipped her. She lifted herself on one elbow, and Enrico ran forward to help her. Tears still smarting on her cheeks, she was half-carried, half-supported forward to meet her audience. Someone snatched a torch from its sconce and held it close to her face so that she could be seen. She flinched at the sparks, at the smoking flame. The pitch acted like sal volatile under her nostrils. And the company itself was shaking her hands, patting her back and head, shouting with the rest.

Bewildered, exhausted, delighted, incredulous, she stood there alone. As her father had said, the monster existed only to be tamed. It wiped its eyes, blew its many noses, clapped its multiple hands, cried, *'Brava! Brava! Brava!'* and belonged to her, as she to it, for the first time.

FOUR

'Pack the trunks!' said Enrico. 'We must move on.'

They carried the sick woman with them through the dust of summer, the rains of autumn and into an icy winter. She played in life a finer role than in art. On the stage she had been held back by a natural timidity and no particular talent; but dying in that Bologna hospital, without lines, properties or rehearsal, she acquitted herself admirably.

Eleonora heard of her mother's death at the end of Act Two. She took a long breath, drew her eyebrows up and back to prevent herself from crying, and carried on. She was almost fifteen.

But afterwards she hurried through the streets aimlessly, driven by sorrow as she had been driven by her transformation that triumphant night in Verona. Along the Strada Maggiore she ran, only this time there was no mother to hasten after her in sympathetic silence. No eventual pleading to come home, no timid questions as to where they were going, no following her through the dark alleys and over the bridges, no arriving at a black square with a church at its heart, no seizing of arms as Eleonora crushed herself against a parapet, dizzied by the cascade of stars in the river below. No one to restrain her if she cried, 'Let's throw ourselves down, Mamma! Let's throw ourselves down!'

The river invited her in vain. One part of her, a loving and beloved part, was dead; but the rest would not be killed too. The rest turned her away from the parapet and the starred black water and urged her homewards.

Life must be lived, work must be done, noses blown. She felt for a handkerchief and her fingers stumbled against Angelica's abominable mending. For in the end she was no needlewoman, though willing, and had bunched the pocket as she sewed. Then in relief the girl laid her forehead against the cold iron of a lamp post and wept for her mother.

They buried Angelica in Bologna, a pauper's funeral since funds were low, and moved on.

From the lowest of the *ingénues* Eleonora had become a leading lady, starring in such popular plays as *Celeste*, a drama of love and mystery, with her name in large letters near the top of the bill. But professionally she remained an enigma. She could never be trusted, for instance, to go through the same motions two nights running. She could be appallingly dull one night and glorious the next.

Talent in such a troupe was a matter of luck, but everyone possessed their full share of temperament. So the ladies were rightly angry when she played badly, and unreasonably jealous when she played at her best. They said, knowing perfectly well that her eight lire for eight evenings could never encompass a complete mourning outfit, that they would feel themselves monsters not to wear black in memory of their departed mothers. One aunt said she would rather sell herself on the streets than fail to pay proper respect to the dead. And another said she thought the lady had done very well in that direction already, with or without reason, though rather long in the tooth to earn much. But the girl looked inward on her loss, with only a black crepe band on her sleeve and a locket about her neck for outward show.

Then Alessandro suffered a last, belated love affair. He had lost his wife, he had ensured that his daughter could scratch a living, and he snatched his chance before old age took it away entirely. He intended, he said, to devote the rest of his life to Art. True, he was no Raphael, but he did not ask nor expect a place among the great wielders of the brush. He would simply pursue that which offered him most happiness. They could carry on very well without him, he said, and he had left them the better part of himself in his daughter. So he packed his bundle and departed on the heels of a dream.

Enrico had entered into partnership with the actor Giuseppe Lagunaz, and the Compagnia Duse-Lagunaz quarrelled and travelled and went hungry much as the Compagnia Duse had done; taking Eleonora with them.

Her performance as Juliet was repeated. The business with the roses was repeated. The monster was re-enchanted. And a critic in the *Revue de Paris* of 1874, a journal so far above Eleonora's place in life as to appear level with heaven, pronounced her to be a find.

Trovato di rosa — a find, a veritable rose find! he wrote, enraptured by the pale face brought forward in torchlight to receive homage.

Trovato di rosa.

FIVE

Without the protection of father or mother Eleonora found life in the new company insupportable. The ladies subjected her to numberless little professional humiliations, on and off stage. The men, on the whole, forgot about her once she had contributed to the performance. She did not possess the experience, the patience or the strategy necessary to combat her tormentors, but fought back openly and fiercely. Her insistence on playing a part according to her own conception of its requirements was set down as wilful arrogance. Reserved and proud, she seemed sly and awkward. Her demoniacal temper, goaded into life, dubbed her a troublemaker and a malcontent. Beset, she looked about her for other work, and on the strength of her long record in the profession, and the cutting from the *Revue de Paris*, signed up with the Benincasa Company.

'*Trovato di rosa?*' said Luigi Pezzana, taking in the excellent carriage, the cheap clothes, the magnificent hair extinguished by a rusty black hat. 'Well, we shall see, we shall see. Smile for me, will you? You're too sorry-looking by half! Who are you sorry for, eh? Yourself? The world?'

He found her a disappointment. Clad in a velveteen dress, so streaked and glossy with age that the other *ingénues* christened it the 'the snail trail', she entered another obstacle race. Her starved face and fanatical eyes, her heavy mouth and air of sadness affected the carefree and disturbed the careworn. Penniless and friendless, without influence, she showed an arrogance above her station. Luigi, hot-tempered and flint-tongued, screamed at her obstinate re-rendering of roles long since stamped into one spiritless mould.

'You!' he shouted during rehearsal. 'You there — with the voice of a cicada — how often do I have to tell you to speak up?'

He smiled round the company, who smiled and snickered with him. He spread out his hands in mock commiseration.

'Why must you act at all?' he asked. 'Why not sell flowers, or yourself?'

'Well — flowers, perhaps!' said one actor, raising a laugh on his own.

Her lips compressed and the light went from her eyes.

'Don't you know?' shouted Luigi. 'Has nobody told you yet, that the theatre isn't bread for *your* mouth?'

But Giacinta Pezzana, upon whose ample shoulders the glory of the company lay like a shawl, was generous.

'Leave her alone,' said Giacinta. 'Now and again she does something in quite a new way — her own way. She will be somebody.'

But he could not restrain his anger, nor his contempt for her ridiculous airs and notions. Forced to hear him out, she nevertheless pursued her own course — then dodged him, sullen and obstinate, as he raged forward after a performance. She struggled through one little company after another, burning her fingers, stubbing her toes, causing them almost as much trouble as she caused herself. And persisted, because in Verona she had assumed the living mask, and glimpsed through *farde* and costume a living art. Now and again, as Giacinta had said, she startled them, but not so frequently that they could bear with her at any price.

Enrico Belli-Blanes, with his shock of greying hair *en brosse* and the head of a young Roman emperor, washed his handsome hands of her. Francesco Ciotti of the rakishly tilted hat and cold eyes gave her up in his turn. Adolfo Drage managed to net Giacinta Pezzana, and on Giacinta's personal recommendation, engaged Eleonora as his second leading lady. His black moustache waved splendidly. His mind was as strong as his features, and as set. He, too, believed in the grand tradition of rolling eyes, of storming and melodramatic gesture and pose. He was also something of a dandy, and he liked his own way, all the time.

'Give the girl a chance,' Giacinta coaxed. 'I know her well, I am a friend of hers. She works with me on stage. A pathetic little thing. She needs only kindness and understanding — a new dress or two — regular meals.'

She appealed to his vanity, which was considerable.

'The other *capo-comicos* didn't know how to handle her!' said Giacinta, and narrowed her handsome eyes under the fetching fringe, and squared her marvellous shoulders.

With misgivings — since Eleonora was nothing to look at, sulky at worst and melancholy at best — he gave her a chance. The rehearsals fell very flat.

'Signorina Duse,' said Drage patiently, since Giacinta was shaking her head at him and pursing her mouth, 'you are supposed to be in a storm, in a tumult, a tempest. What is the use of standing there at the back of the stage, with your head bent so that the audience cannot see your face — and biting your lips? You must rage to and fro, fling your arms to heaven, beat your breast, fall upon your knees. So!'

He raged theatrically, to show her, and waited for gratitude and obedience.

Less shabby, since Pezzana had been very kind in the matter of discarded gowns, Eleonora said, 'But Signor Drage, when I am in a tumult I do none of these things.'

Simmering, Drage noted Pezzana's slight shake of head, and lowered his voice.

'This is not *life*, Signorina. This is *art*. You must exaggerate to seem natural.'

'When I am in a tumult, Signor Drage,' she said painfully, 'I fight *inside* myself — and this feeling is what I am trying to convey.'

Drage shouted, 'By standing at the back of the stage, turned away from the audience, and wringing your hands?'

Only too conscious that her efforts were less than adequate, she replied softly but stubbornly, 'I know, Signor, that I have not yet found out how to show what I feel — but I *am* on the right lines!'

He clutched his head and called upon three favourite saints to sustain him. He thumped his chest, rolled his eyes, and dashed his script to the ground. Shrinking in the wings, watching him, she marvelled that he did not know how unconvincing he appeared: like a man acting anger.

She was almost twenty and life was broadening. They had started in Trieste, still — with Trento — in Austrian hands, near the border of Yugoslavia. Now, on the longest itinerary she had ever experienced, they travelled right down from this north-eastern corner to Naples in Southern Italy, opening at the Teatro de' Fiorentini. Italy was unified by 1878, but a millennium and a half of fragmentation is not altered by the signing of papers or the coming of a king. Naples, gallant and gay, with its own dialect and flavour, its reputation for ice cream and pizza, seemed as foreign as any foreign country. Garibaldi and his ragged volunteers had united the city with the rest of Italy in 1860, though Rome held out for another ten years, and the spirit of nationalism had taken root in more than a political sense. An attempt was being made to found a theatre of national rather than local importance. For still the darlings of Naples were not necessarily acknowledged in Rome, heard of in Turin, or applauded in Milan. So the company's advent was peculiarly fortunate in that Naples was ready for originality and passionately concerned with a new concept of the theatre.

Though Eleonora had known a series of exiles and no settled home, she found the city forbidding at first sight. Strange streets, strange people, strange dialect, and strange food which involved a dramatic quantity of garlic, olive oil and tomato. As a recompense for enduring some of the most Stygian slums in Europe the Neapolitans were blessed with a debonair facade, backed by the phrase *Far bella figura* — 'put a good face on life'. Eleonora retreated under Pezzana's motherly wing, concentrated on her roles and those of Guilia Gritti, whom she was understudying, and kept out of Drage's way.

He, visualising himself as an innovator, and certainly a shrewd judge of his present audience, was producing Emile Augier's latest play, *Les Fourchambault*, with Guilia Gritti in the lead as Maia. Augier, lawyer turned dramatist, had worked his apprenticeship from verse through neo-classical to social dramas. Writing reasonably well, though he had his critics, adapting to the fresh current of thought sweeping its way through revolutionary Europe, he scorned the romantic tradition upheld by Dumas *fils* and his like. His plays dealt with the problems of adultery, of illegitimacy, of the disruption of home life; and *Les Fourchambault* was a splendid vehicle for any company to ride in Naples in 1878. The Neapolitans booked an encouraging number of seats — and Guilia Gritti was taken ill.

Drage announced her unavoidable absence to the audience, begged their several pardons, and, with a confidence he was far from feeling, said that the part of Maia would be played by

Signorina Eleonora Duse. They clapped politely. He bowed courteously. Then, slipping backstage, he glared at Eleonora, who stood white and wooden in the wings.

Relieved to find her in a humble mood he whispered, 'Now *act*, for heaven's sake, and never mind the fancy work!'

She turned a colourless face to his, and said nothing. She had been given the opportunity of a leading role in a new play, and she intended to make the most of it, in her own way.

Her entrance was not conspicuous, but the spectators were friendly and did not expect much. Unobtrusively she eased herself into the part of Maia, and then cracked into life, a formidable firework. Pezzana caught both her hands as she came off, tired and triumphant from the final ovation.

'But what a little savage you are!' she cried, delighted, patting the girl's flushed cheek. 'Who but me would have thought you had it in you? See, you have pleased even *him*!'

And she indicated Drage, mellowed by this unsuspected success.

'Splendid. Splendid.'

Then she draped one comely arm round Eleonora's shoulders and walked with her to Gritti's dressing room.

'But you must practise your hand and arm movements,' she said in a different tone. 'You have beautiful hands — has no one told you? Make the most of them. Now, I'm not being catty — you know me too well for that — but your gestures are limited. The fire, the passion, the abandon, comes through. But you must act with your whole body, so that even if you turn your back to the audience they will *know* what you are feeling and thinking. Drage is right, in one way, you must exaggerate a little — but a *controlled* exaggeration, mind, none of his slapsticks! You're a proud little creature,' Pezzana continued kindly, 'but not too proud, I am sure, to take a few tips from an old professional, eh?'

Eleonora was gazing in on some golden world of her own, and answered from it.

'I should be so grateful to you,' she said. 'I want to learn. I never stop trying to learn.'

Her eyes glittered at the remembrance of Drage's sarcasm.

'I am only proud when I feel that people in authority do not understand what I am trying to do!' she said imperiously.

Pezzana began to laugh, giving her a little push to bring her from her pedestal. Then she paused, and became very gracious with an immaculate man of middle height and neat features, who came forward and bowed over her hand.

'Signora Pezzana,' he said, his voice beautifully modulated to caress every syllable of her name, 'may I kiss the white fingers of a very great tragic actress?'

'You are too kind, too courteous, Signor!' She brought Eleonora forward. 'I hope you admired the little Duse this evening. Nella, you have not met our eminent colleague Giovanni Emanuel?'

'At your feet, Signorina!' cried the actor. 'Naples will be flocking to see you. I am happy to be the first to congratulate you.'

She blushed from neck to forehead, glancing nervously at Pezzana — who smiled like a fairy godmother.

'What roles I see before you!' cried Emanuel. 'And what a combination you will make! The exquisite Pezzana, the mysterious Duse.' He tapped his mouth with one manicured finger. 'We must speak of this later,' he said, smiling. 'I shall see you both often.'

And he bowed and smiled his way out, a master of exit.

He was a perceptive man and a fine actor, original, courageous and enthusiastic. With the material assistance of the Princess Santa Buona he assembled a company, booked a season at the Teatro de' Fiorentini, and engaged Pezzana and Duse as his leading ladies.

'Now you are on the ladder!' cried Pezzana, delighted by her protégée's success.

'Now I can *breathe*!' said Eleonora.

Encouraged, she gave Naples her wild, desolate Ophelia; her gentle, submissive Desdemona; her gutter-tongued sensual Nana; her galled Electra. They roared for her, captured by an element of sadness which clung to almost every part she ever played. The imbalance of her portrayals was resolving itself. Expanding, stabilising herself, she began to act brilliantly and consistently. *Every evening,* one admirer wrote of that season, *she seized your heart and squeezed it like a handkerchief.* Naples, the chaos of alien streets and faces, menacing in its sophistication, now formed into familiar landmarks and brought her her first friends.

At twenty she had come a long way from the poverty of a third-rate troupe. She could eat and clothe herself adequately. *Far bella figura.* She smiled often, she laughed, she teased, she enchanted. The demands of the thwarted child within her clamoured for attention, and she gave them rein. Her hands fluttered to express her feelings. Her speech quickened. She responded almost pathetically to attention and admiration. In repose her face had been sullen, now it was vivacious. At times she appeared beautiful.

'Your little Duse is finding her wings!' said Emanuel, pleased.

'She will be very fine, very great,' said Pezzana.

Naples, as Emanuel prophesied, flocked to see and hear her. Foremost among them were Matilde Serao the novelist and her journalist husband Edoardo Scarfoglio. Matilde, shorter, sturdier, and a little older than Eleonora, sought her out. They shared the same perception but not the same vulnerability, and Eleonora leaned on her. Since she had waved to Déjanira in the square, all those years ago, she had not been able to say of anyone, 'She was my *friend*!' So she put out her hands to Matilde without reserve, and Matilde — strong enough to contain and sustain a river of confidences, fears and affection — returned a friendship which was to last for life. Eleonora, whose mute obduracy had rebuffed many older and wiser people, could turn to her and say with humility, 'I am ignorant. I know nothing.' Tactfully, Matilde set herself the task of filling in educational chasms, taking her beyond the little world of the travelling players.

Pezzana and Duse set the seal on their temporary partnership by engaging in mortal combat as Madame and Thérèse Raquin. Elemental fury met cold implacability, and the audience rustled in their seats, knowing they had been permitted to witness the unforgettable. Duse's feelings became their own. They too, shuddered as she touched the wedding veil. The heavy-lidded eyes and strongly marked brows were theirs. With her they experienced the violence of murder, of illicit love, and the final truth of retribution.

An undistinguished little figure, she threw back her head and extended her arms at curtain call after curtain call, offering them the last of herself.

SIX

Eleonora had, in a profession noted for promiscuity, led a life of convent-like chastity, preserved by a forbidding manner and a total lack of prettiness. But her armour concealed a nature both sensual and intensely affectionate, so far unchannelled and untapped. The Neapolitan spring of 1879 found her adored from a distance by thousands, and known to no man. It was the time for loving, and Matilde introduced the lover.

'Hurry yourself!' she commanded, as Eleonora drooped before her glass, too weary to change, the evening's mask still visible on her face. 'I have somebody coming to supper who worships you — besides being very useful to know. He's a newspaper magnate. Martino Cafiero, director of the *Corriere del Mattino*. Quite young — thirty-five-ish — and exceptionally handsome. So put a smile on your face, Nella, do!'

She thrust a hairbrush into Eleonora's hand and began to unhook the back of her dress.

'We know how greedy you are for good conversation and culture,' she went on, mocking the face in the glass, 'and Edoardo said, "Bring Martino along. Eleonora never eats much supper — perhaps she'll eat him instead!" Oh, but, Nella — just one little warning. He's a fearful rake. Had affairs with half the society women in Naples. He hasn't met the other half yet! Are you listening?'

Reviving under the onslaught of words and assistance, Eleonora said, 'He won't be interested in seducing me, so don't concern yourself!' She stepped out of her dress and rubbed her arms to life.

'I'm not at all sure. You should hear the men in the audience suck in their breath at your love scenes!'

They giggled together, hands over mouths. Chided each other, hurrying to make Eleonora ready for this Prince of Love-makers.

'Edouardo didn't cry a bit at your Thérèse,' said Matilde, impish. 'He sat there as solemn as an owl, while the rest of us wept our eyes out. Just kept saying to himself, "My God! My God!" and suffering in heroic silence. But outside they're all waiting for you — so hurry up!'

Eleonora slipped unobtrusively from the theatre, escorted by Edouardo and Matilde, and little groups of people moved uncertainly nearer, trying to recognise in this soberly pretty young woman the fiery Thérèse Raquin.

The doorkeeper settled their doubts. In broad Neapolitan dialect he shouted, '*That's* her, ladies and gentlemen. That — is — *her!*'

As timid as Angelica, she ducked between them as they called out greetings and congratulations, reached out their hands to touch an arm or shoulder, expressed their thanks. And the doorkeeper, grinning and unrepentant, made a way for her through the press and ushered her into the Scarfoglios' carriage with a bow.

They sat late over their fruit and wine, while Cafiero wove a spell about them. He was gallant with Matilde, brotherly with Edouardo, gentle with the strange girl who had eaten so little and sipped glass after glass of water while she listened. She had created a solitary pool of silence sitting there in the candlelight. A worldly man, he was enchanted by her simplicity, her lack of paint, her withdrawn air. He had known a number of actresses, but none like this one. *Still,* he thought, noting the full mouth, the abundance of hair drawn away from her face in a Grecian knot, the fashionable fringe and neat ears, *she's no nun*.

He told a particularly funny story, risqué without being offensive, and she flung back her head and laughed, showing excellent white teeth. He spoke of modern Italian literature, paying a gracious compliment to Matilde on her own work, linking her with Renato Fucini the Tuscan writer. He raised his glass to Giovanni Verga, who was freeing the Italian theatre from its shackles. He described the aims and ideals of the *Scapigliatura Milanese*, the Italian bohemians who sought freedom from the fogs of domesticity and order. He wrote down a list of their works for Eleonora to read, instancing the works of Giuseppe Rovani, of Emilio Praga, of Arrigo Boito.

'Boito is especially fine,' he said, handing her the note with a smile. 'He is also an excellent musician, and librettist to Verdi — who is his particular friend. You have heard his *Mefistofele*, of course?'

She said she had not, and read the names — which meant nothing to her, reared on scripts of comedies and tragedies.

She was all admiration and humility. Her eyes never left Cafiero as he touched on art and poetry, spoke of the new movement in European drama, and paid a compliment to Eleonora for her portrayals of Zola's and of Augier's heroines. Whenever he looked in her direction she was watching him, with such absorption that he felt himself swimming out of his depth. As he surfaced, pleasurably shaken, he concluded that the little Duse should not be difficult to befriend, and enormously intriguing.

Eleonora never considered whether she was falling in love with him, nor the consequences. Brought up to live from one day to the next, to hope that the future would take care of itself, she simply let go of everything that so far had kept her apart from men, rejoicing. Cafiero's accomplishments were many, hers narrowed within the limits of a theatre in which she was still an apprentice. His way to her affections, physical attraction apart, lay through her hunger for education. 'I must work. I must learn,' had become her watchwords.

So he escorted her all over Naples, lent her books, took her to galleries and exhibitions, wined and dined her exquisitely, and haunted her performances — which he discussed with considerable judgement. In return she listened and observed, acted better than ever in his honour — and showed him, with pleasure, a letter from Emile Zola himself, praising her performance as Thérèse Raquin. She could not read, see, hear, discover, experience, fast enough. She flitted here and there, trying and tasting whatever was offered, afraid it would vanish.

'He is fifteen years older than you. He is mature, he is charming, he is clever, and he is a rotter with women!' said Matilde. 'Are you listening, or are you too busy putting on that flowered hat?'

'I am listening, my dearest Mati, as I always do and always shall.'

Matilde discounted the sentiment and pursued the practical issue.

'If you fall in love with him you will eat your bread in sorrow, Nella.'

'But if I eat?'

'Half the society women in Naples, and a number of charming actresses, have shared the same loaf!'

Eleonora speared her hat with an ornamental pin and drew on her gloves.

'But every day he sends me flowers, Mati. Such flowers — and so many of them. We dine or lunch at the most beautiful restaurants. We drink a different wine with each course.

Imagine, when I first came here I thought there were only two wines — red and white!'

Matilde leaned forward, level-headed and obdurate.

'Tonight, my dear Nella, or tomorrow night, or the night after — since he is not used to waiting so long for ladies to fall into his arms — he will take you sailing in the Bay. Preferably by moonlight.'

The hands drifted down from a radiant face, and clasped each other as though they held something infinitely fragile and precious.

'And he will say,' Matilde continued inexorably, '"My dearest Nenella…"'

'Yes, yes, you are right. He does call me Nenella…'

'"Look at Vesuvius!" the little cur will say. "How placid the old man seems! Just an occasional huff and puff, and yet his heart rages fire!"'

'Rages fire. Yes. Oh, but how very beautiful, how poetic. How well you understand, Mati, being a writer yourself…'

'I am not that kind of a writer,' said Matilde. 'And then the hound will say, "Vesuvius is like my love for you, Nenella. On the surface I am serene, I am gay, I do not care. But beneath — oh, Nenella — what a ferment of desire!"'

'Martino,' said Eleonora, entering on a sigh.

'Listen to me, instead of dreaming like a fool. The next part is very important. He will then tell you that you are young and lovely and incredibly gifted — and he is right! — and will ask you, since you and he love each other so much, to consent to put out the fire! Now do you comprehend what he means by that?'

Eleonora said, almost in reproach, 'You should not speak to me in that way, Mati. Even *you* should not come quite so close.'

'My dearest girl, I only want you to promise me that you will say "No" and keep on saying "No". I'm no pryer into love affairs, no voyeur. I have a good husband of my own. But Cafiero does not, and probably never will, mean marriage. And you will not always be in Naples. Just keep saying "No!"'

One hand touched Matilde's cheek. The other blew her a kiss.

'You see — forgive me, Mati — he is waiting for me!'

She was ready for the affair and circumstances made it possible. Though money was not abundant she could dress a little better; she was sought out as a minor fashionable interest; she had a small furnished room in which she could receive visitors. So she received Cafiero, and discovered that the body as well as the mind has its own language.

Cafiero's interest helped both actress and woman. A person of great urbanity and sophistication, he praised her performances in the *Corriere del Mattino* — partly because they merited praise, partly to press his own interest. Naples knew exactly what his admiration entailed, but it was fashionable to be seen on his arm. Naples thought, on the whole, that the little Duse was very sensible to please him, while she lasted.

Into love, as into a new part, Eleonora lost herself wholly, recklessly and painfully. Her world took on the colour of his moods, her work fluctuated accordingly. In his absences she was lifeless, annoying even the easy-going Pezzana, sending the audience away disappointed of its morsel. On his returns, flinging herself laughing and crying into his arms, she was magnificent. Her performances gained in depth and polish. Her innovations roused admiring comment. Other actresses in *Electra* had swept on garnished like Neapolitan ices. She appeared in white and Grecian simplicity. Her love scenes now burned with such abandon that the onlookers, excited and shaken, felt faintly *de trop*. They shuddered when she shuddered. They watched, hushed and motionless, her fraught silences.

She entered love as a swimmer enters the sea, emerging dazzled and refreshed from Cafiero's accomplished arms. And with an innocence that bordered on folly, expected love to go on for ever and ever.

April, May, June, July, 1879.

The season in Naples was over. But from the northern city of Turin, Cesare Rossi of the Compagnia Carignano offered Pezzana and Duse hospitality.

'What an honour!' cried Matilde, testing the reaction.

'It *would* have been an honour,' said Eleonora, 'but all that is behind me now. No more travelling, Mati, no more dust and noise and jealousy. I am staying here in Naples with Martino.'

'Has he asked you to?'

'Not yet — but of course he will.'

When he, too, congratulated her, she was astounded.

'But,' she said, smiling and trembling, trying to catch his eyes which were so suddenly busy with everything else, 'Turin is so far away, an incredible distance in fact. And, when we have found even an afternoon's absence a hardship, how much more will all those hundreds of miles seem?'

He laughed, and took her hands in his, and said that nothing would ever really separate them, since their hearts were one.

Disturbed, she went back to her lodgings, and — unable to refuse the offer — packed.

Martino really intended to surprise her, she told Matilde. Perhaps he was following her to Turin, one never knew. Or perhaps, at the last moment, he would realise what separation meant and pull her from the train, trunks and all.

'For pity's sake, Nella,' said Matilde, worried for her, 'just forget him. He's a rascal.'

Tears, fury and reproaches. All delivered at top speed and top pitch. Then pleas for forgiveness, dwindling to a quiet sobbing, and back again to that stupid and incredible hope.

Far bella figura. Matilde, at the carriage window, talked of anything but what they were both feeling; while Eleonora played with the flowers Edoardo had presented in farewell.

'I shall write to you every week, and you must write to me,' said Matilde. 'This is not goodbye for ever, Nella, only for a time. You'll be back again with us, rich and famous. And we'll be here to greet you.'

The gloved hands were smoothing, separating, rearranging the flowers in mute choreography.

'Our house is yours,' said Matilde to the downcast eyes, the swollen mouth. 'And whenever you need me, Nella, send a telegram and I'll come. Wherever you are, and for whatever reason.'

Eleonora lifted her head and stared past them to the station clock, whose hands marked the hour of departure.

'I've packed fruit and bread and wine in your basket,' said Matilde, 'and some provolone, that smoked cheese you're so fond of. And cooked chicken. It's such a journey... but between such friends as ourselves what is distance? We can bridge it with letters and remembrances, can't we?'

The first movement of the train struck the girl like a blow on the back. She shivered, tried to say goodbye, and became suddenly lifeless. Dumbly she stood at the carriage window, the flowers drooping in her hands, staring at her friends. Her features seemed to thicken and coarsen with grief. Plain and sad, so that even her clothes were dulled, she clung to the window ledge and could not speak.

Matilde and Edoardo — Neapolitans to the core — kept up appearances, and waved and called and smiled as the train began to draw out of the station. But they evoked no response from that slight remote figure. And the face at the window became, in the end, a white blur dominated by two pairs of dark uncomprehending eyes.

SEVEN

The Compagnia Carignano of Turin was another attempt at unifying the Italian theatre, founded in 1877 under the management of Cesare Rossi, the actor. But any city other than Naples was now exile to Eleonora. And Rossi — mature in years, well-fleshed, a lover of good food and sensual women and perpetual comfort — viewed her foreign appearance with misgivings. Still, he reflected, perhaps the long journey and the weather had changed this young hope of the Teatro de' Fiorentini into a silent dowdy. He shrugged philosophically and lit a fine cigar.

Her rehearsals were makeshift and lifeless.

'Ah, but the little Duse is never much at rehearsal,' Pezzana said, to comfort him. 'Wait for her performance.'

In the vast Teatro Carignano, half-empty and cold, Eleonora made heavy going of a mediocre repertoire, and her performances were rather worse than the rehearsals.

'She needs encouragement,' said Pezzana, worried.

Rossi invited the girl round to his apartment with other members of the cast, and cooked like an angel for them all.

'In the south,' he said, disposing of that languourous territory with a wave of the arm, 'a plate of spaghetti, swimming in oil and tomato sauce, is a banquet. What do I offer you here? A glorious marriage of French and Italian cuisine. I cook only in butter!' He kissed his fingers theatrically, laying a dish before them. 'For you I have created *cardi in bagna cauda*, a famous Piedmontese speciality. Edible thistles in a sauce of butter, of oil, of anchovies, of cream and shredded garlic! I offer you wines fit for the King himself. Had I not been an actor I should have been a chef!'

The girl ate little, said less, and drank water.

The night that she not only spoke her lines inaccurately, but also forgot some of them, he held his head.

'I have been robbed!' he trumpeted, to whoever cared to hear him. 'A hoax has been perpetrated upon my trusting person!'

Pezzana placed one hand under Eleonora's chin and turned the face towards her: all wretched eyes and swollen mouth.

'I grieve for you, Nella,' she said kindly, 'but such things happen to all of us, *poverina*, and yet we do not die. Work and forget, *cara*, work and forget.'

Helplessly the girl said, 'But I'm expecting his child.'

'Then you must tell him,' said Pezzana, after a pause, 'and he must give you money. Such matters cost money, both now and later.'

'But will he not wish to marry me, now? Won't he? Shouldn't he?'

Pezzana said, out of pity, 'Write to him, at any rate. This is his responsibility as well as yours.'

Cafiero's reply, after a long interval, arrived with an air of reluctance. He said how very much he was enjoying living at his mother's villa outside Naples, and that he found the countryside both a rest and an inspiration.

As an afterthought he bade her take courage in face of life's temporary frustrations.

In rage and terror she wrote that she would not come to the villa itself, but must see and speak to him about the child.

By return, he wrote that she must not attempt to journey all the way to Naples. He would meet her in a small hotel in Rome.

Since there was nothing left, hope lingered. She scraped together the money for the fare, and for a new dress and hat with which to enchant him. All through the night, as her train clattered and jolted down to Rome, she rehearsed fascinating speeches to influence him while other passengers slept. In the afternoon, weary and unready, she made her way to the hotel he had chosen.

He was waiting, courteous and relaxed, with a mouthful of compliments and a guard on his eyes. She knew the scene had slipped away from her, that she had been outclassed and outmanoeuvred, and she could not help herself. Her small store of confidence spent, she sat silent, hands in lap, the palms upturned as if in supplication.

Cafiero was charmed by her grace and sadness. He could hardly leave her alone in Rome, and her train to Turin did not go before the morning. So they must pass the time somehow, and be gayer. *Far bella figura!* He set out to smooth the sorrow from her mouth, to make her eyes narrow and sparkle.

'Where's your smile gone?' he asked impishly.

She looked up, lovely with hope, and after that it was easy — lamentably easy. On the double bed in the back room of that obscure hotel they made a little paradise of the evening. And when it was over he wished her all the luck in the world, offered to pay her medical expenses when the child was born, and left her.

She sat by the window until dawn, crippled with shame. She considered throwing herself down into the street. She wept bitterly, twisting her hands, calling upon her mother for comfort. She had nowhere to go but Turin, no money but what she could earn before the child's birth. So she packed her few things back in her suitcase, pulled the veil down over her blotched face, and went out into the empty city. The train did not leave for another two hours.

Driven by misery, she wandered up and down without purpose or direction, needing to keep moving on, somewhere, anywhere. And finally she set down her bag, exhausted, and chafed her aching hands.

The sky grew lighter, and into her range of vision came two words of augury: Teatro Valle. The Teatro Valle of Rome, theatrical hub of the city, stood there before her. Out of her reach, but so tempting that she would have entered it that moment and played out the whole of *Electra* to an empty auditorium, just to have felt those boards, those particularly unattainable boards, beneath her feet. She forgot her trouble, her lover and her coming child. All the disasters, the triumphs, the hunger and tears and cold, the perpetual packing up and moving on, crystallised now into one purpose and made sense.

She marvelled at the confidence of her vision. There was no need to whip up defiance, to swear great oaths, to challenge greater odds. She knew she would return some day in style, though now she left in wretchedness and anonymity.

Turning to a passer-by, as the streets came to life with her, she asked to be directed to the railway station.

The man who informed her thought she looked rather pale and thin, but considered that her eyes and bearing could only be described as magnificent.

'One moment, one very short moment, in my office if you please, Signorina,' said Rossi briskly, and ushered her into a chair and closed the door.

Leaning his bulk against it, surveying the thickened waist that even a corset could no longer control, he shook his head and shrugged. Who would have thought it? Who would ever have thought it?

'Signorina,' he said kindly, but with a half-smile and a twinkle, since sexual matters were at once a source of amusement as well as passion. 'May I, with the utmost delicacy in the world...' and here he sat confidently next to her, in another and more comfortable chair, '...may I suggest, Signorina, that you are no longer in any... condition,' he wriggled his fingers in the air, 'to play the more virginal roles in your repertoire?'

She was downcast, staring humiliated at her hands.

'Look here, my dear girl,' said Rossi, dropping his bantering tone and becoming a comrade-at-arms. 'I wasn't born yesterday, you know. I understand these matters — only too well, in fact! You're pregnant. That's obvious. But why didn't you tell me, instead of waiting until the whole of the company found out for itself?'

Still she stared at her hands, crucified.

'Look, my girl, I'll keep you on the payroll. I suppose the man in question isn't doing much about it, eh? It's an old story. You can stay on the payroll, go off somewhere quiet to have the baby — say, Marina di Pisa, that's a quiet place. And then come back here and start again with a clean sheet. Good Lord, you're not the first actress to trip up, and you won't be the last. What do you say?'

She said, with difficulty, that he was exceedingly kind.

'Not entirely kind,' said Rossi honestly. 'At first I thought they'd passed a dead pigeon on to me, under cover of Pezzana. But now and again, in the last few weeks, I've seen a gleam of something. I expect you had a lot on your mind, that's only natural. Now, when you're better, and back on the boards, I want to see the actress they went mad about in Naples. Understand me?'

She started clumsily to her feet, tears running down her face, and caught his hands, kissing them with passionate gratitude.

'You shall, indeed you shall, Signor Rossi. Oh Signor, if you knew... And I wanted, all the time I wanted, to do well for you. So kind. So very good and kind. Like my father. Like my own father...'

Rossi patted her shoulder and lent her his handkerchief, since hers was wet and in shreds. She was young and fresh and tragic. The feelings he experienced were not entirely fatherly, nor wholly professional.

At Marina di Pisa she was joined by Matilde Serao. With trouble and fortitude she gave birth to a son, and received him in dismay.

'But why does he look so old?' she cried, touching the small grey face, lifting the limp wizened hands.

'All babies look old at first, Signora,' said the peasant woman who attended her.

'But not with such a face, such a *poor* little ancient face. Such a *sorry* little soul to live in such a face.'

Cafiero's son was to know nothing of joy or tragedy; after a short fretful passage he weakened and died.

Eleonora did not indulge in any of the histrionics that Drage insisted were the accompaniments of mortal tempest. In silence she followed the small coffin, in silence threw on a handful of soil, in silence picked a few leaves from the tree under which he lay. Then she said to Matilde, 'I'd best get back to work, Mati.'

The shock of birth and death, following upon the shock of betrayal, had stunned her. Certainly she wept, and smoothed the little clothes, and could not yet bear to give them away. But she had been wounded deeper than that. Cafiero, said Matilde, was Duse's tormentor. So he was, and yet was little but an instrument in the hands of a far greater tormentor: herself. She had her own nature to contend with, and its extravagance bankrupted her. Tears ran again as soon as they had dried, and Matilde sat and grieved with and for her.

Rossi's telegram did not arrive so much as explode. La Pezzana seldom showed temperament, being too well-established and good-natured to indulge in hysterics. And Rossi had discounted this side of her personality, with disastrous results. In a scene, later described with tremendous relish by other members of the company, Pezzana had thrown a tantrum to end all theatrical tantrums, and left Rossi in the lurch.

Would Eleonora, he begged, upon his humble and trusting knees, return as soon as possible? Would she, since he and she had made a compact with each other, and were good friends, step into the shoes of the lamented Pezzana and become his leading lady?

For the first time since that morning in Rome the old excitement possessed her. In a flurry of packing and crying and thanking and paying, she sent a wire to Rossi to say that she would be with him as soon as a train might be caught.

'The leading lady,' she cried to Matilde, 'the leading lady of the Compagnia Carignano. All the best parts. How I shall work for him — work until I drop with sleep and hunger...

Then she sat down quickly, her mood switching.

'But the little one stays here,' she said. 'Always the same, Mati, always the same. The good and the bad together in one cup.'

'Then drink deep!' counselled Matilde, determined not to let her relapse.

'Oh, I shall, Mati, I shall. I was never one for half measures, you know!'

EIGHT

Rossi himself met her at the station, and noted that her figure had improved past recognition. Her movements were slower, more assured, and she had developed a most delightful bosom. He condoled with her, briefly and not very sincerely, on the baby's death, and whisked her off to the theatre.

Together they walked on to the empty stage of the Teatro Carignano. Rossi gestured magnificently at the rows of dusty velvet seats, the four tiers of balconies, the baroque ceiling.

'Turn up the gas!' he shouted, and the house glowed into life: gilded, garlanded, draped, pillared and swagged.

'Now, Nella,' said Rossi, 'Pezzana often told me that you might bring off a risky notion but you were always damned difficult about doing as you were told. So let us understand one another. You do as you please — but fill this theatre for me!'

Neither life nor art works so simply. Eleonora struggled to illuminate the empty comedies, the turgid melodramas, the humdrum farces. But the Carignano remained half full, the applause perfunctory. Any effort on her part to introduce Zola, Augier, Shakespeare or even Dumas *fils* met with Rossi's flat refusal.

'Mother of God, Nella,' he cried. 'We can't fill the place with what they want, let alone what they don't understand. And it's no use saying "Naples" to me. Turin isn't Naples, and I shouldn't need to tell you that!'

'Turin is dead,' she said, with passionate emphasis. 'The theatre is dead. The company is dead. The audiences are dead.' In the grip of depression she added, 'I also am dead, Cesare.'

Torn between his fading box office and Duse's fresh charms, Rossi raged too. He had had few complaints about her acting since her return, but many about her cold nature — which, God Himself knew, could not have been so frigid, or she would never have become pregnant.

'You are young and ardent,' he cried, astonished that she should repel his advances. 'Why not? Certainly, I am no Adonis, but I know a lot about women. I like to please them. I should like to please *you*, Nella.'

'I was in love,' she said, 'and deeply though I respect and admire you, I do not love you.'

'What has love to do with it?' he grumbled. 'Do I ask you for love?' And incensed by her lack of politics, 'I have done you many a favour — you should do me one for a change!'

'I suppose you think I should also extend favours to the other male members of your company, Signor? Thank you, no. If I wished to earn a living on the streets I should have done so long since.'

She walked slowly away from him, head bent, thinking. Since the end of her love affair and the death of her baby her wardrobe had mourned with her. Observing the piled black hair above the plain black gown, Rossi sighed with self-pity.

'Besides,' she said, suddenly vulnerable, 'you should not make things so hard for me. My life is my own when I leave this theatre, surely? I must be quiet, must be alone. I am not strong, Signor. I have a complaint inherited from my mother, I know the symptoms. A childhood spent in hunger and hardship has not improved my lungs. Even now, after my rest in Marina di Pisa, I tire easily. The cold makes me cough until sometimes I can hardly stop. When I mount the stairs to my lodging I draw breath at every flight, and my heart hammers.

At night I find myself feverish and alive. In the morning I am too exhausted to wake.'

He picked up his bowler hat and slapped it hard down on his grey head. She paced to and fro, seeking reasons to placate him, to keep him at a distance.

'I looked upon you as my friend and protector. As my father...'

Rossi expressed disgust at such a role.

'Signor,' she said desperately, 'I cannot fight everything and everyone all the time. You will kill me if you persist!'

'Kill nothing,' said Rossi contemptuously. 'You're a damned sight too tough to die. Save your act for tonight!'

She drew herself up in supreme disdain, but trembled with the effort to stay calm.

'I can get plenty of women, *sensible* women,' said Rossi, flourishing his walking stick. 'I was only doing you a favour. Keep yourself to yourself, but remember this. If the theatre can't be filled I face ruin, and so do you. Remember this, too. I don't doubt your talent. But great actresses reach the top by drawing great audiences. Where are *your* audiences, Signorina? And how long do we have to wait for them?'

A large hand touched her wrist tentatively, as she stood motionless where Rossi had left her. A throat cleared, preparatory to speech.

She turned so rapidly, with such an instinctive gesture of fear, that Tebaldo Checchi said, 'I shan't trouble you, Signorina.'

'If you will excuse me, please. I must go home and rest for the performance, Signor Checchi.'

He was a nice-looking fellow with curling hair and a curling moustache. A dash of the devil would have made him downright handsome, but his nature was milk and honey. Nourishing, wholesome, stable, and entirely void of excitement.

'Allow me to accompany you home, Signorina. My feelings for you...' he paused, but when the words arrived they were not so earth-shaking that he had need to hesitate, '... my feelings are honourable.'

A small-part actor in the company; reliable, competent, and uninspired; she had early on discounted him. Now, observing his good-humoured beseeching eyes, the proffered arm, she laid one hand upon his sleeve and thanked him.

From then on all *tête-à-têtes* with the reluctant Eleonora were severely hampered by Checchi's presence. He loomed everywhere, polite and obstinate. He cleared his throat in gentle warning. He escorted Eleonora to and from the theatre. He saw that her rest periods were uninterrupted. He led the applause when it lagged, and augmented it when it quickened. His eyes beamed upon her from the wings.

'Checchi's got it bad!' one actor observed.

'Oh, I don't think so,' said another cynically. 'He's just getting well in with the leading lady. Knows which side his bread's buttered — like the rest of us.'

Under his protection she began to heal and expand, to throw herself with zest into her performances. When he asked her to marry him she hesitated, longing for the emotional security he offered, honest enough to realise that this was all he meant to her.

'Rossi is only *one* manager,' he said. 'There will be others — other managers, others actors, other admirers, other men, wherever you are. But if you are my wife you will be left in peace — and isn't that what you need? What you want?'

'But,' she said, afraid to hurt him, 'I don't love you, Tebaldo.'

'But you like me? You like to be with me?'

'Very much.'

'I am not distasteful to you — as a man, I mean?'

She shook her head, smiling.

'Then that is all I ask,' he said simply. 'You are a fine actress, Eleonora. You will be a very great one. I am content to love and support you, and your interests, for a lifetime.'

'You are offering a lot in return for very little.'

'The honour of placing your shawl upon your shoulders is not a small one.'

Simplicity moved her where sophistication would have failed, and they announced their engagement. Rossi's behaviour was exemplary. He congratulated Checchi, was roguish with Eleonora. The rest of the company indulged in open or hidden malice.

'Here is the leading lady's husband!' they said to each other, in voices loud enough to be heard.

And behind their hands, whispered and sniggered, 'Here comes the pimp!'

Occasionally some more daring than the others would draw Eleonora aside and, speaking with smiling ill-will, condole with her over Tebaldo's lack of talent.

'But how he works at it!' they would say, in mock admiration. 'He never gives up trying, does he? And always knows his lines by heart.'

Life was restful, if uneventful, and she welcomed it. They married in Florence in the May of 1881, and returned from a brief honeymoon to a comfortable apartment and a little maid who would care for it. Respectability seemed a soothing garment for the time being, and in its warmth sat Eleonora, gathering strength for the next assault on the theatre world, whenever that might be. She received all Tebaldo's hopes for her future with a courtesy she would not have extended to anyone else. For, after all, he was a very ordinary man, and his dreams went no further than tumultuous applause, bouquets of rare flowers, ecstatic press notices, a brimming box office, and her name very large and black upon the posters. Whereas her dreams, as always, scaled mountains she could not name, reached heights she could not visualise.

'It is not enough,' she said to him gently, 'to be adored. Between what I have and what you hope for me is a great chasm to be filled with work. I must work, Tebaldo, I must learn. And above all I must have the right plays. Where *are* these plays?' she demanded, walking to and fro, hands clasped, head bent. 'How can I find them? Cesare is very good, very kind, but when I suggest something a little more interesting he cries, "They won't come to see *you* in *that*!" But they don't exactly flock to see me anyway!'

She stopped at the sight of Tebaldo's puzzled face.

'In here,' she said, placing her hands on her heart, 'I have a terrible longing. I love the theatre, and I'm jealous of it, for it must be all *mine*. Mine in spirit, mine in expression, mine in scope and feeling. Do you understand what I am trying to tell you?'

Then for days she would be totally content, lying on the floor of their living room, one hand supporting her head, the other turning the pages of some new book she had bought. The opening of the door brought her into sitting position, hands gesturing, eyes shining.

'Now tell me,' she would cry, arresting her visitor imperiously, before so much as a greeting could be exchanged, 'what do you think of this?' and begin to read aloud.

Sometimes Tebaldo, mystified, leafing through anything from George Sand to St Thomas Aquinas, would say, 'Why did you buy this, my love?'

'Oh — I liked the cover!'

'Do you always buy books because you like the covers?'

She was uncertain for a moment, fearing criticism, wary of those voids in her education which were to take a lifetime's filling. Then, seeing his placid admiration, she made a face, kissed him on the nose, caught up his hands and danced him round the room.

'Of course! It's the best reason in the world. Besides — I wouldn't know what to choose. I'm so dreadfully ignorant.'

So she danced and smiled and courted his attention. And he, utterly happy, watched her as some sentimental animal lover might watch a lion cub.

CURTAIN RISE

At Athens, in the Museum, there is the mask of a tragic actress: the passion of sorrow seen for a moment on the face of a woman on the stage, is engraved into it, like a seal.
Eleonora Duse

NINE

Having conquered the capitals of the world quite recently, Sarah Bernhardt turned her attention to lesser fry and sent a royal command to Turin. Abasing himself, Rossi replied that the Teatro Carignano was at her disposal for life. Sarah said eight days would be sufficient. He thanked her humbly, stared about him at the Carignano, snatched off his bowler hat, struck it in despair, and shouted for the cleaners. To his company, suddenly bereft of guidance, he confided, '*She* is coming!'

Pushed to the background with the rest, Eleonora watched Rossi's hysterical preparations with interest. Jealous for her small reputation, Tebaldo said that at least the theatre would be fit for his wife when Madame Bernhardt had gone! But Eleonora waved his kindness away. Gracefully, eagerly, she said that her personal dressing room was at Madame's disposal.

'Your dressing room?' cried Rossi, horrified. 'I had forgotten! Let me see it at once!'

'Oh, do please inspect it,' she said dryly, enjoying herself. 'As you observe, I have two hard chairs for visitors and a mirror on the wall above my dressing table. True, the glass is a little blotched, and the table a shade rickety, but one learns to overlook such imperfections. The iron washstand in one corner is only slightly rusty, and I have four hooks for my costumes.'

Rossi slapped his cheeks and moaned.

'How much will Madame Bernhardt draw for the boxes when she performs?' she asked shrewdly.

'Do not torment me, Nella. In her currency — perhaps a hundred francs apiece.'

'One hundred francs,' she marvelled. 'And for me they would pay the equivalent of — five.'

'I beg of you,' Rossi cried, bunching his hands at her and kissing them open, 'do not distress me further. Do not be jealous, Nella. I have many troubles. Possibly I shall go mad. You are most talented, most original — but you are not Bernhardt!'

She dismissed his remark, pushing her fringe aside, folding her arms on the back of one hard chair, surveying him.

'I can see, Cesare, that I am not Madame — only a twentieth part of her, it would seem! And they will pay this price, will they, these dull dogs we entertain?'

'Are you mad?' cried Rossi, opening his eyes to their full extent. 'They will pay twice as much. They will be standing at the back, too close to breathe. They will be fighting in the queues, bribing their friends, outwitting their enemies, cutting their mothers' throats…'

'At twenty times the price they pay to see me?'

'Please, Eleonora, please, please, be merciful!'

'I was not going to make a scene,' she said, amused, 'only to suggest that you can afford some renovations out of your coming profits.'

'But of course! Only — when I think of the theatres in which she normally plays. Paris, Berlin, London, New York…'

'The Valle in Rome…' Eleonora suggested, with a pang of heart and a glint of eye.

'Certainly, naturally, of course. Ah, who am I to entertain such magnificence in my poor little theatre?'

'Oh, *do* stop acting, Cesare — and so badly — get something done as fast as possible. Otherwise Madame might eat you up!'

She showed all her splendid teeth in a grin, and laughed in his face.

Rossi fled.

'When Madame has gone,' said Tebaldo, concerned for his wife's pride, 'you will find the theatre greatly improved — and for your benefit.'

'I don't want her to *go*!' said Eleonora, fascinated, 'I want her to *come*. I must see the woman who can cause such a commotion!'

They brushed the seats and scrubbed the boards and cleaned the draperies. They dusted and shook and washed and touched up the worst of the paint. But the theatre activity was only one ripple in Turin's pond. The hotel at which Bernhardt would stay became a hysterical hive. The station master decorated the station with flags and bunting. The city went gloriously mad.

In one day, in the space of an hour, all the seats for the entire stay — real and imaginary — were sold out. And ahead of Madame arrived her entourage of pets. Dogs, monkeys and parakeets, encouraged to make thorough nuisances of themselves, were treated like royalty. Then came a positive caravan of properties and costumes, of this and that and the other little whim or luxury, without which Madame might at best be desolate, and at worst refuse to perform.

'Goodness,' said Eleonora, intrigued, 'and what is Madame going to play first, if she *does* condescend to play?'

Rossi kissed his hands to the empty boxes.

'La Dame aux Camélias!'

'Ah!' She was silent for a moment, since Rossi would not let *her* tackle Dumas *fils*. 'Tell me,' she asked seriously, 'beneath all this flummery, what sort of person is Madame?'

'She is not a person,' said Rossi humbly, 'she is a goddess.'

'And how long,' said Eleonora, feeling insignificant, 'does it take to become a goddess?'

'Divinity has nothing to do with time,' said Rossi simply.

The company stood in a respectful palpitating line, listening to Rossi oiling Sarah's progress in the distance. Tebaldo looked anxiously at his wife, who had turned extremely pale.

'We shall soon be through with all this nonsense,' he whispered, not comprehending.

She flashed him a glance which was almost hatred.

'Please,' she whispered back sharply, 'I am trying to *concentrate*!'

He stepped away, hurt. She was sorry, but could comfort him later.

'Madame Bernhardt, I beg most respectfully to introduce my company,' said Rossi, bowing low. 'My leading lady — Signora Duse-Checchi. My second leading lady, Signorina…'

Eleonora was conscious of being dazzled and dismissed. A pair of exceedingly knowledgeable blue eyes glanced off her. A mouth, scarlet with paint, smiled and smiled at no one in particular. An extravagant aureole of frizzed red hair challenged the fights. The gown, of Parisian cut, was very young in style for Sarah's thirty-eight years, but set off her boyish figure to advantage. She glittered with jewellery, and must have been wearing a little fortune on her neck and arms alone. She was being utterly charming to Rossi, and loving every scrap of homage, every minute of playing the queen.

'We look forward,' said Rossi, 'to the unutterable honour of watching Madame's first incomparable performance!'

She laid one brilliantly ringed hand upon his arm, smiling like a tigress.

'If I am recovered after the journey,' she said tenderly. She kissed her fingers to the assembly and swept away.

'*If* she is recovered after the journey?' Rossi repeated, in a terrible whisper.

He clasped his cheeks.

One of Sarah's minions crept noiselessly back.

'Do not worry, monsieur,' he said kindly. 'Madame has never missed a performance in her life, only — she has a great sense of humour.'

Ruin receded.

Hysterical with relief, Rossi cried, 'Of course, of course. A wonderful, a superb, a marvellous sense of humour — *formidable*, in fact!'

He had never been so frightened in all his life.

The company broke ranks, while Rossi wiped his hands and forehead, chattering, exclaiming, full of adulation. Sarah had risen on them like the sun, and they warmed their hands reverently in the beams. But Eleonora moved quietly away to digest what she had seen and heard. The test of Sarah, in her mind at least, was yet to come, and she would be there to judge. *Because,* she thought, *the magnetism is so impelling, the trappings so sumptuous, that cool judgement might possibly be overlooked.* And if to be a great actress meant such a show of power then she herself could never be one. *Because,* she reminded herself, *though I may occasionally glow, I never shine.*

She said nothing to Tebaldo, who put her mood down to damaged pride and was especially patient, which she did not notice.

The Carignano held its crowd manfully, though extremely hot and pressed for space. And several minutes late, just to make sure that they were all humbled and ready, Sarah allowed the curtain to go up.

Even before she spoke a change came over Eleonora's face. The magnetism drew all eyes to Sarah: scarlet mouth laughing, blue eyes crinkling, her fantasy head aflame with hair. And then she spoke and the theatre became absolutely still. Her voice was first of all a pleasure to the ears, a warm lucid golden flow which made one long to listen, without caring what was said. But she had worked on that initial gift until she commanded a most magnificent instrument, which soothed and tore, and pierced them with joy, and drowned them with sorrow, and lost them somewhere beyond the baroque ceiling. She used them without mercy. In the death scene she was possibly the only person in the theatre with dry eyes.

The number of curtain calls was prodigious, becoming almost another play, with Sarah in lonely grandeur, occasionally requiring the strong arm of her leading man. Eleonora observed Sarah's showmanship wistfully. Each rise of the curtain revealed that arrow-like figure standing perfectly still, hands on cheeks or clasped under her chin, gasping from her exertions. And as the audience burst upon her, wildly applauding, she extended her arms straight before her in gratitude. Never for one instant did she allow them to forget she had bankrupted her strength in their service. The leading man was kept, barely visible, in the wings. And as she faltered towards him he supported her for a few moments, and then returned her inexorably to her adorers. And each time she did return, somehow, until the last foot had ceased to stamp, and the last pair of palms struck ecstatically together, and the last hoarse cries of *'Brava!'* and *'Viva!'* rung through the house.

The people of Turin might meander along to see the local talent, but they knew how to treat an international star. The stage looked like a flower shop, and from her sea of blooms Sarah rose, a modern Venus, weeping with surprise and pleasure. Flowers, she intimated, had never come her way before. And even after the final curtain the show was not yet over. The outside of the theatre became as packed with spectators as the inside had been — and Sarah, apparently at point of death, gave herself up once more to her public. The horses were unharnessed from her carriage and a score of young men escorted her to the hotel, where later — in response to further acclaim — she showed herself upon the balcony, and kissed her hands to them all.

'Please don't speak to me!' Eleonora said to Tebaldo, as the last curtain fell. 'I cannot come back so quickly.'

He respected her wishes, as always.

Each night Turin begged to be massacred, with any play Sarah chose. And each night Eleonora sat in her seat and marvelled and watched and wept. On the last night she begged an interview with Madame, though the crush at the dressing room door nearly turned her back. But Sarah, feeling kind, sent everyone else out and allowed Rossi's leading lady a private word, with Rossi to translate.

Eleonora faced the cerulean eyes, the scarlet smile, the tired woman beneath the paint, and went down on her knees.

'Oh, do get up!' said Sarah, good-natured.

'Madame,' said Eleonora, trembling, 'I beg of you. I cannot pay homage sitting. Madame, you have taken possession of us. You have honoured Turin with your presence. You have played with superb artistry. You will go away like a great ship, leaving a wake behind you that will never be forgotten. And do you know what I thought, Madame, while I watched you?' she cried, putting out her hands in a gesture of humility. 'I thought — a woman has achieved all this. A woman has made Turin into a living, breathing audience with her great art...'

'You are very gracious, Signora.'

'But above all, Madame,' cried Eleonora, fired, 'you have given me courage. You have released me. In my small way I have tried to free myself. Now I know I was right in what I sought and what I dreamed. The theatre must breathe, Madame. We must not go on playing the same mediocre plays, we must have courage. I beg your pardon,' said Eleonora, suddenly diverted, 'that I am unable to speak your language, but I shall learn it, if only because it is your own.'

'You are most charming!' said Sarah, touched. 'Most charming. Thank you, Signora.'

She held out her hand, which Eleonora kissed reverently. The audience was over.

'Now that's a nice little woman,' Sarah said to Rossi. 'What did you say her name was?'

'Signora Duse-Checchi, Madame.'

'She'd better stick to the Duse bit — the other's a mouthful.'

'Signor Checchi is her husband, Madame.'

'Well, she'll either change her ideas or her husband,' Sarah commented.

Luminous, wet-cheeked, Eleonora placed both arms round Rossi's fat neck and said, 'Oh, Cesare! I quite forgot to tell Madame how wonderful I thought she was as Marguerite Gautier. I went every evening — and cried!'

'All good things come to an end,' said Rossi gloomily, as the last parrot rolled off across the continent with Sarah. 'I suppose we must make the best of it.'

He patted his thighs and brooded, twisting his moustache. He found himself in the unenviable position of a man who has conducted a national orchestra, and is now reduced to the fumblings of the local brass band.

By his side, though rapt in her personal vision, Eleonora read his thoughts accurately. Touching his arm, she said impishly, 'Lift up your eyes, Signor! *I* am here!'

'I know you are, my dove, my lamb!' he replied, patting her absent-mindedly. 'I'll tell you what,' he said hopefully. 'We'll rehearse a new play. You were quite right, Nella, the old ones have been done to death. What about a little something by Gherardi del Testa? *The Reign of Adelaide*, for instance!'

Her eyes narrowed. A note of Sarah sounded in her soft voice. 'It will be Lionette in the *Princesse de Bagdad* — or nothing!' she said firmly.

'But that would be unheard of — the most difficult of roles — only Bernhardt has attempted it successfully. And Croizette was hissed off the stage in Paris. And after Bernhardt — another Dumas *fils* seems cheeky. Surely?'

'She didn't play the *Princesse* here!'

'She plays Dumas *fils* better than anyone in the world. But you…'

'I intend to play the part of Lionette.'

'Hissed off the stage! *Hissed* off! Sophie Croizette, mark you. La Croizette. Not Eleonora Duse-Checchi — La Croizette. Hissed off!'

'Another good reason for doing it.'

Astounded, he stopped gesticulating.

'I want the *Princesse de Bagdad*,' Eleonora repeated inexorably, 'and if I do not have that play, and others of my choice…' She swept one arm in a superb arc, indicating that all would be over. 'I leave the company!'

Rossi shouted in hysterical wrath, 'And where will you go, Signora? Where will you go?'

'*Chi lo sa*, Signor Rossi?' she said, enjoying a flash of power. 'Who knows?'

He said, shrugging, 'I can only be ruined once. I am not rich enough to be ruined twice. Do as you please.'

Left with her own way and sole responsibility, she was very frightened. But she set herself to study the play minutely, knowing some of the pitfalls, sensing others. Her literary and artistic faculties were not yet sufficiently developed to carry her over all theatrical shoals, and to a major extent she relied upon instinct. So, revering the name of Dumas *fils*, she did not see the hollowness of the play, the reliance upon dramatics rather than genuine character-building and genuine emotion. Yet she knew she must convey the drama in some subtler way than by ranting. In the key scene, where Lionette attempts to prove her innocence, Croizette had ranted, her voice rising to a crescendo of 'I swear it! I swear it! I swear it!' delivered at top pitch, in a great clarion call. It was at this point that the Parisians hissed her off the stage.

Eleonora flung down her script and paced her apartment, putting her hands to her temples, muttering disconnected phrases of self-reproach.

'*Why* do I do it? *How* do I do it? What a *fool*! What an *idiot*! Oh, so superb, so clever. Bernhardt plays Lionette, so this unknown one can play it! Of course. What folly, what arrogance, what pride!'

She sat down again, her feet propped on another chair, the play in her lap, trying out the sound and shape of phrases, her ear cocked to test the note of truth, of conviction.

Sarah had done much for her already, and was to do more. When Rossi groaned at the rehearsals of *Princesse*, Eleonora drew herself up. Tartly, she said, 'You should know by this time, Signor Rossi, that my rehearsals are only makeshift affairs while I find my way. If you wish to employ some other actress with a method more to your liking — please do so!'

He was silenced.

Turin was amazed. Enslaved by Sarah, they found the prospect of little Duse-Checchi falling flat on her face, in one of the goddess's most difficult roles, too entertaining to miss. They flocked to the Carignano for the first night, almost in Sarah-numbers, and continued to flock for very different reasons.

Sarah had sustained the play by force of personality. Duse-Checchi made it credible. She took Croizette's unlucky scene very quietly, with fervour rather than volume. Twice she cried from the heart, 'I swear it! I swear it!' and then, turning to her small son who stood near her, placed one hand lovingly upon his head and with utmost simplicity said, 'I swear it.'

Rossi accepted the congratulations of Turin, and the personal letters to himself and Eleonora from Dumas *fils*, with a wave of his cigar and several chuckles. To all those who expressed astonishment he was condescending.

'No, no, no,' he said, shaking his head from side to side, incredulous at their lack of perception. 'I always said so! But one must let her have her own head, you know. That's the secret of handling her. Let her have her head!'

The Carignano became, in its provincial way, quite a Mecca for the faithful in the next months.

'So we tour,' Rossi stated. 'Turin must bewail your absence, Nella. It will whet their appetite for our return. And we tour. Venice, Milan, Florence…'

'Rome?' she asked hopefully.

'We shall see. At Rome the big lions live. We must make sure you are a Daniel first, before we try those teeth!'

'I should love to play at Rome,' she said childishly. Her chin set. 'I *shall* play at Rome!'

Each town, each city, was a little victory. In the great wake of Sarah sailed the small ship of the Compagnia Carignano, finally broaching Rome itself as Bernhardt was winding up her Italian tour in the September of 1882. Fired by the prospect of playing at the Teatro Valle, ambitious, fearful, obstinate, Eleonora added a new role to others in her repertoire, another Dumas *fils* failure — *La Femme de Claude*. Rossi held his breath.

Humbly he said, 'I trust in you, Nella, but only Desclée succeeded in this part — and even then they didn't like the play! May I not beg you to wait until we are home again? Turin loves you. In Rome you are just another stranger.'

He sighed and shrugged at the obstinate mouth, the fanatical eyes.

Seeing only what she wanted him to see, Tebaldo said fondly, 'You will have Desclée's dressing room, Nella. Think of that!'

And in an instant the impending storm cleared, became a harmless mood of the moment. Sparkling, laughing, she linked arms with Rossi and Tebaldo, smiling into their faces.

'What an omen!' she cried, delighted. 'I am to have Desclée's dressing room. I shall breathe the same air, play on the same stage as she did. Ah, poor Desclée is dead, but the dead help the living, truly. My mother has always helped me — or I shouldn't be here today.'

'Of course, you are right!' said her husband fondly.

'I pray God and the Virgin Mary and all the saints in heaven that she is!' said Rossi.

She started from her sleep in terror, and lay awake oppressed. Always the new role began in formless darkness and she felt her way blind.

'You will be a great success,' said Tebaldo. 'You will be a very great actress. I know it.'

She laid her head upon her knees, wrapped her arms about them, uncomforted.

'So alone,' she said. 'Always so alone.'

'Not alone, Nella. I am here.'

She gnawed a knuckle savagely, staring through a black curtain of hair.

'I am *always* alone!' she said imperiously.

He smiled upon her, wrapping a shawl about her chilled shoulders, making coffee in the early hours.

On the first night the theatre was almost empty. A scattering of students and youngsters applauded vociferously and stamped their feet as the curtain ran up. In the wings, having spent the day on water, Eleonora stood white and sick.

'Cesare,' she said at last, 'I am very much afraid.'

She was not nearly so afraid as himself, but he kissed her hands.

'You will be magnificent,' he replied.

The students received her rapturously. She had followed Pezzana's advice on physical suppleness and the use of body and limbs to express emotions. Though not particularly tall, her bearing gave her the illusion of height. And she could bend backwards, arms outflung, in a pose almost acrobatic. To the part of Césarine she brought the splendour of a queen and the feelings of a woman. And on the second night the Teatro Valle filled, and Rossi turned many away, drawing their attention to the fact that Signora Duse-Checchi would be playing on other nights. They came, and the Prince Napoléon, mindful of that other actress who had died the year Eleonora was born, said quietly to himself, 'Rachel!' as Eleonora crossed and re-crossed the stage.

But in her dressing room she laid her head on her arms and wept.

'Brilliant!' cried Rossi, cried Checchi, cried the company, cried the spectators to each other outside.

Eleonora shook her head to rid herself of them and the performance. She had put on a wonderful display, and the centre was empty.

'I captured their admiration — not their hearts!' she said, and as Rossi flung up his hands and signalled astonishment with his eyebrows she said to herself, 'It is not enough to be accomplished. Tonight I broke some law within me.'

Rossi was too busy counting the takings. And Tebaldo walked up and down the entrance of the Teatro Valle, savouring the size and blackness of the letters that made up his wife's name.

Still they came, and so did the critics. And this time she attempted the role with fewer histrionics, emphasising the woman in Césarine: weeping, suffering, loving.

In the end she could not find her way back through the shout of joy that greeted her curtain calls. The Bernhardt method of receiving rapture could never be her own. The flowers blurred and shivered before her eyes. She was grateful for the supporting arms which led her forward. Tears of real exhaustion shone in her eyes. So she stood before the footlights, remote and withdrawn, brows lifted to give a semblance of composure, and let the waves break over her.

The Marchese Francesco d'Arcais, editor of the Roman daily *L'Opinione*, reviewed her wonderfully well, and gave a reception in her honour. Students unharnessed the horses from her carriage and drew her home with torches and plaudits. She lived in a daze of flowers and praise and felt the ground move beneath her in warning. With her usual courtesy she sat down and wrote to thank d'Arcais and the other reviewers. Recognising, in him particularly, a fineness of appreciation and an understanding of her aims, she wrote with the same frankness that she would have written to Matilde.

I must work, she scrawled across the paper, scoring the t-strokes, and underlining for emphasis. *I must find release from an inner longing. My love for art is too great, and so is my jealousy of it.* She paused, and was honest, setting egoism by the side of altruism. *For I desire it should be mine, mine in feeling, in spirit, in expression, in scope. Woe betide me if it were not so.*

She recollected that first night of *La Femme de Claude*, when technique had made a fool of feeling.

I should be able easily to indulge my hopes, but my inner satisfaction would soon be over. Then I should feel no longer this dissatisfaction which does me good, the desire that haunts me, the longing for help such as I need from you now.

She faced her failings, the knowledge that display was not art, that showmanship could blind herself and her audience to defects of portrayal. She knew that she must somehow accomplish the hardest thing of all: forget herself in the pursuit of something she could not define, but so far saw as art.

Humbly she wrote, *For I am terrified lest I take the wrong way.*

As though with this remark she let loose temptation, the flesh and the devil appeared before her in different forms.

First, Joseph Schürmann, Bernhardt's own impresario, sat in the theatre one evening, his chest glittering with medals. He had watched Eleonora's faithful attendance on Sarah with amusement. Now he watched her own performance with interest, and craved a private word. She sat at her dressing table and listened, playing with the red silk scarf of Césarine.

'Allow me, Signora,' said Schürmann, 'to arrange a European tour for you. I have some little influence.' He inflated his glittering chest.

'Signor Schürmann,' she said composedly, 'you are deceiving either yourself or me. I am not ready for Europe. Besides, I speak only Italian. It would take a genius to surmount the difficulties of a foreign audience as well as the role. I do not possess that genius.'

He was even more interested.

'But you are ambitious, Signora? Do not deny it. You are gentle, courteous, but you are also very ambitious — otherwise, why all these Lionettes and Césarines in the face of public opinion?'

'I am very ambitious,' she said, tired, 'but I am not a fool, Signor. I am not yet ready for a European tour.'

Secondly, a very young man waylaid her in the wings one night.

'Gabriele D'Annunzio, Signora,' he said, lingering over the syllables. 'A poor poet, at your service.'

'Oh, but your poems are beautiful,' she replied courteously, trying to recollect what she had heard of them and him. 'You are very much loved and pampered by a great friend of mine, Edoardo Scarfoglio,' she said, as he continued to gaze on her. 'I believe he helped you to establish your present position on his journal, *Capitan Fracassa*.'

Still he looked at her with his hypnotic light eyes, almost feminine in their beauty. The down on his cheek could scarcely be called a beard. His fox-brush hair seemed alive, his lips were as soft and red as those of a girl.

'All Rome knows of your poems,' said Eleonora kindly, but she was a little tired, and wished that he would speak and go. 'You are quite the rage. I, too, admire the pagan loveliness of the Greeks, who obviously inspire your work. Though I am afraid you are rather a wicked and precocious young celebrity!' she finished teasingly, looking round for Tebaldo, who would surely rescue her from this silent admirer.

Catching up her hands and pressing them to his lips he whispered, 'Make love with me!'

'Signor?' said Eleonora, incredulous, remembering other rumours about him.

'We should make a heaven of even one night,' he whispered. 'You and I, Signora. I sense that you are a woman of many passions — some of them unfulfilled...'

'You know nothing of me!' she cried, enraged, and tried to pull her hands away as he kissed them rapidly and lightly on back and palm.

His blue-green eyes were uncannily shrewd, piercing through her husband's bread-and-butter love-making, stirring feelings that only Cafiero had aroused. Eleonora's first impulse had been to laugh at this girlish youth whose reputation for lechery was keeping pace with his poetry. But now she was terrified to find in herself a response to his impudence; a longing to go with him now, anywhere, and let him take her like a whore.

'Let me be, Signor!' she demanded, softly and emphatically. 'I am not interested in your proposition. You do not know to whom you are talking. You are impertinent.'

She hurried away from him to reach the security of her dressing room, and then trembled and wept for some time afterwards, remembering.

Lastly, the most seductive homage of all, honest homage. Accompanied by her leading actor she stood up in the carriage and waved her handkerchief to the crowd who had come to say farewell.

'*A rivederci!*' they cried. 'Long live Duse! Long live our Duse!'

One very young man in the press moistened his lips, staring as though he would devour her. He almost drank in the white face, the crown of black hair, the tremor on the mouth. She did not see him. She was reminding herself that she must not be carried away by adulation.

'Oh, thank you, thank you!' she called, as the students prepared to pull her homewards for the last time, and a procession of flaring torches lined up behind the carriage to follow her.

With the shyness of Angelica she cried, 'It's too much, you know. I don't deserve it!'

TEN

Tranquility cloaked her in Turin.

'You are happy because you are home again!' said Rossi, sentimental with pleasure.

She smiled at him.

'I am happy, she said, 'because Tebaldo and I are expecting a child.' Then, seeing his face fall and try to right itself into congratulation, she laid her hand on his. 'I shall work as long as I can, and be back as soon as I can. But the rest will do me good, Cesare. I am not well again.'

She sat down on a property basket.

'There is a cold that I cannot shake off,' she said worriedly. 'A cough that my mother used to have. You must have noticed, Cesare, that I have no voice left after a performance. At night I fling off the covers and dream wildly and feverishly, so that Tebaldo wakes up. Ah, such dreams! And such headaches! And the other night, back from the theatre, I looked up our flight of stairs and it seemed long and steep enough to take me to heaven. In the end Tebaldo carried me up because I had no more strength.'

Rossi's concern was doubled.

'Pregnancy has these effects, too,' he assured her, knowing she was concerned about her lungs. 'You simply need more rest.'

But she was worrying, sitting on the property basket, hands in lap, thinking.

'Bernhardt suffers from tuberculosis,' she said, comforting herself.

She lay for hours in a long bamboo chair, a shawl about her shoulders, a rug over her legs, a series of cushions at her back; turning over the pages of a book, dozing off, growing heavier, losing her tensions.

The baby was a girl, and Eleonora exclaimed over the perfection of fingers and toes, naming her Enrichetta. For weeks they were caught up, one with the other, the baby sleeping in her basket, Eleonora reclining in her long chair.

'Tebaldo, I don't want Enrichetta to go on the stage. We can earn enough, you and I, to give her something better than that.'

She had voiced a wish that her own mother cherished, until she had seen Eleonora walk on to a stage at the age of four, clinging to the hand of an aunt.

'As you will,' said Tebaldo, content to please her, busy enough with the career of one actress.

'She must be brought up in the country and grow fat. But near us, near Turin, so that we can see her often. We shall find good people to take care of her, and pay them well.'

She ruffled the pages of the book in her lap, her face registering losses of the past.

'She shall go to a good school, then to a finishing school. She shall be properly educated. She shall be a lady, Tebaldo.'

'Whatever you say, Nella.'

'No one will point a finger at *her*,' said Eleonora.

A ragged child in bright clothes scuttled home to the lodging house, pursued by cries of *Figlia di commediante! Figlia di commediante!*

'She shall always be warm and well-clothed,' said Eleonora.

A child pulled her coat up to her chin, cold beneath the thin blanket.

'She shall never go hungry.'

A child stole polenta, giggling and afraid, scooping her fingers round the bowl to catch up the last scraps.

'She will have everything I always wanted. Enrichetta.'

As Tebaldo stroked the baby's head, Eleonora reached for his hand and put it to her cheek, and then to the baby's cheek, in gratitude.

But Rossi fretted as the weeks passed, tempting her with new roles and old flattery. Unmoved, she lay in her bamboo chair or sat on a rug on the grass in the sun, nursing her child and herself. Tebaldo, loving and solicitous, added his pleas to those of Rossi. She attempted to explain.

'You see I am not well yet, though I'm so much stronger — it's as though all the wrinkles were taking time to iron out. And I am content here. I want to remain content. Besides, away from the theatre I'm such a *good* person — haven't you noticed?'

He said, laughing with and at her, that she was the source of all goodness to him.

'No, Teo,' she said, near tears. 'I am better here with the child. All my life I have travelled, I must sit and do nothing for a little while longer, just for a little. I sit here hour after hour while Enrichetta sleeps, watching the mountains and the sky, and I become so wise, Teo. Did you know I could be wise? I begin to realise what life is all about. I see myself and the whole world as though we were at the wrong end of a telescope — very small, and miles away. I fly above everything like an angel, just as I used to when I was a child on the roof looking at the stars. And I'm filled with pity, Teo. I know in those moments, as in no others, that God is just, that even the most wretched existence has meaning — something, I might tell you, that I've often doubted! And it's like being in heaven. So just a little longer, Teo.'

He was sympathetic, but practical, and eventually obdurate.

'Are you forgetting yourself?' he asked, as she still clung to her long convalescence. 'Turin is waiting for you. Italy is waiting for you. Rossi wants to show you off, and so do I. You can't stay at home with the baby like other women. Give Cesare a date for your return — and rouse yourself, my darling. Enrichetta can stay here with these good people, and grow happy and fat without you.'

'I want,' she said, trembling, 'to be fat and happy *with* her.'

He said, 'Her future depends upon you, and all those fine schools will be daydreams if you stay much longer. Rossi is willing to take you on as a partner in the company.'

She turned away her head without answering.

But the next day she said, 'You can tell Cesare that I am ready to come back at the end of the week.' Her eyes lit with anger, she added, 'You know, of course, that I shall be a devil again when I start work?'

He shook his head, smiling.

'Yes, I shall,' she said, softer and sadder. 'I shall leave my country self behind with Enrichetta. I shall wake you up in the middle of the night, terrified because I don't know how to utter some solitary line. I shall rage at you and at Cesare over nothing. I shall be, at times, disgracefully rude to everybody. I shall put all of myself into each performance, and come offstage frozen and sick with tiredness. And on some of these days, Tebaldo, I shall have pushed myself too far and then you will see how ill I really am. You and Rossi set it down to temper, I know. But I have seen my mother with this weakness of the lungs. I know how it can be. But what is the use of telling you? I am quite alone!'

He said, 'You are never alone, Nella. I am always with you.'

She did not answer, looking in on some troubled image of herself. But an hour later she was full of new ventures.

'Tell Cesare that now I am a partner I shall put on new plays, original plays, plays that will frighten him to death! Tell him that I intend to produce Verga's *Cavalleria rusticana*, with myself as Santuzza. Tell him *that*!'

Rossi, rejoicing in her imminent return, said, 'She can paint herself black and play Othello in English if she wants to!'

Every parting was anguish. Rended by the tearful farewells over the child's head, Tebaldo nevertheless perceived that life was serving as fuel for art.

Rossi received her with flowers and condolences.

'She has suffered a great deal,' Tebaldo whispered.

Rossi's eyes shone shrewd and black and bland. 'But of course,' he whispered back, understanding. 'Of course she has. We must give her a change of scene, new audiences, fresh places. We must give her something damned difficult to set her lovely teeth in and hold on!'

To her, standing mute and white, he spoke in hushed reverence, insisting that she went straight to bed.

'I shall take no script with me!' she cried.

'I forbid you to take even the smallest look at a script,' said Rossi.

'And I have been thinking,' she continued, 'that my performances in *La Femme de Claude* were monstrous. Quite monstrous and overdone.'

'And yet the Prince whispered "Rachel" when you stormed across the stage!' said Tebaldo unwisely.

'Stormed? Stormed? Yes, you are perfectly right. I *did* storm. I over-acted atrociously. I betrayed myself. I caught them with professional tricks!'

'The house rose with one great shout when you finished that scene…'

Heavy-mouthed, she replied, 'I caught them with trickery. I did not play from the heart.'

Tebaldo began to speak again, but Rossi gestured silence and his tone was smooth. 'Next time, Nella, you *will* play from the heart. But now, I beg of you, rest a little.'

Tearing out her hat pins and casting them at his feet, she cried, 'I shall never play that part again. Never, never, never!'

'Certainly not,' said Rossi, knowing her better than she knew herself. 'I shall strike it from the company repertoire.'

Later, keeping very quiet over a bottle of Barbola in the next room, they heard her trying over and over again the lines she felt she had misconstrued. Patient, admiring, Tebaldo clicked his tongue between his teeth and reached for his newspaper with relish.

On a bitter January evening in 1884, Giovanni Verga, too afraid to go near the theatre, sat at a café table near the Carignano waiting for news of his play. The applause reached him before his friends could, and he stood like a sleepwalker as they ran across the snow to clasp his hands and beat his shoulders in good fellowship. Signora Duse-Checchi wanted him to join her on the stage and share the success. He paid for his drinks and hurried back with them.

She was triumphant in her weariness, reaching out her hand to pull him into the bower of bouquets.

Recovering, as they applauded him too, Verga said quite sincerely, '*Cavalleria* belongs more to you than to me!'

It was a night of looking into the future and back to the past. Arrigo Boito begged to pay his compliments. She remembered his name being mentioned by Cafiero, five years before, at the Scarfoglios' dinner table. She stared at his blond hair and high cheekbones, inherited from a Polish mother, and charmed him almost mechanically. But Boito, Verdi's librettist and ex-leader of the *Scapigliatura* – the movement known as 'the unkempt ones' – had put away unkemptness as his literary stature grew. He courted, she flirted, but afterwards Tebaldo – who never missed a tremor – asked her what was wrong.

'I fell in love with his green eyes!' she cried, opening her own, laughing.

'For a moment I thought he reminded you of someone. I saw you shiver.'

Inwardly damning his watchfulness, she said lightly, 'A goose must have passed over my grave — that's all!'

Giovanni Emanuel, her former director at Naples, had been playing opposite her, but he left for another engagement. Into his place slipped an actor a little less subtle, but quite as polished and more handsome. His name was Flavio Andò, and he was adored and admired by female audiences.

'We must give the part of Turiddu to Flavio,' said Eleonora, making the most of her new eminence. She surveyed his beauty with impish satisfaction. 'I'm sure he will make a marvellously unfaithful lover!'

Her teasing covered an uncomfortable personal moment. Just for a few seconds she had felt herself shiver in his stage embrace, felt his arms tighten, felt the theatre rock pleasurably about her, and recovered. Her husband was good to her, her daughter deeply loved, and a lifetime of work lay ahead. She must, she reflected, keep Flavio at a seemly distance. And yet in those few moments she had experienced a return of Neapolitan nights with Cafiero.

To quieten her conscience she praised Tebaldo extravagantly for his portrayal of Alfio in the play. He pondered her words with bewildered satisfaction. He had done his best, as usual, but surely nothing more?

'Not a town in Italy,' said Count Primoli, elegant in her hotel room, eyes half-closed with pleasure, 'not a single town that has not heard of you or seen you, Signora. Success upon success. Known by thousands. And now Dumas *fils*, mindful of your great performances in *La Princesse de Bagdad* and *La Femme de Claude*, has written a new play and sent it to me, hoping you will find yourself able to illuminate the role. Yes, that is the word — illuminate.'

'What is this play?' Eleonora asked, eyebrows raised.

'*Denise*, Signora.'

She was very fond of the Count, and his air of ease and worldliness infected her. Without knowing it, she became in his presence easier and more worldly herself. Reclining on one elbow, she waved a hand as her signal for the reading to begin, and prepared graciously to listen. Count Primoli adjusted his eye-glass and smiled to himself, knowing of some incident in her past that Dumas *fils* did not — and had, by chance, most happily hit upon.

The restless fingers clasped and unclasped, smoothed her dress nervously. Her eyebrows came together in a dark frown. The Count smoothed his whiskers with pleasure, and read on. First act, second act, third act.

But she has lost a son, thought Eleonora, and was suddenly still. The Count read well, with sufficient feeling to set free her own interpretation. She watched him, moving her lips, eyes glittering. Sprang to her feet and paced up and down, twisting her handkerchief, wringing her fingers. Then disappeared behind a screen. The Count still read, imagining those tormented hands and eyes, and as he finished the scene his reading was punctuated by suppressed sobs. He smiled, knowing she would accept the play.

They began rehearsals in Rome in the spring of 1884. Driven by the memory of that first dead child, Duse drove herself also. Sleeping badly, running a slight temperature in the evenings, raving at Rossi, snapping at Tebaldo, she pulled the part to pieces and rebuilt it. An unrehearsed collapse in her big scene surprised no one. Respectfully they waited as she raised herself uncertainly from the floor. Waited for the outcome of this new idea, expecting her to writhe and moan and abandon herself in staged grief. Then Tebaldo ran forward, horrified. She was coughing up blood, on her splayed hands, down her white dress, over the dusty boards. They wiped her face and mouth, lifted her on to a couch, called a doctor.

Count Primoli dipped his pen into the ink and composed a letter to Dumas: *Yesterday she was very near leaving this world, and even today it is not certain that she will live.* But Eleonora improved, drawn back to life by the thought of the première. Outwardly she lay white and listless, but inwardly the force which discounted health and circumstance demanded that she get up and work. To Tebaldo, hovering at her elbow, she said dryly, 'I can die later. Just now I haven't the time.'

Conserving her energy, she crept back to rehearsal. The company clapped spontaneously at her first appearance, and were further mollified by her mildness.

Rome expected much, and was not to be disappointed. For five nights, sustained by champagne and cognac and a vigilant husband, she played Denise with fire and pathos. They applauded the paper face and smudged eyes, demanded her back, curtain after curtain.

A double knock, subdued but demanding, on the door of her dressing room, roused her. Rossi and her husband tiptoed into the room.

'There is such a crowd outside the window,' Rossi whispered, 'going quite mad for you, Nella. Look here, my dove, if Teo and I take an arm each you can show yourself to them.'

She moaned and shook her head wearily from side to aide.

'Only for a moment,' Tebaldo pressed her. 'You need say nothing, my darling. Just appear for them. Listen! They are begging for you.'

Smiling, wrapped in their own worlds, they took her arms, led her unresisting to the window and threw it open. The crowd surged forward as though they would touch her. She heard her name called over and over again: unsmiling, shivering, swaying in the grip of the two men, the death of her son and of Denise's son still upon her.

A face formed on the blank wall opposite and she frowned slightly, trying to bring it into focus. It was small and toothless and grey as an old man. Had she been alone she would have shrieked aloud, but she was bound to her public. For a few moments longer she gazed, and then fell forward in the arms of her two cavaliers.

She held Rome captive for nine more days, then collapsed again. Hearing the doctor say she must rest for a long time, and hearing Tebaldo mention the mountains of Piedmont and small Enrichetta — who was being despatched to comfort her mother — Eleonora wept with relief. The lights of the city could burn on without her. In the next few months she caught up with herself. She wrote to her friends of the landscape, the weather, and her own thoughts. To her admirer and critic d'Arcais she scrawled:

It's a heavy day, it rains and rains and rains. The mountain seems to be coming nearer under the rain, and the valley of Ivrea and of Chiusella is nothing but mist... The poor women in the plays I have acted so get into my heart and mind that I have to think out the best way of making them understood by my audience — as if I were trying to comfort them. In the end they comfort me! And though everyone else may distrust women I understand them perfectly. I don't bother whether they have lied, betrayed, sinned or been lost from their birth, once I feel they have wept and suffered, whether sinning or lying or betraying, I stand by them. I stand for them. And I burrow, burrow into them — not because of my thirst for suffering, but because woman's capacity for sympathy is greater and more many-sided, gentler and more perfect than man's.

She learned French, becoming fluent, but never losing her faint Italian accent.

'The next time I meet Madame Bernhardt,' she explained, excited, 'I can address her courteously in her own language.'

She was calmer, happier, not working. Tebaldo's references to her return brought a passion of tears.

'How can you talk of it?' she cried. 'When I think I must go back to that distracted and chaotic life I feel such *pity* for myself. I have almost forgotten the stage. *Acting!* What an ugly word! And yet,' she added honestly, beginning to know herself and her divided nature, 'I may well be the first to want to go back!'

Then she spent the afternoon on the carpet, playing with Enrichetta.

'Such a little creature,' she murmured into the soft short neck, 'aren't you, my baby?'

And she knelt up on her couch for hours, face in hands, staring out at the mountains.

'What are you doing now, Nella?'

'Oh — supporting my elbows and my thoughts on the window ledge! Do you remember Gabriele D'Annunzio asking me to sleep with him? I read his *Intermezzo di Rime* the other day — it was quite as sickening as himself! I saw him again in Rome just before I was ill. He was walking arm in arm with his wife. She was the daughter of the Duke di Gallese, you remember, and a friend of Matilde, and there was a most terrible scandal before they married. A nurse was walking behind them holding their baby son. And D'Annunzio is hardly twenty-one!'

'You say his poems sicken you?'

She made a face. 'He was so astonished at their bad reception that he tried to excuse himself. He said the poems were not pornographic, they were the result of a temporary mental weakness! *I* found them destructive of love, *and* decadent.'

'And does the illustrious Boito sicken you, too?' asked Tebaldo, amused.

She threw back her head, running her hands through her hair, smiling.

'Promise me you won't shoot him for being a little in love with me!' she said.

'I expect every man to be in love with you,' he replied gently. 'I should perhaps shoot them if they were not!'

'Promise me you won't be jealous!' Eleonora demanded, queenly, knowing that he was not. 'I was in my green *frappé* velvet dress,' she reminded him, and narrowed her eyes. 'Who could have resisted me?'

Tebaldo chuckled, prepared to fall in with every mood.

'The scoundrel asked for your picture, and in your husband's presence. In the presence of your leading man!' he said, joining in, playing his part.

She was smiling, shining. 'He wrote to thank me, and said there was no need to answer. So at once I answered, and said how *very* politely he had shown me the door. But, I added, it would be so much nicer if he sent me some small souvenir. A photograph of anything — Milan cathedral, if he liked. And he sent — please bring my box, Teo, and I'll show you.'

'You must rest, Nella,' he said. 'Lie on the sofa and I will cover you. Then you shall show me.'

She yawned, losing strength and vivacity in seconds, her eyes beginning to close even as he carried the box reverently to her.

'Here we are, see? I had written to him, *May is on the wane — how sad a thing!* And by return he sent me the May page from a French calendar. A fluffy yellow chicken, see how sweet! And a four-line verse which made a play on the French *"mai"* and the Italian *"mai"* which means "ever". Now isn't that pretty?'

'And how is this great love affair progressing?' asked Tebaldo, tidying the box of souvenirs and putting it neatly away.

'Oh, dear me!' said Eleonora, eyebrows raised. 'It seems, like May, to have waned!'

'These fiery matters soon flare up and out,' said Tebaldo sensibly.

She was back at work too soon, drawn by the bait of her success with *Denise*. But in October one old fiery matter flared up with frightening abandon. Cafiero died while she was acting at the Valle in Rome. Instinctively, Tebaldo left a note for the maid, telling her to keep the morning papers out of sight. Then, fearful that she must learn the news anyway, he asked a young friend of theirs to spend the afternoon with her while he himself kept tactfully out of the way.

Edouard Rheinhardt arrived to find Eleonora huddled in a

shawl at one end of her couch, feet tucked beneath her, eyes dark and pathetic.

'My dearest Eleonora…' he began.

She threw herself into his arms, ugly with grief, sobbing, 'I read that note before she did. I read the papers. I read all the papers.'

Throughout that afternoon, while Tebaldo walked the streets of Rome and nursed his own trouble, Eleonora relived the affair of 1879. Rheinhardt was young, devoted and wholly trustworthy. He encouraged her to talk and sob herself out. And as the time approached for her evening performance she seemed for the first time to compose herself, touched his cheek, said, 'Edouard, dear dear Edouard. Thank you. Thank you a thousand times.'

He ordered coffee for them both, saying gently, 'Eleonora, how *good* Tebaldo has been!'

She recollected her husband, and looked about her for that self-effacing man who respected every mood and whim, supported her weaknesses of health and temper, served her and thanked her for the service. She wept again, only quietly this time, and for him.

ELEVEN

Eleonora was ill again that winter. She fled to the country and turned her face away when Tebaldo spoke of work. She played with Enrichetta and sat for hours with a book open in her lap, looking out on the Tuscan hills.

'Better now,' she would say. 'Much, much better. Out of the dust and the noise. Away from people. I'll never go back, Teo. We must manage somehow, the three of us.'

He waited with obdurate patience, and early in 1885 placed a petition before her, signed by Rossi and every member of the company. Only his name was absent. She read it through, troubled.

'A contract for a tour of South America, *dolcezza*,' he said, 'but only if you go with the company.'

'It is not *fair*!' she cried passionately. 'Not fair, Teo!'

'You are too good an actress to let poor Rossi down,' he said. 'You cannot lose them such an opportunity. And, mark this, Nella, South America has stipulated *your* presence — not Andò's, for all that his reputation is so great. Besides,' he added, 'you can open in Rio de Janeiro with *Fédora*, think of that!'

He coaxed her as an artist, flattered her as a woman, to draw her back again.

'The Adriatic spring has wafted two new loves into your orbit,' he said, paying laborious compliment while they rehearsed for the closing season in Trieste. 'You have conquered not only the handsome Flavio but the young Diotti too!'

'Flavio courts every woman,' she observed dryly, 'and Diotti is merely another dear baby of mine.'

'But the handsomest actor in Italy at your feet, Nella!'

'Poof!' she cried, not displeased.

At the final rehearsal of *Fédora* an occupational hazard occurred, and Tebaldo tapped the leading man on his broad shoulder.

'Pardon, Signor,' he said stiffly. 'May I beg of you not to hold my wife quite so closely?'

'A thousand pardons, Signor,' Andò replied blandly. 'Your wife acts so divinely that for the moment she carried me away!'

He took Eleonora into his arms again, and continued the scene.

'You seem a little breathless, Nella,' said Tebaldo, placing her mantle exactly.

'It's my lungs!' she cried angrily. 'My poor lungs, labouring away for you — so that you and Rossi can drive me to death on these dusty boards!'

He apologised, worried. But she buried her face in a posy of spring flowers.

'Who has given you those?' he demanded.

Eyebrows raised, looking sternly past him, she replied, 'An admirer. Have you any objections — you who have never had any before?'

'No, no. Of course not.'

He watched her, afraid. She was too good in the love scenes. Far too good. He was relieved when they sailed and she became so sick that they lapsed into their old roles of protector and protected. Later she kept to her cabin, demanding long afternoons alone. Mollified, he left her tucked up in her bunk, the script of *Fédora* on her knees. And Flavio Andò, lounging at the ship's rail greeted him courteously with enquiries as to his wife's health.

'She needs the afternoons to rest, she tells me — and I agree that this is sensible,' said Tebaldo, uneasily.

'Very wise,' said Andò, 'very wise of you both.'

'What a dandy!' Tebaldo muttered to himself as they parted.

His duties on Eleonora's behalf prevented him from watching the leading man as closely as he wished, but on the following afternoon some conjugal sixth sense drove him to break in on his wife's sacred rest period. He opened the cabin door, gaped, and shut it violently behind him. After a few minutes Andò appeared, composedly adjusting his shirt front.

'You are a scoundrel, Signor!' said Tebaldo, shaking. 'I should challenge you for this!'

Andò's expressive black eyes were contemptuous.

'Nevertheless,' said Tebaldo, swallowing his humiliation for her sake, 'the tour must not be interrupted. No one must know of this, and it must never occur again — do you understand me?'

'I would not harm her reputation by so much as a whisper,' said Andò, furious. 'I am a gentleman, Signor. And you should know, Checchi, that this is no sordid entanglement. I love her — and she loves me. Kindly let me pass!'

Tebaldo pushed him aside and re-entered the cabin. On the floor, in a disarray of dark hair and white chemise, Eleonora sobbed with rage.

'I forgive you, *dolcezza* — absolutely,' he stammered, humbled as always by her presence. And was silenced by the fury with which she attacked him.

'Forgive?' she cried. 'I am not *asking* for forgiveness. I am no statue to be worshipped and fawned over, and made to work in your interests! I am a woman, Tebaldo, a woman — and *he* knows it! Kindly leave my room and mind your own business.'

'Eleonora!' he whispered, aghast.

He observed, in jealousy and terror, that she was flushed, alive and beautiful as he had never seen her except on the stage.

'At least,' he said, finding words with difficulty, 'be discreet. For your own sake. For the sake of your professional reputation.' He put out one tentative hand and touched her. 'These things pass, Nella. I quite understand. But these things pass.'

She flinched away from him, picked up a script and threw it at his head. When he could feel himself able to put one foot before another he went out, and walked up and down the deck trying to make sense of madness.

Rossi, though smiling privately into his moustache, patched up the surface.

'We have a tour to make,' he said, wise over a bottle of wine, 'and we don't want to arrive flying our dirty linen, now do we?'

On that, at least, they were all agreed. Andò kept his distance, and Tebaldo continued to share his wife's cabin — though neither of them spoke to each other, except in public. The company gossiped among itself, diverted by Eleonora's sudden switch from respectability. And Rossi, chuckling to himself, was friendly with Andò, sympathetic with Tebaldo, and just a shade too correct in his behaviour with Eleonora.

Exasperated by the twinkle in his eyes, she cried, 'I am in love, Cesare!'

Bowing over her hand, he replied, 'Of course.'

Days later she was enraged by quite a different matter, and wrote to her friend Matilde of the cavernous theatre her voice had not been able to encompass.

A complete failure for your little Nenella, she mourned, driving the pen across the paper. *I felt quite small and helpless.* Still angry, because she was afraid that her voice had betrayed her, she added in an annoyance flicked with humour, *I should have had to cry 'I love you' in the same voice as one usually says 'Begone!' for my voice to have carried!*

Fédora had failed to reach, let alone arouse her audience, but *Denise* on the second night made them sit up and pay attention, and on the third evening she conquered them with *Fernande*.

But on that third night her triumph was spoiled by concern when she realised that Diotti, her adoring baby, was weakening from a fever contracted on the voyage out. She turned instinctively to Tebaldo, standing stiff and polite beside her in the wings, and broke the silence between them, looking for comfort.

'Poor baby, he must not die, Teo. He must not die.'

As the company glanced nervously in her direction, for she was on the stage in a moment's time, she fell upon her knees.

'Holy Mother of God,' she whispered, 'be gracious unto us, and save this young man's life. Do this. Do not let him die. Save him.' Then, offering all she possessed apart from her daughter, she said, 'Let me fail for ever as an artist, but save this poor young man.'

That evening she wrote again to Matilde, swollen-eyed over Diotti's death. *You never told me that life was common,* she scrawled. *You only, sadly, agreed with me that it is hard to bear.*

But there was more to bear than the death of a young Italian actor in a strange country, and it was not borne by Eleonora.

Tebaldo Checchi, in a short space of time, had struggled against the suspicion that his wife was attracted by another man, then with the realisation that she was unfaithful to him, and lastly with the bitterness of her refusal to give up Andò.

Each revelation cost him a ransom of suffering. Each aspect of the affair was made harder by the knowledge that the company found his betrayal comic rather than pitiable, and even Rossi's condolences were accompanied by a twinkle.

Alone, while his wife and her lover triumphed in public and embraced in private, Tebaldo went over and over the situation, seeking an honourable solution. He had no wish to be vindictive, to make a scandal of her good name and take away the child. Divorce was not possible. Therefore, he concluded, it would be best if he withdrew completely from her life, leaving her to pursue her career and her lover untrammelled by the embarrassment of a husband.

He knew his small worth as an actor, but he was intelligent and hard-working and clever enough with a political pen. He had Italian friends in the Argentine who were influential enough to find him a minor diplomatic position. From there he could manage by himself. So he approached Eleonora and told her he was staying behind.

She could not comprehend a life lived anywhere but in Italy.

'You will be exiled from *home*, Teo!' she said, conscience-stricken.

'I am exiled from you,' he said simply, 'and it will be easier to live where you are not.'

As her eyes filled and her hands went out to him he gently repulsed her.

'I wish you nothing but good,' he said. 'You must go your own way, Nella, wherever it may lead. I shall ask nothing of you, make no trouble over the child. She is yours, and you are free.' He added, 'I have been happy with one of the greatest women it has been my honour to know — with one of the greatest women any man *could* know. For these four happy years I thank you.'

The breadth of his kindness, the depth of his generosity, brought Eleonora to humility. She could find nothing to say in response, so put her hands together and asked his forgiveness.

The Italian newspapers reported that Signora Duse-Checchi, idol of the Italian theatre, had left her husband behind in South America laden with her debts, and returned with her present lover Flavio Andò. In a passion she took up her pen and scorched into print:

Art and my own resolution will come to my assistance. Art, which always, in the worst times, has been my shield, my comfort, my refuge and my solace!

Gone the long lazy days in the hills of Tuscany, the reflections on life and death, the warm afternoons coaxing smiles from Enrichetta. She reverted to the name of Duse, and for the moment Flavio's glowing eyes and the homage of the audience were enough. But debts accumulated and she struggled under them, afraid of hunger and poverty.

'To be able to live in accordance with my own ideas,' she said. 'I must be more conventionally correct than everybody else.'

Only close friends knew that she spoke from some inner moral code. Outwardly, with her theatre life and theatre lover, she trod convention underfoot daily. She had outgrown Tebaldo and now was outgrowing Rossi. Once his imposing countenance and curly-brimmed bowler had inspired respect; now they only annoyed her thoroughly.

To the Marchese d'Arcais, her friend and mentor, she wrote, *Rossi is just the same. He refuses to understand that I am not a chattel but a human being.*

She wronged Rossi, who had been kind to a shy little actress and now found a tempestuous artist on his hands. He knew that their partnership was unequal, even laughable, since she never listened to what he said. He missed Tebaldo, who was his friend and had interceded many times on his behalf. And when Eleonora spoke of chattels she wilfully mistook the situation. Rossi was the chattel, and she rated him as less than a human being because she saw further than he did, and was going to be greater than he could imagine, and must therefore be rid of him.

So for a while he argued with her, and lost the argument; or agreed with her and was treated with contempt for having no mind of his own. And then in the following year she broke her partnership with him, and took the company on to her own shoulders. A little older, a little greyer, Rossi dusted his bowler hat with his sleeve and offered some advice. He said that she was taking a risk.

'Remember *La Princesse de Bagdad* — and then talk to me of risks!' said Eleonora, triumphant.

But when he had gone she felt sad, and cried for a while.

Again to d'Arcais, she scrawled:

I have come to a final conclusion — that the greatest force in the world is work — and once one has made that one's own and felt all its torments and blessings, then one will hold to it tooth and nail (even if one is *a woman) as one of the most precious discoveries of life, and prize it as highly as the responsibility one has for one's own future and that of one's dependants.*

Lounging at her side Andò said hopefully, 'And what shall you call your company, Nella?'

She glanced at him briefly, noting that his vanity expected some link of names, and said, '*La Drammatica Compagnia della Città di Roma!*'

The City of Rome Dramatic Company. She had not forgotten, as she never did forget, any slight, any humiliation. Walking those Roman streets at dawn and smarting with rejection and anonymity.

'Perfect!' said Andò, and kissed her fingers.

His good looks, his polished performances, and his almost imperturbable good nature, were to maintain him a director of that company, and leading man, for a decade. He had not quite worked out what compliment was intended for him in the title, but never doubted there was one.

'How exceptionally handsome Signor Andò is, Signora!' said a young *ingénue*, ready to make a fool of herself over him if the opportunity offered.

'Oh, *exceptionally* handsome,' said Eleonora cordially, and to herself with a grin, 'and exceptionally stupid!'

Years afterwards she dismissed him with the comment, '*Il était beau mais il était bête!*' and, 'He was the folly of my youth. I was a seeker after knowledge, and a woman who loved love.'

No longer ill, now that all depended on her, she toured Italy without respite. In Turin she placed Enrichetta at a respectable boarding school, thanking God that the child's surname was not Duse and therefore linked with the actress. She charged the school to keep her profession a secret until the child became older, and bowing their heads they took her money, understanding and approving the request.

In Chioggia she visited her father, who was turning from picture to picture, inspecting the second-rate with reverence. She heard from him how some really fine painting had been sold at such-and-such a market stall, and how he contemplated one picture which would put all the rest of his work to shame. Eleonora knew little about art, but sensed that between Alessandro Duse, painter, and the great artists lay a formidable gap. Nevertheless, she praised him, kissed his cheeks, and felt a child again.

Looking upon her fondly, in her trim costume and broad-brimmed hat, he spoke out of ignorance, so long away from the world of theatre.

'You seem very smart these days,' he said. 'Are you doing nicely, then?'

If he had struck her across the face she could not have suffered more. His lack of interest flayed her. But spearing her hat, drawing on her gloves, she answered lightly.

'Oh yes, thank you, Papa. I am doing nicely.'

TWELVE

She was enjoying her power. Unhampered by Rossi, Checchi or Andò, she chose Renan's *Abbesse de Jouarre* for her opening in Rome. The company followed faithfully and doggedly at her heels, opening their eyes and mouths at some of the more daring lines. The critics applauded her audacity. The ladies in the audience raised their fans to hide their blushes, but did not cease to listen and watch. Night after night the theatre was packed... and the young D'Annunzio, with pale eyes like a cat, watched her spellbound, from his seat in the stalls. In last year's Roman Carnival he had crept into the privacy of a grove and taken off his fine clothes to feel the air upon his skin. And was discovered, clad only by leaf shadows on this warm moonlit evening, by a woman in search of adventure. Their coupling savoured of religious martyrdom, and in his mind he subjugated the actress also and ravished her in the dappled grass.

That summer Eleonora and Enrichetta spent their holiday in a pink box of a house near the sea. A grape vine grew beneath the window. A mendicant friar called daily for alms, smiling his thanks, walking on unsandalled feet. A peasant woman cleaned and cooked and washed for them. And in the blessed quietness, protected even from the contact of a newspaper, Eleonora rested and healed her troublesome lungs. In a flurry of thanksgiving she wrote to a friend: *I am writing with one hand and reaching toys for my delightful tot with the other. She is the only achievement in my life which has cost me no work, no worry and no effort of will.* Surprised by this discovery, she added: *That is worth noting!*

But as summer faded she grew restless. The holiday was over, work beckoned, all the sweeter for being set aside awhile.

'I am a vagabond,' she admitted, in a flurry of packing and planning, 'a nomad. I was even born travelling.'

Mother and child parted in tears, but the trains covering province after province, the dusty roads warm with autumn, the trunks heavy with properties and costumes, filled her with an ecstasy bordering on the mystical. Something of great significance, she felt, portended in each arrival and each departure. As a child she had longed to stay and become part of somewhere. Now she moved on in jubilation and from inner necessity.

In the spring of 1887 an old admiration flowered. Arrigo Boito, seventeen years older than she, already famous as Verdi's librettist, courted her — and she responded. For almost a decade, since Cafiero had shown her a new and shining world across the dinner table, she had worked and educated herself in a vacuum, knowing no one in her narrow theatre life who could lead her beyond it. Ahead of her in the international category glittered Bernhardt. But Sarah's excellencies were not Duse's own, and Eleonora strove to express and create her roles without professional guidance, feeling that those about her could not see as far or experience as deeply. And yet she longed for someone who would see further and plunge more profoundly.

With his reputation sealed by the libretto he had written for Verdi's *Otello*, Boito was working on *Nerone*, and promised to translate Shakespeare's *Antony and Cleopatra* into Italian for Duse. Finding her avid to learn, he began to educate and instruct her in a literary sense, and horizons of which she had not dreamed began to open before her. She saw that if the material of a play was poor, even the best work would not redeem it, and she looked more critically than before at her own dramatic and popular repertoire. Together they studied in what she called *un febbrone d'arte*, and Andò's animal charms were discounted by this fever of fine words and fine feelings.

Boito was committed to the invalid Fanny, and Eleonora was not free to marry anyway. But neither of them considered marriage, at first, finding their way in a relationship so honeyed as to bemuse them both. He had sat with Verdi in a box, and asked if Duse would see him during the intermission so that he could pay her homage. Few words passed between them. They smiled. She noticed the flower in his buttonhole and he proffered it. She laid her hand in his, and he put it to his lips, bowed and left her.

That autumn she went to his apartment in the Via Principe Amedeo in Milan, and tapped upon the window pane. He opened the window and handed her a little key, beginning a love affair more profound than she had ever known before. In the early flush of this liaison Boito travelled with Eleonora whenever he could, from city to city, and joined her on a Sicilian tour. Away from each other, they wrote letters part-tender, part-philosophical. She was re-kindled, transported by love, and she abased herself before him:

I am in my dressing room during my free act. I have brought with me a white sheet, a white inkwell and a white quill: and here I am — all white — in the presence of my soul.

And:

Before Milan this winter, and after Brosso that summer, I would sometimes in the night, in sleep or in dreams, try to say in an undertone, 'Arrigo'. But I would hear that 'never' you gave me for the May of that year, and the name would be snuffed out in my heart.

And over and over again, scrawled before a performance, scratched during an intermission, penned after the last curtain call:

I love you and love you and love you… What peace, what sweetness, what torment, what agony, what rest, what hopes!

They spent that August in a small white hillside house near Bergamo. And here Boito began his translation, his labour of love and art, *Antony and Cleopatra*. Excellent at allowing an artist to create, even when he was her lover, Eleonora kept quiet while he worked. *Arrigo is in his room working,* she wrote to one friend. *Lenor is in her room, keeping very quiet and thinking of Arrigo.*

Personally, he longed to regularise the union. He spoke of the possibilities of marriage, thinking of the small Enrichetta.

'Three heads at one window, Lenor. Three heads at one window.'

But the obstacles were insuperable, and something within her feared to be tied down again. Marriage, to her, seemed the enemy of surprise, of rapture, of poetry: an unwieldy harness of which she might tire. And Enrichetta, after all, was happy in her boarding school at Turin.

On 24 November 1888 Eleonora performed her subtle, passionate Cleopatra. The audiences thronged to see her. She was just past thirty, an established celebrity in her own country, a stranger outside it. When she worried, Boito encouraged her.

'Up, up, up, towards the vision!' he said, smiling at her frets and frowns and terrors.

Confidence in his judgement gave confidence to her.

'You'll see!' she cried, 'you'll see! And oh,' putting her arms round his neck and laying her cheek to his, 'I *love* you!'

He had broadened her knowledge, enriched her capacity for beauty, whetted her appetite for a larger stage. And devoted to her interests, as Tebaldo had been, he arranged for his friends, the Volkovs, to see her perform in Venice, suggesting that Russia might share their enthusiasm. But the invitation for a tour frightened her. Such a distance, such cold, such a language barrier.

'Art knows no frontiers!' Arrigo reminded her, 'and when you return from Russia you will say, "Ah, how soon can I go again?"'

Intent on personal imperfections, she said at random, 'But I'm afraid it will take a lifetime to fill the gaps in my education.'

And as he spoke encouragingly of the coming Russian tour she moaned at the onset of winter.

'My ideas are frozen up inside me. This cold weather has taken away my will. Do you know how my day is spent? Twelve hours in the theatre and twelve in bed — with a cold to match!'

Something else was wrong with her, was beginning to go wrong with them. An emotional claustrophobia attacked her.

'I'm locked in a room without air!' she cried in terror.

She sat in a chair, hands in lap, head bent. The attitudes she had studied so patiently, so consciously, were now a part of herself.

'Oh, what's wrong with me?' she asked. 'Every day I make up my mind to do something, but days go by — and idiocy comes nearer!'

He was troubled, but did not say so. They had been together for almost three years.

On the eve of the company's departure he kissed her goodbye, as she stood booted and furred against the bitter weather, taking what was left of their personal summer with her.

'Until we meet again, Arrigo,' she said, empty with fear, stiff with cold.

'You will come back?' he asked, meaning back to him.

She chose to ignore their private communication line.

'What else should I do?'

He looked intently at her, as though to remember what might be lost to him.

'Three times,' he said hesitantly, 'three times since our love began, three times at parting, I had the impression of *farewell* in your voice and in your face. You were not saying "farewell", you were saying "until we meet again". But your tone said *farewell*.

'I am going into Russia with my company,' she cried fiercely. 'Into the middle of a Russian winter — and you know how I dread the cold. I am afraid, too, of failure. I wake up at night and wonder how I shall bear the silence of total incomprehension when I perform in a strange language. How I shall endure applause that is only politeness. I shall be quite alone out there. Far from home and responsible for all of us. And I am not well. I am not well. I am not strong. And you talk of my *tone*, and the *quality* of my farewells…'

'Forgive me,' he said, placing both gloved hands upon her muff in supplication, 'but for a year, for exactly a year, we lived in a dream.'

He longed to say that he, too, was afraid.

THIRTEEN

I am going to work alone and far, Eleonora wrote to a friend, as though the expression of her solitude and distance from home might mitigate her fears.

She huddled in one corner of the carriage, her feet wrapped against the cold, as the train rattled and jolted across Europe with its cargo of players and equipment. Already she was running a temperature, and the journey had become a nightmare of snow and desolation. One Eleonora coughed and racked her lungs as flurries of wind and white flakes descended on her, as she waited at borders, waited at stations; another Eleonora saw the train itself, a minute black snail crawling through wastes so vast and icy that it was the only moving thing on an eternal landscape.

A German troupe joined them, also bound for St Petersburg. Unknown to each other, having only their profession in common, they exchanged polite bows. But one young German actress, Jenny Gross, saw that the little Italian woman was ill and offered her assistance.

'I am afraid you are not well,' said Jenny, pitying the flushed cheeks and brilliant eyes.

Eleonora translated the kindness, though she could not comprehend the language, and laid one dry little hand over Jenny's warm fingers. And through the night, as she coughed and moaned, Jenny sat by her, administering brandy and words of comfort. Towards dawn she drew up the blinds and wiped the window clear, and breathed a little circle of heat on to the glass so that Eleonora might see Russia in the grip of winter.

'The home of snow,' whispered Eleonora, despairing.

'You'll be all right,' said Jenny, understanding the fear beneath the language, 'there's something strong about you, Signora, for all your frailty. Be of good cheer, Signora. Of good cheer.'

The black eyes lost some of their feverishness. One hand crept from the muff to touch the girl's cheek.

'You give me new hope,' said Eleonora, slowly. 'I don't know what you're saying, but what you mean comes through. And I thank you.'

At the Customs, a little apart from her company, la Duse, as her public had taken to calling her, stood silent and thickly veiled, shivering in the cold sunlight. Jenny pointed her out to Hermann Bahr of the German troupe. 'That poor creature has been ill all night,' she whispered. 'And she is also playing at St Petersburg.'

Bahr beat his hands across his chest and stamped his booted feet, pursing his mouth, raising his eyebrows. 'Poor creature indeed,' he said, sorry for her. 'She looks like nothing — nothing at all.'

'But she has great courage,' said Jenny, 'and I like her so much. We must see them if we can.'

'She is one of the players, you say?'

'She is the star. The actress-manageress. Very fine, I believe, in her own country.'

He shrugged sympathetically, and turned away to haggle over the trunks.

Eleonora Duse, the celebrated dramatic artiste! said the Russian poster, but St Petersburg had not heard of her and the theatre was half empty.

The city froze in a halter of ice and snow. The opera, the ballet, the circus were more attractive than a troupe of actors speaking only Italian. But the critics, who had come to the Maly Theatre, urged on by the Volkovs and their friends, were captured. Supported by brandy and the new challenge, Eleonora played Juliet, in spite of her thirty-three years and the fine fines already etched about her mouth. Her entrance was greeted by an astonished silence that so plain a woman, no longer young, should attempt the part — and without paint.

'I make up my soul, not my face!' she said arrogantly, in answer to the hints and prompts of colleagues.

So, though her hands and arms were exquisite, holding that cloud of white flowers, they were disappointed — until she spoke, and laughed, and dropped twenty years in an instant. When the curtain fell they were on their feet, shouting; and the second night the theatre was full.

The critic Ivanov spoke of her as 'Her Holiness'. And Anton Chekhov sat down at midnight to write to his sister, Maria Pavlovna:

I have just seen the Italian actress, Duse, in Shakespeare's Cleopatra. *I don't know any Italian, but she acted so well that I felt I understood every word. What a superb actress! I've never seen anything like her.*

The Russians took her to their hearts. Whole stalls and boxes were bought up for friends and relations. They gave her receptions, begging her to attend, overwhelming her with thanks. The streets were strewn with rose petals when she passed, and the barrier of language was broken by loving kindness. Both personally and professionally, Eleonora responded to them, and years afterwards said they were the best audiences she ever played to, since they really understood what she was trying to do.

After one reception, the Countess Levashova took her by the hand and led her through her great house to a private room. Eleonora looked at the girl lying in her bed, helpless and incurable, away from the noise and life.

'My daughter,' said the countess, indicating by gestures that the child wished to see la Duse in the flesh though she could never see her on the stage.

Sitting by the bed, holding the small hand, Eleonora thought of her own daughter so many miles away. And as the countess smiled and nodded and chattered in Russian, and the child replied excitedly and touched the heavy satin of the actress's dress, Eleonora said, 'Now I know that words are not the most important thing in the world.'

'I love you *all*!' she cried, standing up in her carriage so that they might see her. 'You have taught me so much!'

A dozen students unharnessed her horses and prepared to pull her home.

'Remember me,' she said. 'Remember me.'

But at Moscow she must begin all over again, for the intellectual capital disregarded the plaudits of St Petersburg and reached their own judgement. She made her début with *Dame aux Camélias* before a group of hostile critics, and conquered them. One elegant woman waited night after night outside the theatre door to open Duse's carriage door. Her autographs were sold for extraordinary sums, and the proceeds given to charity.

The Russian tour, after the disastrous journey, had been another milestone. The German troupe coming to watch her play were quite overcome and made fools of themselves. One man, Mitterwürzer, sobbed outright.

'Oh, she is fine,' said Hermann Bahr, 'very fine. I shall write an article on her. The Italians and the Russians shan't have it all their own way. She must come to us, to Germany, mustn't she, Jenny?'

'*I* am not astonished,' said Jenny Gross. 'She was so much when she was ill — how could she be less now?'

One Russian admirer was to worship Duse anonymously for thirty years. Whenever he could, he followed her, and never once asked for an introduction. In their old age she heard of his devotion and offered him a box for the evening performance, and a meeting afterwards. He accepted the box with gratitude but sadly declined the meeting, saying it was too late.

She journeyed back across Europe in honour, leaving behind her the last remnants of the old florid Italian style. She had proved herself.

Fame had its drawbacks, and even in her own country she did not please every critic. Reinhardt of Germany might applaud her. Stanislavski of Russia could praise her. But Tommaso Salvini, patriarch of the Italian theatre, wrote dryly:

What is there for her to lean on — in explanation of her startling results with so scant a repertoire — except the fact that she is a bundle of nerves? For the Duse does not command even the first principles of acting. It is her remarkable personality that permits her to convey instinctively what others can do only after profound study.

'Take not the slightest notice!' said her friends, indignant. 'If an angel descended before him he would criticise the shape of its wings!'

But she pondered the criticism painfully.

'He is quite right,' she said at last, brooding. 'My repertoire *is* small and dreary, and I *am* a bundle of nerves. But what he does not see is that I try every single time to create a new role.

Just as nothing in life is ever repeated exactly, so nothing in art should be repeated exactly. Perhaps — I give him a point there — perhaps I do not act well enough. But the intention is pure, and I shall work and learn and watch all the time.'

In 1892, perhaps in search of that warmth which had been given her so profusely, she made her second Russian tour, and broached the cold in good heart.

They had not forgotten; they were waiting for her, with torchlit processions, baskets and bouquets of hothouse flowers, crowded theatres. They unharnessed her horses, hauling her carriage through the streets. And Ivan Ivanov, dipping his critical pen in the ink, endeavoured to set down her magic on paper for the *Artist*.

Her Holiness, he wrote reverently, *of her performance in Cavalleria rusticana, plays an abandoned girl, with a voice. Her despair is natural and convincing: the cry of this poor trampled creature sounds like that of a stricken deer!*

And on 15 September, after her performance in Sardou's *Odette* at St Petersburg:

She enters: her appearance and way of dressing make her seem an elderly and rather ailing widow. She stumbles along, barely able to keep on her feet, but her eyes burn with a light as if dominated by some fixed idea… She starts to speak in an altered voice, and falters: under the weight of this faltering her shoulders bend, her back curves over… These difficult parts suit her best.

But during a performance of *A Doll's House* she received a telegram.

'Bad news, Signora?' one young actor ventured, seeing a tremor of mouth.

'My father is dead,' she said, with iron composure, 'and I was very fond of him.'

She clasped her hands for a moment, then went on stage, prompt for her cue.

She saw Alessandro as she played: laughing her out of the *smara* and giving her a rose, swinging her up in his arms, following her patiently from mood to mood, sitting in dumb wretchedness after Angelica's death. Then in his old age, painting, pottering, enclosed in the dream he had at length been able to enjoy. She heard him say, 'And are you doing nicely now, Nella?' when everyone in Italy but himself must have known the answer.

Her throat was dry, her tongue swollen, her eyes smarting. But she carried on until Nora, too, reached the death of her father. Then she burst in such a passion of tears that the audience wept with her. Together they mourned, for different reasons.

Back in Rome she bought violets from an old woman at the foot of the Piazza di Spagna, talked to the ragged children who swarmed about her, milking her easily and painlessly of money. She gossiped with the cabbies, mimicked the dialect, giggled with her friend Matilde. Then she brooded, at a standstill, not knowing what to do nor where to go next.

The news that her company was not to be included in an international theatre festival in Vienna brought her sharply to life. She had assumed that such an important event would require Italy's leading actress to represent her country. Instead, invitations had been extended to Giacinto Gallina's Goldonian Company and Sonzogno's 'Opera Italiana'.

'So they think we are merely clowns and singers?' she cried, enraged. 'Who is to represent *drama* for Italy?'

No one, apparently.

'*Who* has dared to exclude me and my company from the festival?'

The Princess von Metternich, patroness of the event.

'And *why* have I been excluded?'

Because, though this of course was an absurdity of the greatest magnitude, and the Princess more to be pitied than blamed, and someone must naturally have made an appalling mistake…

'Why? Why?'

It had been suggested that la Duse fell short on renown — international renown, that was. Only renown, not ability, one understood. Not having, as yet, played in Paris or London or New York, or even Vienna itself.

'What is this nonsense about renown?'

What did it matter to the Signora? The Signora did not play to pigs. Vienna was the capital of Austria, and not long ago the Austrians had been soiling the plains of Northern Italy…

'I can say what I like about myself,' said Eleonora in a tempest, 'but nobody, nobody else, says *anything*! Where is the address of that agent Tänczer who wanted me to play in Vienna? Send him a telegram. Send him three telegrams! Tell him I will come tomorrow if necessary, and play in the marketplace if he can find nothing better. Be quick! I detest procrastination!'

Tänczer was young and brave. He had read Hermann Bahr's article on Duse in the *Frankfurter Zeitung*. He divined, correctly, the real reason for her coming to Vienna, and applauded her determination. By return, he wired that the Carltheater was at her disposal for four nights, from 19 February. Wisely, he did not attempt to explain that the theatre was in the second rank of Viennese play-houses, was extremely old-fashioned, and usually offered a popular bill of minor operettas and low farces. Nobody warned him, either, that la Duse was apt to start off in a half-empty theatre, looking exceptionally plain and uninviting.

'I am either made or finished with this venture!' said Tänczer, and he was not joking.

'Are you going for the right reasons?' Boito asked her gently, aware that pride and professional vanity were two of her more turbulent vices.

'I am going because I must and will,' said Eleonora briefly. 'Can you think of better reasons?'

'And what have you chosen for your début?'

'Dame aux Camélias.'

'Is that wise? You are playing to one of the most sophisticated audiences in the world — and Bernhardt has been to Vienna. They have seen her interpretation, and it will be closer to their understanding.'

'What is faulty with *my* interpretation?'

'It is your own, my darling. Pure and simple and good. But recollect that Dumas wrote her as a coquette, a girl of the streets. Witty, heartless and gay — *that* they understand.'

She stared at him for fully half a minute, eyebrows drawn back, nostrils inflated. He frequently annoyed her nowadays, and especially when he was right.

'Then they will learn something new, won't they?' she said.

'But you make life so difficult for yourself, my love.'

'I prefer it that way. It is so much more interesting.'

He turned away and shrugged. 'I wish you nothing but good, Lenor. And I am here whenever you need me.'

The suggestion that she might fail, when she herself knew the risk, was the last betrayal.

'You have given me a raging headache!' she cried.

And she wept with anger, and broke precious things whose absence would sear her in calmer moments.

'I very much regret, Signora,' said Tänczer, young and pale, 'that the house is not as full as it might be. But I see a few critics out front, and the gallery is absolutely packed.'

'It is not important,' said Eleonora, whiter than he.

He looked at her in dismay: at the eyes ringed with exhaustion, at the restless lovely hands, the heavy mouth, the fine lines on her face. He walked away, and stood in the shadows, hands in pockets, so that she might not observe his nervousness. She was far too occupied with her own. Now, as always, temporarily bereft of pride and ambition, she asked forgiveness for her importunity and begged the strength to go and do what she could.

Just before the curtain rose she heard Tänczer say something so solitary and desolate, so wrung from his youthful heart, that the tone registered though the words did not.

'Not even lipstick!' he told himself, and then with some philosophy, 'I am ruined!'

Before Vienna stirred properly awake on the morning of 20 February, he was skimming through the papers for reviews, and shouting for coffee.

'Good news, *mein Herr*?' asked the waiter, benevolent and curious at his jubilation.

'The best in my life!' cried Tänczer. 'She's a success!'

And he was so tired that he could have fallen asleep over the steaming cup.

He had suffered before la Duse arrived, at the wicked hand of Zasche, the cartoonist, who had drawn the Italian actress as a pedlar in the Prater, slicing off pieces of salami labelled *Nora, Frou-Frou, Fédora*, and so on.

'Zasche can eat his cartoon!' said Tänczer with relish.

The first night had yielded only 800 crowns. The next one brought 9000 into his pocket.

And before she left Vienna a gracious invitation came from the Princess von Metternich, begging Signora Duse to take part in the International Drama Festival. On 15 May, when she returned three months later, the Carltheater sold out every night for three weeks, and Eleonora prepared to advance on Berlin. To Tänczer, her newest slave, she was most kind.

'Forgive me, Signora,' he said, bowing over her hand, 'but the first impression — if you understand me — is no indication of the glory that is to follow!'

'I know,' she said, with a smile whose brilliance Sarah might have envied. 'My strength lies in my ugliness.'

'But the Signora is excessively beautiful,' Tänczer stammered, remembering the illumination that was almost a miracle.

'I can be if I want to be,' she replied composedly, 'and that's the best kind of beauty to have. One can put it on and off, like a mantle.'

FOURTEEN

Her first American tour, arranged by Tänczer and managed by the Rosenfeld brothers, appalled her. The stormy crossing matched a superstitious storm within her: fear of death in the wild, icy waters, or in a country far from home. She slipped ashore unnoticed. The noise of wheels, the welter of people and buildings, the size and profusion of advertisements, alienated her. A nonentity in the ebullient crowds, she took a cab to the Murray Hill Hotel and locked the door of her room.

On the pier Carl and Theodor Rosenfeld peered and stamped doggedly until the last passenger had disembarked, looking for some miraculous vision which never appeared.

She was drinking coffee, trembling with fatigue, seeking contact with home by letter. Across the paper she scribbled her terrors to Corrado Ricci, the art historian: *I longed to get back on that stormy sea at once, and return to Italy right away…*

Later, she sat by the window, breathing on the pane, rubbing it clear with her handkerchief, possessed by a sadness she could not explain.

The Rosenfeld brothers, hats in hands, were polite and puzzled and anxious to do their best for her. New York, they explained, wanted to know all about her.

'What about me? Why must they know?'

'Human interest, Signora.'

'What is that?'

Bewildered, she confronted the press through a harassed interpreter. But her reluctant acceptance of this duty turned to rebellion as she caught the purport of their questions.

'Now then, Madame Doozy, what do you think of the USA?'

'I have only just come...'

'Madame Doozy, have you gotten a favourite recipe for spaghetti and meatballs?'

'Spaghetti?'

'What do you think of Madame Sarah Bernhardt?'

'A very great actress. I first saw her in Turin —'

'Do you learn your lines out loud, or in your head?'

'Is that important?'

'Who do you think make the best husbands? Americans or Europeans?'

'I have not been married to an American. What do you mean?'

'What country do you like best, Madame Doozy?'

With dry irony she said, 'The journey there!' Then, in a rage at this assault on her privacy, she cried, 'I am not a curiosity! You!' to the hapless interpreter. 'Tell them I will not tolerate such impertinence! Tell them that in my country the press discusses art, not meatballs. Tell them to go away, at once, and leave me alone! I wish — I wish to go home. I wish I had never come. Bring a doctor. Quickly! I must rest. My lungs burn, my head aches, I am ill, sick at heart. *You*, you stay with me until the doctor comes, and then you can tell him what is wrong with me. Tell him — tell him I shall die in this terrible city...'

'Now that is a very excitable little lady,' said Carl Rosenfeld, abashed.

'Who is going to cost us plenty if she won't talk!' said Theodor, replacing his hat.

For the moment the press had enough to work on. She had scalded them, and in their turn they mocked her as 'the Hermit of Murray Hill'. Her performances were poorly attended, not only on the first night when she usually surprised her critics, but on following nights as well. She gave her best to the theatre, hurried back to her hotel room, and hung a notice on the door saying *Do not disturb — Doctor's Orders!* When they dared to penetrate the sanctum she dressed up her maid in her clothes and retired to another room, trembling and hysterical.

Her managers pointed out that her mute resistance to publicity was losing them money. Her reply was frigid.

'No power on earth will make me see a reporter now!'

'But indifference hurts them…'

'They have hurt *me*, and in a much more damaging way.'

'You are capricious, Signora…'

'Listen to me. I believe there is in the United States a public which is cultured, educated and important — and that is the only public which interests *me*!'

'Madame Bernhardt co-operates…'

'That is Madame Bernhardt's business. I have the utmost admiration for her, but I form my own judgements of what is right for me.'

'But publicity is the most important factor…'

'Only work is important,' she cried, 'the rest is trivia! Let them come and see *me*!'

'But if they don't know about you, Signora, they won't come.'

She turned her back on them with a superb shrug of the shoulders, her eyes glittering with tears. 'Then they must stay away.'

'Will you receive just one lady?' Carl Rosenfeld asked, after a long and awkward pause.

As she shook her head, and the tears dropped faster, he said even more gently, 'Her name is Mrs Helena Gilder. Her husband is the editor of the *Century* magazine. I reckon she's one of those cultured ladies you were talking about just now, Signora.'

'Very well,' she said, controlling herself. 'She is a woman, at least. She will understand me. Please show her in.'

Helena Gilder, easy of manner, sympathetic by nature, was astounded to find herself the object of an impassioned appeal.

'Signora,' cried Eleonora, eloquent and desperate, 'you will comprehend. You are a woman like myself. You understand, perhaps, what it is like to be in a strange country, to be subjected to impertinence. Signora, I believe you have seen my work. I put all of myself into each role, without stint. You see me now, after an evening performance. Look at me!' She spread out her hands. 'I am tired, I am ill, I wish only to go to bed, to sleep. Even your workers, Signora, only work so many hours a day. The rest of the time they have to themselves. Is this not so? They are not required, when they are weary and sick, to answer questions about meatballs and American husbands. Why am I set apart? Why should I not have privacy?

'Signora, to give so much of myself I must rest and recuperate between one night and the next. I am not an organ-grinder's monkey to be obliged to perform on every street corner! I beg of you, as you are kind, as you are a woman, to tell the women of your country, at least, the truth about me. I am not proud, Signora, I am not capricious. Only, my health is not good. I *must* be quiet, *must* have my sleep...'

Helena Gilder said, pitying her, 'I'll tell them, Signora. Now don't you worry one little bit!'

As a result of her efforts the theatre filled, and then the praises came, as before. But the tour was hard and long. New York, Philadelphia, Chicago, Boston. The Gilders became good friends, keeping the door of their house on Clinton Place always open for her, making it home. She, in turn scrawled vibrant letters to them from every stopping place. Her fear of America overcome, she saw the funny side of both the country and herself. And after one successful evening, in high spirits, scribbled to Helena Gilder, *Come to Boston! Bankrupt yourself! Life is short!*

Eyes bright, eyes brooding, eyes wet with tears, eyes closing in fatigue, she swung from mood to mood. In each unknown town, with each performance, she started again from nothing, and produced magic.

America had been a turning point. Though she seemed to act impetuously, her impetuosity sprang from months and even years of stoking small private fires, which finally sprang into some great eruption. She had, in the last two years, conquered Russia, taken Vienna by storm, besieged the German theatres with her flagrant Nora. And even over this one role she had fought and argued Ibsen's cause.

Perhaps Ibsen would not be such a force in theatre if it were not for the soul, rather than the play, he was interested in? she wrote to one journalist. *Perhaps within ten years all the theatre will be so! What a shame not to be there!*

Painters and sculptors, trying to capture a momentary expression, translated her into pigment and stone. The Russian Ilya Repin had done an engraving of her reclining in her chair, gloves on lap, thoughtful, ironical. Franz von Lenbach, the German society painter in Rome, had drawn her more than thirty times in pastels. They transmuted her on to paper and canvas, the eye of the artist producing an image which looked deeper than the surface, refining the nose and mouth, exaggerating the dark hair and intent eyes, and yet producing something indefinably herself.

And Hugo von Hofmannsthal, the critic, observed that she played what lay between the lines, played the transition.

She had given all of herself, a different way of walking for every part, a different face for every character, with a hundred different expressions and movements. She had delved into roles until she knew more about Nora than Nora could ever have known. When psychological motivation was missing in the play she could supply the lack, make the indifferent credible, and the credible miraculous. And suddenly she had had enough, enough of everyone.

On her return to Italy she broke up the company, finished her long professional partnership with Flavio Andò, and retreated to the country. And here she rested for some months, pondering on the change taking place within her. This new eminence in the theatre had left her amazingly empty. Certainly, London and Paris remained to be conquered, but opportunities would come in their time. And at the moment she was struggling in an old bondage, which could not wholly be blamed on the *smara*. Everything had become too easy, and praise tasted of gall. She needed not success but the freedom to expand. The first European raptures were over, and her life seemed tawdry and false as the paper scenery her parents had carted patiently over Northern Italy, all those years ago.

'I am *humiliated* by the roles I play,' she said to Matilde, who had been permitted to break her privacy. 'And my repulsion is so great, the protest of my conscience so strong, that my physical powers might fail. I can use neither my ears nor my understanding any longer. I am sunk in stupidity.'

'This,' said Matilde, 'is the beginning of some new project, Nella. Mark my words!'

Eleonora clasped her hands behind her head, threw herself back into her long chair, and reflected.

'I have at the moment one consuming desire,' she said, narrowing her eyes, 'to put out the footlights and try something different. I am no longer content with past and present work. Something new is growing within me, and all the old self is decaying — or dead. I want — I long for — I desire some fresh artistic form. I am tired of playing to people who come to the theatre merely to digest their dinners!'

'The middle thirties,' said Matilde, knowingly, 'are the age for stopping and reckoning…'

'I am drawn to the Greek tragedies,' said Eleonora, not interested in hearing the reason for her discontent, 'or to the early medieval mystery plays. But they are no answer for a modern world. In order to become great, each age must discover its own expression, and its own laws — and *that* is my problem.'

She turned her head and smiled at Matilde, acknowledging not only her presence but the years of friendship. She walked over to the window, rested her elbows on the sill, looking for a reply in the mountains.

'Well, *thinking* about it is no use,' she said at last. 'It will have to be lived through! But remember this of me, Mati, I never sought success in art, I sought refuge.'

'Oh, come on, Nella! You enjoyed the success as much as anyone.'

A flash of eyes and teeth.

'I loved it — all of it!' she admitted, stretching and yawning, 'and now I have it I know it is not what I was looking for!'

Walking in the Italian spring, she said, 'I hear they have just published a new novel by D'Annunzio, called *The Triumph of Death*. I must read it, and so must Arrigo. This is a poet we love — don't you, Mati? Perhaps all life is the triumph of the end. Imagine!'

'I thought you loathed him, or you could have met him a dozen times. Edoardo knows him very well — but he's a little unsavoury.'

'I am speaking of his work, of course,' said Eleonora in quick distaste.

But her frown turned to a smile, and the smile to a laugh.

'That *infernal* D'Annunzio,' she cried. 'All of us poor things think it is *we* who have found all the words. But that infernal D'Annunzio knows them all, too!'

'His reputation…'

'Oh, I'd rather die in a corner than love such a soul. I *detest* him, and yet — do you know what I mean? — I adore him, too.'

'A most *feminine* judgement!' said Matilde, grinning.

One morning Eleonora slipped out of bed as the sun rose, walked the garden in her wrap, head lifted, eyes alight, nostrils keen.

'I'm better,' she told herself, exulting.

For the benefit of the birds and mountains she tried out a few favourite speeches, and heard her voice respond without a trace of hoarseness. She breathed deeply. Her lungs no longer burned. No tension troubled her. And the beauty of trees crowning a hill brought tears that were pleasurable, not fatiguing. But their importance to her over these months of rest and thought was already fading.

She heard the hush that fell as the curtain rose. Saw the trains rolling out over Europe with their cargo of players and properties and costumes and scenery. She smelled dust on velvet and greasepaint in closed rooms, sensed the ghosts of old theatres, waiting for a cue that would never be given, felt the dry thin paper of telegrams. She tasted an air profoundly different from this fresh sweet country breath that had healed her.

Recharged, she cried, 'Get me an agent! I don't care on what terms! I must go back on the road!'

FIFTEEN

Bernhardt, of course, had set foot in England long, long before Duse, in 1879. She had vanquished the country painlessly, treading over an armful of lilies laid down before her by the young Oscar Wilde at Folkestone, accepting a single gardenia from Forbes-Robertson. She had played at the Gaiety, at a French fete in the Royal Albert Hall, and had returned again and again. In 1882 she had married Aristide Ambroise Damala in London. She had been entertained royally by Henry Irving in the Beefsteak Room of the Lyceum; was on terms of easy friendship with Ellen Terry, Lillie Langtry and Mrs Patrick Campbell; had enjoyed conversation (and, rumour hinted, other favours) with the Prince of Wales; had been interviewed by the best newspapers and magazines; had been lauded, loved and honoured; and she regarded the Metropole, the Carlton and the Savoy as second homes.

Sarah was playing at Daly's Theatre when Duse landed, seasick and forlorn, to be received with the politeness always accorded a foreign actress of some distinction.

A long, thin, red-headed, red-bearded Irishman laid down his wicked pen and came to watch Duse at Drury Lane. George Bernard Shaw had been having a wonderful time ripping the London theatre productions apart and examining the shreds. Only the week before, he had observed that bad though *Fédora* was, Mrs Patrick Campbell had been worse — in fact, a masterpiece of failure. He was boisterous over Sardou, and had coined the word 'sardoodledom' to describe the lath-and-plaster melodramas, the stale and mechanical tragedies. And he was not surprised, he said, that Madame Bernhardt's exhibition should be flagrantly vulgar and commercial, nor hackneyed and old-fashioned — it simply surprised him that anyone should go to see it. And *how* Mrs Pat ruined her leading man's clothes! he said with delight. Why, she knelt at the feet of Mr Beerbohm Tree and made a perfect zebra of his left leg, clasping it in her whitewashed arms. Before the act was over, he observed, a gallon of benzine would hardly have set him right. And might he suggest that soap and water were excellent cosmetics, and would not mark coats? But he was extremely kind to Mr Jerome K. Jerome's *Pinder's Progress,* capitally acted.

Reasoning more, quipping less, he discussed a WH Henley and RL Stevenson play, *Macair*, in the *Saturday Review* of 8 June 1895. Then he put his clowning to rest and began very simply and quietly:

The appearance of Duse at Drury Lane on Wednesday in La Femme de Claude *is too recent for my judgement to have recovered from the emotional disturbance produced by such an appeal as she made to my passion for very fine acting. The furthest extremes of Duse's range as an artist must always, even in this greatest art centre in the world, remain a secret between herself and a few fine observers. I should say without qualification that it is the best modern acting I have seen,* – here he paused, and added impishly, *were it not that the phrase suggests a larger experience of first-rate acting in this department than I possess… Duse is the first actress whom we have seen applying the method of the great school to characteristically modern parts or to characteristically modern conceptions of old parts. Her style is not, to the attentive observer of the stage, entirely new: nothing arrives at such perfection without many tentative approaches to it.*

But his admiration could not be sustained so long, and he turned his ebullient wit to more obvious targets. He wrote, tongue in cheek:

I remember years ago, when The Lady of Lyons *was first produced at the Lyceum, being struck with two things about it: first, the fact that Henry Irving, after much striving, and if I may be allowed the expression, not a little floundering, had at last discovered the method of heroic acting. Duse has been helped to her supremacy by the fortunate sternness of Nature in giving her nothing but genius. In Duse you necessarily get the great school in its perfect integrity because Duse without her genius would be a plain little woman of no use to any manager —* Duse, with *her genius, is so fascinating that it is positively difficult to attend to the play instead of attending wholly to her.*

His grasp of an actress's art must have delineated, stage by stage, Duse's own experience. He described the enthusiastic beginner, seizing upon half a dozen good points in the part, learning her apprenticeship by making these points smoothly and letting the play carry on unhampered between them. Then the finished actress becoming a great actress who makes many points, and makes them well. And lastly the great artist, who integrates all these points into a continuous whole, until she appears not to be acting at all, but living the role.

He dissected the business of Marguerite Gautier tying up her flowers in the third act, and called it *the final development of a highly evolved dance with the arms.*

There are years of work, bodily and mental, behind every instant of it. Work, mind, not mere practice and habit, which is quite a different thing. It is the rarity of the gigantic energy needed to sustain this work which makes Duse so exceptional; for the work is in her case highly intellectual work, and now for a little serious fun, *and so requires energy of a quality altogether superior to the mere head of steam needed to produce Bernhardtian explosions with the requisite regularity.*

Sarah Bernhardt has nothing but her own charm, for the exhibition of which Sardou contrives love scenes — save the mark.

But back again to Duse, enthralled, enchanted.

Duse's own private charm has not yet been given to the public. She gives you Césarine's charm, Marguerite Gautier's charm, the charm of La Locandiera, *the charm, in short, belonging to the character she impersonates; and you are enthralled by its reality...*

And having spent some eighteen hundred words discussing her, he added, *I must leave discussion of the plays she has appeared in this week to my next article.*

In his next instalment he spoke of her delicacy of touch upon her roles, of her sleepless vigilance over beauty of thought and feeling and action, of her prodigious industry. He sliced at Sarah, calling her plays pinchbeck and her acting poor, suggesting that London expected first-rate acting not mere reputation. And he respectfully urged Madame Bernhardt to add a complete set of strings to her lyre.

But though he wondered at Duse's ability to blush in the part of Magda, in Sudermann's *Die Heimat*, Shaw's eyes were sharp, his ears attuned, his admiration for her unbesotted. At another time he was to mourn her absence from the London scene, but write a marvellously funny description of Eleonora turning away the press and thereby gaining even more publicity than Sarah — who courted every reporter as though he were the answer to a prayer. Sarah, said Shaw, was a babe-in-arms compared to Duse, who knew that the way to stay in the news was to stay publicly out of it.

ROMANCE OF THE POMEGRANATE

Some day remember — the deepest love is the love one gives another.
Eleonora Duse to Gabriele D'Annunzio

SIXTEEN

As *La Dame aux Camélias* advanced, so did the enthusiasm of the audience: not a noisy nor a jubilant adulation, but an increasing weight of sadness in the toils of *her* sadness. They faced Armand's father with her, nobly serious, and mutely accepted his demand that Marguerite should give up her lover. They were suffocated by her pain, pierced by her three cries:

'Armando!' with resentment.

'Armando!' with entreaty.

'Armando!' with anxiety.

They stirred in their seats, unwilling to go on with her, unable to leave.

She had begun so gaily in her long dress splashed with vivid flowers, and as the colour fled her cheeks so it fled her costume, until now at the end she lay upon her couch all in white, reading old love letters taken from beneath her pillow. A white nightgown, a white négligée trimmed with heavy white lace, and the lace upon her pillows and the rug beneath her feet and the cover on her bed, all white; with her own supernatural pallor to match it. A scene set for death, and only death himself awaiting entrance.

Sarah had made the most of this, moaning and coughing, the consumptive absolute. But Duse was gentler, less life-like, and infinitely more poignant. No sound disturbed the silence on stage or the silence in the auditorium. Rapt as acolytes, they approached the end, which must come soon, and Armand waited with them.

She moved slightly, and they held their breath, following the direction of her stricken eyes. And there, invisible, stood death itself, seen by an eye sharper and clearer than the senses. They saw death in the folds of the curtains, gliding across the silent stage, vanishing through the door, and he was paramount.

'Armando!'

The last sound, the last whisper, the last tremor of the lips, the last drift of the head upon his shoulder.

I have the deepest devotion for her sensitive hands, wrote Gabriele D'Annunzio. *They are hands that tremble with joy when they touch beautiful lace or velvet and linger there with a grace that seems half-shy of being so languid.*

He closed his eyes and mused, hypnotised by his own words and the vision they evoked.

Her hands were not visible in the photograph he kept on his desk. Shoulders heaped with a collar of thick soft dark fur, dark hair pulled back into the nape of her neck, she looked into some distance the eye could not penetrate. A staid portrait for such a sensual man to preserve. A nocturne of a study, sad and delicate and subtle. An aura of much to be discovered, to be quickened, to be exploited. He raised her image to his lips, remembering her as Marguerite Gautier in Rome that year, coming offstage with death still upon her face. Waiting for her, he had noted that her white robes hung upon her like cerements, imbued with her own exhaustion.

How many men in how many audiences, he thought, must have felt her mouth upon theirs as she kissed Armand? How many men, after each performance, courted her in sleep? What loves and what dramas did she arouse on stage and off, in herself and others? What springs of bitterness watered her genius? He himself had experienced pity, horror and the threshold of death that evening through her. He had seen the traces of a hundred masks in her face, and sensed her body, saturated with caresses, laden with voluptuous knowledge. He had heard that unforgettable voice carrying words to a multitude of people, and he made his way behind the scenes to speak with her again.

In his exultation he caught a silk fold of her gown in his hand, to detain her as she swept past him.

A white frown of displeasure, a gesture of sheer tiredness, prevented the flow of words always at his command.

Stammering a little before that imperious face and presence, savouring the struggle between attraction and distaste in her eyes as she recognised him, he cried, *'Oh — grande amatrice!'*

Venice faced autumn with undisturbed serenity. A city of green waters and sun-warmed palaces; of narrow alleys hung with washing; of sunsets and markets and carnivals; of beauty and decay. Solitary trees burned with colour. The walls were velvet with lichen. On the lagoon a boat, laden with grapes, trailed seaweed in its wake.

Eleonora had taken a small flat on the top storey of the Palazzo Barbarigo on the Grand Canal, a haven of white walls, old furniture and few pictures. Released, impregnable, in her eyrie she scribbled ecstasies to friends.

I have arranged a little home for myself… under the roof, with a great arched window that looks over the whole city. This autumn is calm, the air is pure, and I have peace in my soul.

Peace was never a permanent lodger, and Venice — as her father often told her — harboured the *smara*. An oppression she could never trace nor define drove her out into a

September evening. The city became a hallucination of the senses: shapeless, endless and foreboding. Wrapping her black shawl about her head and shoulders, anonymous in her trouble, she took a gondola and told the gondolier to go where he wished.

Only that morning she had picked up two crimson leaves and felt their colour warm her hands. Now, even the memory of them smouldered, portentous and terrible. Teetering perilously on the brink of unplumbed depths, she was losing all sense of personal being. Breathing became difficult. She gasped for relief, and the autumn air flowed moist into her lungs. The season lost its charms, and imposed its message upon her. The gardens darkened, the mountains vanished. They passed houses, lighting up one by one, and sailed out into the lagoon beneath the stars.

Patient and uninquisitive, the gondolier plied his oar, whistling softly under his breath, magnetised by the even splash and pull, bearing the silent woman out to nowhere.

Life returned in the smell of boats laden with fish, in the flap of sails, in the touch of a morning breeze on her chilled shoulders, in the taste of salt on her lips, in the vision of Santa Maria della Salute gleaming in the first light of day.

As the gondola bumped against the landing stage, another drew swiftly beside it. Eleonora held her shawl close about her face, paying the fare, too raw to cope with recognition or respond to empty pleasantries, and was aware of his particular presence by his stillness. She turned towards him because he willed her to do so: hypnotised, fearful, conscious of her clothes, crumpled by a night's vigil, of the dripping wool fringe, of age and exhaustion.

D'Annunzio had lost some of his thick reddish-gold hair, but this loss only set a fine forehead to advantage and enhanced his

Roman profile. His beard and moustache bristled with life. His cat-like eyes shone. He was neat and compact and vital. Clasping her cold fingers he kissed them reverently.

She tried to frame some apology which would enable her to escape him, but her voice had deserted her. She stood imprisoned in his own enchantment with her, feeling the warmth of his hand, finding herself again in his admiration. Her back straightened, her head lifted, the draggled shawl hung now in regal folds. They spoke no words, forming between them a silent pact of alliance. First they smiled in recognition, then laughed, then began to walk away together, suddenly eloquent as people are who have met after a long separation.

Fanny died too late to save an old liaison.

Eleonora brushed her lips lightly with the tip of her quill pen, pondering. What to say? Not what he hoped, nor expected, that was certain. And how like Arrigo to assume a love affair would keep at high temperature for eight years. But she admired him, owed him much, would be kind.

I am no longer young, she wrote, feeling every day of thirty-seven autumns in her bones, *and we ought not to go against life but with it.*

Three heads at one window? Too late for Enrichetta as well, now a leggy twelve-year-old staying with a family in Dresden. Too late for all of them. Much, much too late. And then she was angry with him, with herself.

My life, she wrote, driving her pen across the paper in steep blobbing strokes, *is worth as much as another's.*

Worth quite as much as Fanny's life, for instance, who had made her wait. But had she truly waited? Would she, even if she could, ever have married him?

... yet you have never feared nor dreamed that I might die.

Though he knew the frailty that dogged every tour, every performance.

Her lips were cold and heavy, her complexion wax, her eyes fixed and enormous as she dealt the *coup de grâce*.

And so you have compelled me to leave you.

Dumas *fils* died: that short, thick-set old man with the head of crisp white hair and the ponderous belly. Years earlier he had risen clumsily but courteously to greet Eleonora Duse, who had travelled to his retreat to make his acquaintance. His husky voice was still powerful, his turn of phrase gracious, as he paid compliments to this latest lady of the *camélias*, with her pearl face and luminous eyes, dressed all in white for his especial pleasure.

They had entranced each other: the old playwright, the young actress. He had ordered his garden to be stripped of roses, and sent every single bloom post-haste to her.

She had wept with delight, her arms full of roses, her hands pricked by thorns. And now she must weep again, all these years afterwards, because Dumas *fils* was dead.

Before her sat the quaint and lovely gift Arrigo had presented to her in the first year of their dream: a machine that was set in motion only by the rays of the sun. Lacking light, it confronted her in mute reproach as she wrote to D'Annunzio.

6 September 1895

My soul is with me, all of it. I no longer feel removed from it, and it is no longer impatient to go beyond my body. Again I have found harmony — oh, bless, bless, bless, blessings on him who gives. How long have I been struggling to hold back my soul. Today, at last, if you look at me, if you see me, I am what I feel myself to be, and then I live. If you believe, I shall be. I have felt your soul and I have again found mine. Alas! I don't know how to tell you, but — do you know? Do you see? Clasp my hand tight.

Eleonora.

In his diary D'Annunzio wrote, *Amori et dolori sacra. 26 Settembre, 1895.* His pen was as prophetic as it was prolific. Then and afterwards, this day was sacred to love and to sorrow.

'Signora, I have used every vase, bottle and bucket in the apartment, and more are on the way!'

Her maid and the two Venetian messengers were smiling, conspiratorial, fascinated at the ambush of flowers. Up and down the stairs they hurried, bearing their crimson burdens. The scent was sweet and heavy, catching the throat. The blaze of colour almost overpowered her vitality. Eleonora took the card, written in a fine italic hand, and walked about the grove of her room smiling. Banked against the white walls, making an altar of the great arched window, springing from makeshift containers, daunting the furniture, spilling on to the carpets, were hundreds and hundreds of wine-red roses.

'The Signora,' said her maid, overcome, 'usually prefers *white* roses!'

'But these,' said Eleonora, 'are like *him* — and *he* has sent them!'

Arrigo's words begged her from the paper. His comely face rose before her, eyes lit by a mind both fine and gracious, full of fair promise.

One word, Lenor, he had written, *one good word.*

She crumpled his letter in her hand. Then she smoothed it out and slipped it into a drawer.

'Do you know of any other place like Venice?' said D'Annunzio, smiling. 'Stimulating at certain moments all the powers of human life. Exciting desire to the point of fever. Ah, she is a terrible temptress!'

'You really should write for the theatre, Gabriele,' she said, the velvet ribbon about her neck feeling like a noose.

'Oh, I have had no music for months, but that of the sea — which is too awesome — and my own, which is too confined as yet.'

She saw the stars glittering, the trees swaying, through the open window that led on to the balcony. A breeze ruffled the curtains, agitating the flames of the candelabra and the flowers upon the table. He smiled, a boy trying to please, but his eyes were as clear, as pale, as cold as purpose.

'How beautiful your mouth is,' he said idly, 'like the entrance to a hive moist with honey.'

'I am growing old, you know,' she replied, stifled. 'Often, very often, I feel completely lost.'

He missed no tremor of the lips, no movement of her bare shoulders above the velvet dress, no pulse in the throat. He ate and drank her image. But the word 'lost' arrested him. Lost. The lost woman. The wandering woman. The woman unknown, to be found again.

'Perdita,' he said. 'Perdita.'

'There is a vast difference in our ages,' she said loudly, and played with her fruit knife.

'Five years is hardly a vast difference.'

'It is a great difference between a young man and a middle-aged woman.'

He said, pitying her, 'Do you feel the autumn, Perdita?'

She said, suddenly tired, 'It is upon me.'

Her lids lowered, and were motionless. She sat, hands clasped on the table before her, absorbed by some interior vision.

He began to talk, with charm and then with vehemence, of Persephone captured by Hades. His voice, limpid and penetrating, built image upon image: the girls threading chains of flowers in the meadows, the black chariot drawn by black horses and driven by the lord of death; the abduction, the shrieks, the weeping mother walking the face of the earth, the seeds of the pomegranate.

'I shall next write a trilogy of novels called *The Romances of the Pomegranate*,' he said, 'and the finest of them, Perdita, shall be about you.'

Moving from her to Persephone he asked, half-boasting, half-wistful, 'Don't you think that black Hades forced his bride to eat the six seeds on purpose — to furnish me with the subject matter of a masterpiece?'

She shone, softened, laughed. She even put out a hand to touch his cheek, teasing, almost maternal in her amusement.

'You find me an entertaining slave?' he asked. 'For I *am* your slave, Perdita. I have heard, in the silence of the theatre, that incomparable voice — and my heart has stopped beating. You sit before me now, a mortal woman subject to the laws of time, and I cannot believe in your reality. It is as though I were Pygmalion when Galatea stepped from her pedestal, and the marble turned to living flesh. I have worshipped you in my soul, and it is as part of my soul you come to me. A nocturnal creature, forged from dreams and passions on an anvil of gold.'

He had dropped to his knees, clasping her waist, murmuring into the warm velvet of her dress. And she, hypnotised by his voice and the flow of images, stroked his cheek.

'When you speak, Perdita, the words hang in strange shapes in the air. One remembers, long long afterwards, a gesture or movement, created once and for ever. Your shawl — did you know? — drops from your shoulders and retains the impression of your mood. If you are sad it hangs in disillusioned folds. If you are gay it lies carelessly. If you are ill it droops.'

'You *must* write for the theatre, Gabriele,' she said, and, savouring his phrases in her mind, added, 'You must write for *me*. I have been looking so long for a poet who will write plays. Perhaps I have found him.'

Stammering, exultant in the vision of their two minds, he cried, 'Such a theatre we shall build between us. Such a place of fire and poetry as will draw the world. But do you know what it costs me to write?'

She might have told him what it cost her to act, but did not. He twisted his head to observe her, bending over him, and was the child protesting to its mother that the work is too hard, the effort too great.

'For days and weeks, without pause, I am cloistered like a monk in my room. I sleep little and eat less. My hands and feet grow cold with concentration. I *become* that pen and that sheet of paper. And often I see terrible and beautiful things about me, and sometimes feel as though I am struggling in the grip of a nightmare.'

'I know, I know,' she said, soothing and rocking him gently. 'I know, Gabriele, I know, my love.'

'Because when they come,' he continued, staring past her at some fearful recollection, 'I am no longer there. I have become something written down, and there is no strength in me. And then I am at their mercy. And it is terrible, Perdita, terrible.'

'My son,' she said, stroking his face lightly and softly. 'My little son. *Mio figlio. Mio figlietto.*'

Letters and telegrams flocked upon her ripening love, a horde of locusts. From Matilde's lemon-sharp pen to Boito's kind timidity they sounded the alarm. On no account, and for no reason good or bad, was she to encourage Gabriele D'Annunzio. He was on the downgrade both physically and spiritually, they said, drained by excess. At this very moment he possessed, and was not possessed by, a wife and three sons, a mistress and one daughter, and a troop of lesser enchantresses. Everything bad she might hear about him was the truth, possibly mercifully understated. Anything good she might hear was either imagination or his own invention. He ate women like other men ate grapes. Above all, they warned, did she not know that he used his ladies as models for his books? Did she not realise that every embrace, every sigh, every smile, was mercilessly recorded — first by that sleepless machine of a brain, and secondly by that tireless hand on paper? Did she not understand that she ran the risk of losing her heart, her reputation and possibly her career?

Eleonora, Nella, Nenella, Lenor — we beg, we beseech, we implore you. Implore you.

On the fifth of November that same year she was an unobtrusive spectator in the Benedetto Marcello Academy of Venice, applauding the neat slim figure ascending the platform. In the host of rustling dresses and gleaming jewels, in the heady vapour of scent, she sat in simple unadornment. The other ladies, drawn by D'Annunzio's shocking reputation, were waiting to be seduced with words. Hands clasped, head inclined slightly forward as she listened, she came to hear the paean of praise on Venice which crystallised their few weeks of friendship.

D'Annunzio seemed small and cold and self-contained on the rostrum. His strong nose, his heavy-lidded eyes and high forehead were muted in the great hall. He touched his pointed beard, his close moustache, much as a woman touches her coiffure to make certain that all is well. And as he began to speak, a tremor of aversion and attraction passed through Eleonora. She was aware of fans stilled, of stoles pulled over bare shoulders, of a general hush and expectancy which echoed her own reactions.

He was comparing Venice, the sea-city, to a woman in the harvest of her beauty, lit with desire. A woman in love, who held out her marble arms to the autumn and gave herself up to a wild god. He described the green marriage feast, the boat in the lagoon laden with grapes, like a wine-press about to be trodden. He compared the city, the woman, to a fine bow drawn by a strange hand that knew how to use the weapon for conquest. He plucked words out of the air to play on them, as one plays cat's-cradle with a length of string, forming and re-forming shapes and images. The hall became an immense love duet between poems and poet, between poet and audience, between himself and her. He had wooed her in private, now he wooed her in public. And a little multitude of women waved their languid fans and listened in a spell that approached a swoon of senses.

She waited for him by a pillar, afraid of meeting. She watched him come through the press of admirers, seeing with cancerous jealousy the proffered hands, the mouths forming compliments: unaccustomed to a success that marked him as other people's property. Nevertheless, she kept her own praises warm for him.

A girl, white-skinned and red-haired, brushed past Duse to greet him. The gleam in his eyes scorched her, and she felt the pressure of his hands on the girl's fingers, stared from his face to hers, trying to guess what they meant to each other and what they were saying. And when at last he turned away to find her, she could not dissemble her fear and envy. He measured the extent of her involvement with him, and she discerned triumph as well as delight in his expression. But he began, with infinite tact and patience, to coax her back to happiness. She responded, and was again confronted by his demands. She brought up her poor weapons of age and apprehension, her terror of disgusting him by so much as a wrinkle of skin, a fold of flesh; while he called her Perdita, his lost one, his goddess, his soul, his muse, his heroine, his love.

The candles guttered. Logs drifted to ash in the grate. Outside, the rain beat as insistently as his voice. They were together again over the litter of a half-eaten meal. Her glass of wine had been pushed away, untouched. The remnants of an orange, more peeled than eaten, glowed on a green plate.

'I shall possess you in a vast orgy,' he was whispering. 'I shall shake you like a bundle of thyrsi. I shall shake from your body all the divine and monstrous things that weigh on you. Both what you have accomplished and what is still in travail. Ah, it will be good to have waited so long.'

She was quite still, with the stillness of an animal that has run its course.

He had unpinned her hair and drawn it through his hands, weaving ideas as he wove the strands through his fingers, mesmerising both of them.

His eyes glittered, fierce and pale as a cat's.

'The impurity of many loves,' he said, savouring the phrase on his tongue, 'the enchantment of poets, the applause of the crowd, the wonders of the earth.'

He kissed her cheeks, her eyes, her throat, still murmuring.

'The patience and fury, the footsteps in the wind, the blind flight, the evil and the good — and the fullness of night that is to come.'

Stifled, trembling, she placed one cold hand over his mouth to stop the source of her enchantment; but was already lost.

The bell of San Marco tolled out its measure in sonorous bronze, rousing her though he still slept. She sat up and wrapped her arms about her knees, seeking something she had momentarily forgotten and now remembered. She had dreamed of a mirror of dark water in which her image shone like a pearl. There it was, on a wall in one corner of the room, shimmering in the morning light.

Silently, she crept from his side and gazed into the glass, and saw such a wild sad face that she pressed a corner of her shawl over it. Then she drew it back and looked again, fascinated. It was the face of a woman no longer young, and very much afraid; the face of an actress who had played queen the evening before, and was now cast in the role of servant; the face of a mistress who had loved, it seemed to her, beyond human limits, and was now sick of love. In mortal dismay she searched the glass for comfort and found none.

Her secret self stared back at her, retreating already from invasion and total possession.

SEVENTEEN

And here was Schürmann, who had managed and lost Bernhardt, very resplendent about the chest, very smiling.

'So you broached and conquered Europe without my help, Signora?' he said, in reproof. 'Now let us join forces and vanquish the last stronghold — Paris — together!'

Ambition fought with uncertainty, and lost.

'Paris is Madame Bernhardt's province.'

'But not her exclusive property, I believe? Well, well. Another time, perhaps. America would welcome you again with open arms.'

'Not again. America assaulted my privacy and misunderstood my work.'

'A particle unfair, Signora. That was only the first visit. You found a multitude of admirers and some very good friends, if I recollect aright. Besides, they will pay astronomical sums of money for the privilege of a tour. And are you not thinking of building a national theatre?'

She took the problem to D'Annunzio, who promptly bore it and her away on his own wings of fancy.

'We must find a site for the theatre,' he said. 'I see it in the open air, fashioned from great slabs of marble. I see noble columns towering into cerulean sky. I smell the rich dark odour of cypress, and hear your voice speaking my words into the clear air.'

'We can take in London *en route*,' said Schürmann, practically. 'They prefer you to Sarah, in London.'

Into their private visions she cried in terror, 'I shall die in some brutal city far from home!'

The echo of real anguish caught D'Annunzio's ear. Shut up with his notebooks he jotted down her words, and wove a dark fantasy about them.

The brutal city, he wrote, and pondered, then scribbled, altered, crossed out, re-wrote. *Blackened by coal, bristling with weapons. The crash of sledgehammers, the cranes' shriek, the groan of iron.*

Wholly captured, he improvised further: *Houses with deformed eyes, theatres filled with breath. Her name and portrait on walls full of advertisements, on boards, on factory bridges, on the doors of vehicles.*

He was replete with her public image, the power and beauty and tragedy which he embraced with such worship and such sacrilege.

He wrote, *The wandering woman,* and sucked the tip of his quill reflectively.

The wandering woman.

The notes were of no use to him at the moment, but would be corn to the mill later. In her book, perhaps, or in another book, or in many books. He comprehended the sea-surge of her art, the desert of her old age, the fires that consumed her, and the fire itself. *Il fuoco.*

Across the page he wrote in an elegant sloping hand, *Il Fuoco.* It smelled of title. And she? The bow in the hand of the archer. The bow.

In the grip of his own art he wrote at random the words of Heraclitus:

The name of the bow is Bios, and its work is death.

Eleonora moved from room to room in her apartment over the Grand Canal, selecting the books that must go with her and the books that must stay behind. Blinds were drawn down, covers slipped over furniture, carpets rolled. She mused over, and packed, the most familiar volumes: books bought at random, dog-eared, with scribbled margins and underlined passages, their pages marked by a pressed flower, a blade of grass from some remembered summer.

Her box of mementoes which always travelled with her contained other symbols of devotion or death: an earring, a seal, a key, a doll's foot, a silver heart, a small ivory compass, a watch without a dial. With them she placed her mother's photograph, the scales of her zodiac sign, and the locket of dusty leaves that was Cafiero's son.

'But how shall I live without you?' she cried to D'Annunzio.

'I kiss your lovely hands,' he said.

They embraced each other gently, as if sealing an unspoken compact.

'I shall follow you in my heart,' said D'Annunzio. 'My thoughts will travel with you every step of the way. My dreams will be only of you. I shall await your return.'

This time London, too, was waiting. Bernhardt had preceded her as usual. And Schürmann, still finding his way with this strange woman who could leap from humility to arrogance in a moment, attempted to quieten Eleonora's sensibilities.

'No matter where you go nowadays,' he said cheerfully, 'you run into Sarah! I swear that woman never stays at home!'

But Sarah made no difference to Duse's triumphs, and Shaw returned to worship with uncharacteristic adoration.

Even the critics are debauched, he trumpeted, bringing down his shillelagh on the heads of those who still preferred Sarah's open courtship of the public heart and pocket, *there is no mistaking our disconcerted, pettish note whenever a really great artist — Duse, for example — whilst interpreting a drama for us with exquisite intelligence, and playing with a skill almost inconceivable when measured by our English standards, absolutely declines to flatter us with any sort of solicitation for a more personal regard.*

The Queen was in the sixtieth year of her reign. Still she kept up with the times and fashions from Windsor, had seen many things and places and people, and intended to see many more. She commanded the presence of Eleonora Duse, the celebrated Italian actress, now playing briefly at the Drury Lane Theatre before leaving for the United States. Knowing that Her Majesty was a model of domesticity, Eleonora searched through her repertoire for something more suitable than, say, Cleopatra. She consulted with the Queen's daughter on the possibility of a scene from *La Dame aux Camélias*. But how would one explain who Marguerite was, and why she was dying in the arms of an unmarried gentleman?

The Princess suggested watering down the story to digestible Victorian proportions. Marguerite, she suggested, could be an innocent young girl called Daisy, who had waited faithfully for her lover Armand. He returns to marry her, but too late… she dies in his arms. After all, the Princess pointed out, as Eleonora pondered this novel interpretation, the death scene was a model of propriety and pathos. Who should guess *what* the lady had been, provided she died with decorum? In the midst of their good intentions the Queen sent a royal command for 'something cheerful', and unwittingly solved the problem.

'Something cheerful?' said Eleonora. 'Why, *La Locandiera*, of course!'

La Locandiera harked back to her grandfather's days of glory in the Venetian theatre: a sunny, slapstick, Goldonian comedy whose coquettish heroine, Mirandolina, was wholly her own creation. For this part she even condescended to wear lipstick. In her pink-striped skirt, her lace-edged bodice, her linen fichu and be-ribboned cap, she became the incarnation of gaiety. Eschewing her usual quiet elegance, jingling with beads, hands on hips, she prepared to enjoy herself and entertain them also.

Received in the White Salon at Windsor Castle, la Duse dropped one curtsey too many, and silently cursed her nerves as she bobbed decorously before the old lady. She was worried, too, about the acoustics. The high ceiling, the thick carpets, the heavily upholstered chairs and long curtains would smother her soft voice. Her attitude to royalty in Italy was of the cavalier variety. She had excused herself from attending Queen Margherita in the royal box with a polite, but equally royal, excuse about being seen in the corridors in her costume. The message began, 'Your Majesty will understand…' The King of Wurttemberg, attempting rather too obstinately to gain admittance to her dressing room, was informed that the play would not proceed until His Majesty returned to his seat. Only the King of Sweden conquered, by saying he was the humblest of her servants.

But in England she was not on her native ground and shyness came uppermost. Also, she reflected, noting the old mouth firmly set, the shrewdness in those slightly protuberant blue eyes, the grey hair scraped back into a bun, this was not a woman to be flouted. The Queen had loved deeply, even obsessively, and that Duse understood. So it was on her best behaviour, and with considerable trepidation, that she prepared to amuse Her Majesty with a rollicking Venetian farce.

Mr Gladstone was there, very spruce and correct, watching every kick of the satin shoes, every flourish of skirts, every mischievous sideways glance, with unalterable courtesy. Not the easiest of audiences. But they made her feel young and silly and inconsequential. And she observed them smiling more than once.

Presented to the Queen again, Duse dropped the correct number of curtseys, and stood polite and smiling. Her Majesty thought, apparently, that Eleonora was an *amusing* little actress, very droll indeed. Nothing in questionable taste, nothing that the family could not enjoy with impunity. And what a very pretty costume! She liked that. All the ribbons and flounces and so on.

Eleonora caught an echo of remembered youth. When one was eighteen, and newly a Queen, one danced until two and three and four in the morning, especially as no one could refuse. Dancing, at the beginning of a great reign with all the world ahead of one, and waiting to see what would happen.

The eyes filmed, the mouth lost its firmness, the head trembled very slightly. The audience was over.

The Princess smiled. Mr Gladstone murmured something suitable in Italian. She was taken away.

But Venetian humour is all-pervading. The sadness Eleonora had felt, just for an instant, at the old woman remembering youth, fled. Here she was, she reflected, one-time one-frocked Nella of a third-rate Italian troupe, presented to the Queen of England. Alone in the room allotted to her as a dressing room, soaking up the atmosphere of the castle, feeling not a day over eighteen herself with the general Goldonian effervescence, she turned three pirouettes, stuck her hands on her hips and grinned into the long mirror.

EIGHTEEN

Leaving from Liverpool she wept without control. She wept because she was physically and emotionally impoverished by her successes, because she had left a lover behind her at home, whose reputation promised infidelity and heartache, because she plumbed solitude and knew that she was alone and that love was a rare and fleeting thing. And she wept also because, superstitiously, she felt the ship voyaged towards death.

Schürmann had gone ahead of her to prepare America for her advent. He intended, since she declined publicity, to make an asset of her nun-like seclusion, her terrible silences, and her bursts of artistic and personal rage. And she followed behind, her depression deepened by the iron shore and black skyline of Liverpool in winter weather.

The company stood a little apart, eddying on the waves of her grief, which gradually receded and stilled. She wiped her eyes and cheeks, adjusted her veil, and boarded the *Majestic* neither turning nor looking back: a plain little middle-aged woman of no importance, whose dark clothes took on the limp and dulled aspect of their wearer. The gang plank was taken up, and other travellers waved farewell until the ship's outline blurred, and the watchers on the shore were faceless, and the wake of the *Majestic* creamed a black sea.

Schürmann met her on the quay, chuckling.

'I have news for you,' he said, noting signs of tension and determining to ward off those he could. 'A dentist liked the look of your teeth, Eleonora, and he's offered 500 dollars if you'll let him say they're false and that you bought the set from him!'

'You did not — you would not dare…'

In a moment she would be in tears of rage. He held her at arm's length, laughing, and gave her a friendly shake. She began to smile, then laughed with him.

'It's not a quarter as rough as poor old Sarah's publicity,' he said, on the way to her hotel. 'The penny-dreadfuls said she had seduced every crowned head in Europe — including the Pope. And the cartoons were pretty awful. She found one lot of people rummaging in her costume trunks, trying to guess how much she paid for them. And they had Sarah Bernhardt candy and cigars and perfume and eye-glasses. Oh, and a brewing company brought out a before-and-after billboard, to show how six months of drinking their beer had improved her figure. And you've heard about the man who owned a cod-fishing fleet, haven't you?'

'No,' she said, entranced.

'He persuaded her to walk on the back of a dead whale, and pull out a bone as a souvenir. Slippery experience, I should think, but Sarah's game for anything. And then every morning and evening paper in Boston produced a picture of her, with a caption that ran, "How Sarah Bernhardt gets the whale-bone for her corsets!" And the cod-fishing fleet fellow reproduced it as an advertisement on billboards. He thought she'd be pleased, but she smacked his face! Oh, I could go on for hours — la Duse's false teeth are a mere bagatelle, I can assure you.'

He cleared his throat, having coaxed her into a mellower mood. He was pleased with himself.

'But I've given you quite a different line,' he said. 'I've stressed what a lady you are — refined, shy, dedicated to your art and all that. And President Cleveland and his wife are giving you a reception, my dear girl, in the White House! They wouldn't give old Sarah a cup of water at the back door, I can tell you. What about that?'

She was smiling, her hands busy with the nosegay of flowers he had brought her. Schürmann observed her with admiration, respect, and a twinkle. He knew how to cope with actresses, even at times with this one.

'I thought you'd be pleased,' he said, satisfied. 'I have a hunch this tour is going to be a lucky one. I've given you the right image — and they look as though they're going to lap it up.'

Though determined not to be subjected to the attentions of the press, she felt perhaps she should meet her new public halfway, and had a fretful interview with Schürmann over the possibility of learning English well enough to act in their own language.

'If it's not one thing it's another,' said Schürmann, to himself, not yet hardened by years of capricious leading ladies. To her, firm and good-humoured, he said, 'Don't bother learning English, Eleonora, or you'll ruin my business! Can't you see that they want to meet you *because* you're different?'

She succumbed without a scene, even leaned on him a little, since he was shrewd and stable and would not be bounced by fits of temperament. Relaxing, comforted by her smattering of English, protected by her inconspicuous appearance, she eavesdropped pleasurably on hotel lobby conversations. Came away giggling over her new names — Deuse, Dooz, Doozy.

The tour began in Washington on 17 February 1896 at the Lafayette Theatre with a performance of *La Dame aux Camélias* before the President and his wife — who had transformed her dressing room into a bower of white roses and white chrysanthemums. Schürmann was triumphant over her professional and personal success, with the reception, at which she behaved exquisitely, and with the box office returns. They grossed 5,000 dollars that first night. The Clevelands attended every performance, accompanied by members of the Senate and their wives, by foreign ambassadors, and every local dignitary. And Mrs Cleveland, charmed by Eleonora's modest dignity — so unlike that of Sarah — gave a tea for her in one room at the White House, while in another Schürmann passed an august hour with the President.

On 23 February, they opened in New York. And, while Duse glowed beautifully at the Fifth Avenue Theatre, Bernhardt gave a firework display at the Abbey and grossed smaller receipts. Dazed and disarmed, the public flocked distractedly between the two of them, backing their favourites. Four newspapers also took sides: the *Times* and the *Tribune* hailed Sarah as the *nonpareille*, while the *Sun* and the *Mirror* were for Eleonora.

Schürmann purred over the dollars, though he had shaken his head ruefully at a bumper collection in Boston, which was passed over to the city kindergartens after a benefit performance of Goldoni's *Pamela*. He was, however, heartened by an eloquent tirade from a Boston pulpit on Italian actresses who crossed the Atlantic in order to corrupt the spotless American soul; which, in his eyes, evened up matters considerably, though Duse was deeply hurt. He observed, too, that she aroused the admiration of both sexes. Women sensed sympathy for women in her portrayals, which was by no means militant, and often sought her out to confide their hopes and problems. Trouble had been her breeding ground, and she always responded, combining kindness with personal philosophy.

'Work!' she said. 'Work! Don't ask *support* from any man, only *love*. Then your life will have the meaning you are looking for.'

Bernhardt's portrayals, becomingly clad in tights, of Zanetto the boy minstrel in *Le Passant*, of Zacharie in *Athalie*, of the young Due de Reichstadt in *L'Aiglon*, failed to rouse in Duse any desire to follow in her guiding star's footsteps. She pronounced herself to be disgusted, not with the actress she so respected, but at the notion of herself in a masculine role.

The movement for the emancipation of women, too, left her cold.

The mistake of the women's movement, as it is understood and carried on among us resides in this, she wrote, *that it immediately turns into a battlefield of petty bickerings and small victories. Consequently it gives the impression that the sexes are two hostile parts, each of which can win only at the cost of the other — but the solution of the problem must be sought in a reciprocity of trust and respect, in the realm of the most exalted human virtues and powers. Education is the first essential of any progress, education for both men and women.*

Knowing the need and importance of love in her own life, and the equal need that it should be a part and not the whole, she added, *Besides, love is far too important, far too rare and exalted a contingency for either sex to make it the point of reference for every word and act of their lives.*

Her early lack of protection and guidance, in a profession where love affairs were frequent and casual, turned her thoughts in yet another direction. Shrewdly, she wrote, *The tremendous expectation in regard to sexual love, and the shame in that expectation, distorts all perspective for women beforehand.*

But Schürmann, unconcerned with wider issues, remarked, 'A feminine success, in the best sense of the word, is the most lasting of all — since an enthusiastic woman generally carries along her husband, her husband's friends, and all her relatives to the box office!'

Eleonora was thirty-eight. Eschewing the peacock colours of her youth, except for theatrical requirements, she dressed simply and well in either black or white. Her fastidiousness had grown. A distaste for frills and ribbons and fuss, and the financial ability to buy the best, drove her to the fashion house of Worth, who designed and executed her wardrobes both on- and offstage. She detested scent, except in flowers. Described as the actress of a thousand faces, and a different walk for every role, her own face was serious and refined, her carriage graceful. The reading campaign, begun two decades earlier, now swept from Plotinus to Goethe, from Sophocles to Ibsen. She could never resist a flower shop nor a bookstall. Step light, tensions vanished, she sallied forth in the American morning in her black Worth *tailleur*, and sniffed and rummaged with abandon, bearing her trophies home. Or, at nightfall elegant and anonymous, her veiled Gainsborough hat garnished with a small black ostrich feather, her gloved hands clasping a black leather purse, she walked the city and absorbed the outer world.

Schürmann, whose instinct for publicity never failed him, sent a complimentary ticket to Thomas Alva Edison, and effected an introduction so that Duse might visit the old man in Orange Park. He recorded her voice on his phonograph and she listened with rapt interest. It was a quieter reception than the one Sarah had accorded him in 1880, when she and her company had dropped in on him after midnight, and she shrieked with laughter at the playback and was thus mistakenly entertained. But Sarah was Sarah, and said to be the greatest actress in the world, so could do as she pleased.

Edoardo Gordigiani painted a portrait of Duse in changing tones of opal, one lovely hand supporting her head, the other lying gracefully in the satin folds of her gown.

Duse at nightfall on Broadway, crying, 'Show me the Milky Way!' to an old Italian with a telescope for hire.

'It's five cents a star!'

She searched her purse among the unfamiliar money and gave him a dollar. Directed from the North Star across the heavens, she found the Pleiades and loosened the bonds of Orion, back in her childhood among the gods.

'I'll have another dollar's worth, please!'

He had recognised her as she became animated, and with a smile directed the telescope on to Broadway. The trams rolled by, sparkling caterpillars, each winking its little galaxy of publicity at the crowds hurrying along the sidewalks.

'Look there, Signora!' he commanded her in her own tongue.

On the sides of the vehicles, in brilliant letters of light, New York advertised her presence:

THE PASSING STAR. ELEONORA DUSE.

NINETEEN

D'Annunzio in his solitude scribbled a note: *The enormous vessel heading for Liverpool — all black, under a huge red sun.*

Eleonora was weeping for joy, her cabin a tumult of flowers and gifts and farewell telegrams. She had triumphed and was going home again. The milk-and-honey land of Italy awaited her: the olive groves and white-capped mountains; the vineyards and stiff cypresses; the blue enchanted haze of Umbria; the towns full of silence in the morning sun. In Fiesole, on its crescent of a hill, grew a wisteria as old as it was huge; the branches and blossoms falling from terrace to terrace. And submitting to the ministrations of the stewardess, releasing Schürmann to brood enjoyably over a bottle of wine, she lay between the sheets in peace, and closed her eyes. Between waking and sleeping the wisteria assumed numinous qualities, and made its meaning clear to her.

'Of course,' she said drowsily, to herself, 'the houses stand still, but the creeper grows and grows and cannot be contained. Just as the body has its limitations and the spirit flowers. And though I shall rest for a while, I shall — I must — go back to work. And this time, this time at least, I shall do something really new, really splendid.'

Into D'Annunzio's world had slipped a young and spiritual girl of twenty, an accomplished pianist whose family were personal friends of the actress. On one or two occasions Duse had taken the girl on tour with her, as a substitute daughter, loving Giulietta for her grace and simplicity. And Giulietta loved and worshipped in return, but could not help being drawn to D'Annunzio, and yet drew back again when she thought of Eleonora. Then, while her brother Edoardo painted Duse in New York, Giulietta Gordigiani began a tremulous and virginal affair with Duse's lover.

She was, D'Annunzio decided, the perfect foil for Eleonora in the novel he intended to write. Spring and autumn, youth and middle age, Giulietta and Eleonora, *Donatella Arrale* and *La Foscarina*. In art as in life, he felt, one must have the promise of delight to come as well as delight fading and gone.

Giulietta prepared to give her heart, but refused to give her body, begging for a union of souls — a union which D'Annunzio often lauded, but found unaccountably flat without the bonus of an affair. Intrigued, he brought all his charm into play and received for his trouble three prim sweet notes which thanked him for gifts of fruit and flowers. He besieged, she retreated. He pressed her, and she broke. She was flattered to rival la Duse in his affections, she was desperately attracted to him, but the cost in self-esteem and Duse's friendship was too great. Innocent, heartbroken and steadfast, she withdrew from the contest.

The affair was over before Eleonora returned, but she hunted it out and confronted D'Annunzio in a hysteria of betrayal. Missing the finer points of infidelity, he said that nothing had come of it. She summoned Giulietta, imperious as a queen with a flirtatious maid-in-waiting, and quailed her with a glance. The girl's explanation, delivered in sobs and disjointed sentences, disarmed her. Embracing Giulietta, drying her eyes with her own handkerchief, she proclaimed her a sister in spirit, and forgave her completely. On consideration, she forgave D'Annunzio too.

With two main characters and a ready-made conflict to hand, he began to write *Il Fuoco* on 14 July 1896. The flame guttered. Crackling off in another direction, under tremendous pressure, braving exhaustion and hallucinations alike, he wrote his first play, *La Città Morta*, in six weeks, and laid down his pen, exultant. Though the encouragement and inspiration had come from Eleonora he did not intend her to produce it, since his first play must surely be given to the finest public by the finest actress of the day. And who could do the writing of D'Annunzio justice but the most important star in international theatre, Sarah Bernhardt?

Absorbed by her present Italian tour, expecting to be handed the play as soon as he had finished it, Eleonora was unprepared for his deviousness. She agreed with him, puzzled, that her company was not yet composed of the players who could interpret his advanced ideas.

'But by the time it is finished,' she said, knowing nothing of D'Annunzio's capacity for concentration, 'my company will also be ready.'

'It *is* finished,' he said.

She was silent, and a small suspicion crept like smoke between them.

'If that is so, then of course I must look about me at once for the right actors,' she said, disconcerted.

'Oh, there is no need,' he replied absently, turning away, 'Since this is my first play I must do the best I can for it. I have sent it to Bernhardt.'

Her face became peculiarly colourless, even for so pale a woman, and his vanity attributed this to only one cause.

'But, *dolcezza*, you don't imagine that I'm in love with Bernhardt, surely?' he cried, flattered.

'In love?' she said, barely able to frame the words. 'In *love*?'

'I am not giving this play to Bernhardt the woman, but to Bernhardt the actress.'

'To the actress. Yes.'

'And she has accepted it. At least, she says nothing about a date, but I have this telegram from her.'

Admirable! Admirable! Admirable!

He held it out to her, good-humoured, not understanding why she did not take it from him.

'The *woman* is here before me,' he said persuasively. 'The play was given to the *actress*.'

The words dropped one by one like stones.

'It is as an *actress* that I speak to you now,' she said slowly.

And as he stared at her, she cried, 'The woman was betrayed and has forgiven you. That is her role. But the actress has been betrayed and she will *never* forgive you. Oh, sweet *God*!' she said, soft and bitter, and yet her training did not desert her. Anyone else would have ranted unforgivably. '*I* was the actress you wrote that play for. *I* encouraged you and believed in you. What does Bernhardt know of you? Nothing. What has she done with your manuscript? Lost it in a litter of other manuscripts from other playwrights, somewhere in her dressing room under an avalanche of shoes. What would I have done with it? Taken it all over Italy with me, read and re-read every word, put my own money into the production of it, taken the risks, cherished it, loved it, created it in the theatre as you created it in your room. It would have been the seal on our friendship, the best of both of us, set together in one indestructible bond.'

She held her jaws with both hands to conceal their trembling, and stammered with pain.

'Why,' she said, controlling herself with difficulty, 'you have treated me like a street woman. Is that what you think actresses are for? To take to bed for a few hours of animal pleasure? Do you see in us something corrupt and filthy, then?'

'I am not saying,' he broke in humbly (though he was) 'that Bernhardt is a *finer* actress, only better known — better able to present my poor work in its best light...'

'Your *poor work*? I would not lie about the quality of my work in order to cover up what I was doing. What of *my* work? My *good* work. You thought your work too fine to waste on me, and so you gave it to someone else. And it is not hers,' she cried, in a tempest of tears, 'it is *mine*. It belongs to the *Italian* theatre, not to the French. It belongs, if not to me, to an *Italian* actress. We are one nation, now, Gabriele. Your play belongs to Italy. Afterwards, she can have it. Afterwards.'

Believing she had spent her anger on him, he replied sullenly, 'You can't possess me body and soul.'

Her arms dropped at her sides. Miserable, aghast, she turned away from him.

He said, 'Come my love, my lost one. Perdita. Forgive your poor slave who has displeased you.' He built on fancy, with charm. 'But how can a slave displease a queen? He is unworthy of her notice.' He threw a late sop to Cerberus. 'You shall have all the others.'

She said between her teeth, 'I shall have *this* or none!'

He shrugged, impatient of her.

'Bernhardt has accepted. I can hardly ask her to send it back, can I?'

She looked at him until he looked away. Then picked up her hat and gloves.

'The actress is leaving you, Gabriele,' she said, with a finality that disturbed him. 'And the woman goes with her.'

In the October of 1896 she left Italy on tour, taking Giulietta. Professional pride supported the actress, but the woman turned to an older and kinder love, and scrawled pages to Arrigo Boito.

Of the girl whose devotion moved her, whose presence pained her, she wrote:

Giulietta comes with me. Another joy, it is true, but another sorrow. The poor child distresses me so, but since this is what she wishes...

Giulietta, loving both Duse and D'Annunzio, scarred both and was scarred in turn. Once, driven by the demands of love, she sent a note to D'Annunzio in Venice. He, like so many other rakes, had been captured by his captive's chastity. Unable to fathom her, he sealed all her letters in an envelope. A few years later Giulietta erased his image by marrying Robert von Mendelssohn, the German banker, escaping D'Annunzio's net without wholly casting off Duse's silken chains. For Robert von Mendelssohn was an old admirer of the actress, and continued to be her financial adviser.

Arrigo, now in his middle fifties, welcomed the ghost of Eleonora's affection, and wrote back without reserve: consoling, sympathising and unselfish. His generosity roused her compassion and regret.

'Whenever I see anything green,' she wrote, 'whenever I touch roses, I cry like an idiot. Whenever I come across two individuals who seem to agree, my heart contracts.'

Shame at being one of D'Annunzio's victims struggled with the emptiness she experienced at his loss.

'Oh, Arrigo, I must try to make you like me again... I *must* find again the inner harmony that you recommend.'

Later, with only her work to sustain her, she scrawled, *The strongest is the loneliest, and the loneliest the strongest.* Then, repentant, for she was after all only using him, *Forgive me if I disrupt your peace.*

D'Annunzio filled his private notebooks with impressions of Duse, reproducing descriptions and conversations, building up the character of his ageing actress heroine, *La Foscarina*. But he lacked some union of the soul which she undoubtedly had given him, the body being more easy to replace. He wrote:

I am in travail. I don't know why. I no longer know anything about myself; I should like to find someone who knew everything about me and told me. Does love help? Does love enlighten me? A while ago, did not the noble woman whose eyes are filled with tears and infinity desperately withdraw from me? Always in her sad step I heard the rustle of laurel leaves...

Her sadness, which he was incapable of feeling, haunted him. He was bereft, not because he had hurt her but because he needed her as a gardener needs earth. Love affair and book had been cut off alike, before he had more than begun either.

Remembering, he put pen to paper again.

She had tied a hair round each of my fingers, as I talked with her beside me. I was tied by five hairs, and I began to feel the hurt as if the five hairs were five chains... She does not release me and says, 'Break them! Snap them!' The hairs break but the knots remain round my knuckles... She takes my hand — I feel her tears falling. An obscure anguish binds us, fibre to fibre...

Disciplined, solitary, dedicated, Eleonora worked and learned, recovering a measure of serenity. The business of losing herself in a part, she began to comprehend, must be extended to daily life if she were to survive. One morning, achieving this freedom, she awoke as from a nightmare and saw Venice with detached clarity: languor and beauty, sensuality and decay.

'The whole city is coloured by that man!' she said, and walked her rooms, arms folded.

She terminated her lease, found new tenants, dismantled the eyrie which had first brought her peace, then passion, and finally disruption. Exulting in her release, she asked Count Primoli if he would store her furniture while she found another retreat. Playing with the idea of setting up a theatre outside Rome, since that joint theatre could not now materialise, she prepared to set out for the capital, full of plans. A glow of colour caught her eye. She stood back, hands on hips, staring in amazement at the opulent red velvet hangings in the entrance hall.

'What are those doing there?' she demanded, sensing them to be out of tune with her, to be strange and curiously intrusive.

'The Signor chose them for you, Signora,' said the maid timidly.

Eleonora turned to her new tenants, who had come to measure the apartment.

'You may have these, if you wish — with my compliments!' she said, gracious and imperious at once.

And as they thanked her, delighted, she smiled and said to herself, 'They are just like *him*!'

Count Giuseppe Primoli, last descendant of the Bonapartes, kept open house to the most original men and women of the day, and documented his period with the skilful and extensive use of the camera. Subtle and worldly, an early admirer of Duse's art, and of D'Annunzio's also, he regretted the disintegration of a union which he felt to be of immense value to both parties. But he stored Eleonora's furniture and bided his time.

The challenge of Paris arrived in a confusion that was never wholly explained. Eleonora chose to believe that Bernhardt, in professional liberalism, had invited her to appear at the Renaissance theatre for a short season.

'Sarah never asked her to come to Paris!' said Schürmann, amused at the notion. '*I* rented the Renaissance theatre from her — and on leonine terms, I might tell you!'

A third rumour whispered that Sarah had at first declined to let la Duse enter her private territory, and had only changed her mind when Victorien Sardou said that the Italian actress would never succeed in Paris.

However it had come about, Eleonora insisted outwardly that Sarah had recognised her and offered the hand of friendship. It was Duse's spiritual strength that she could work herself without mercy in the service of her art, physically frail though she was. It was an emotional weakness that she could not detach herself sufficiently to observe her ambitiousness, which was mighty, with an entirely honest eye. Dragged from a background that had made her what she was, and conversant with the tricks and politics of the theatre world, she knew that this talk of sisterhood and friendship was simply talk. She intended — had she dared frame the words — to challenge Sarah on home ground. She rated herself, with justice, an artist of greater sincerity; subtler and more profound than the

French show-woman. And an old rivalry had been intensified by D'Annunzio's gift to Sarah of that treasured first play.

Ambivalent as always, she prayed humbly that she might triumph for the sake of her art — and intended to show Sarah how that art improved on Sarah's own.

She turned to Count Primoli, seemingly for advice on a difficult issue, but he had contrived a little Machiavellian plot of his own by arranging for D'Annunzio to interrupt them by accident, as they conversed in the library.

'Ah!' cried the Count, smiling, touching his black beard. 'You come at the right moment, Gabriele. Our exquisite artist has been offered a season in Paris, and does not know whether or not to accept.'

Disturbed, but proudly in command of herself, Eleonora avoided D'Annunzio's eager eyes, and handed him the telegram.

'But surely,' he cried, 'you are not hesitating?'

A delicate flush betrayed her, but she continued to speak evenly and composedly. 'The French are accustomed to such a perfection of *ensemble*, and,' she transfixed him with an arrow of reproach, 'to such a *personality*!'

He absorbed the snub.

'Accept at once!' he commanded, and conveyed adoration in the command.

Hesitating, she said shyly, 'If I might play *La Città Morta*...

But she must not stand between himself and his work.

'*La Città Morta* is — regretfully — reserved for production at the Renaissance theatre,' he said gracefully.

Rebuffed, she said lightly, 'It is precisely at the Renaissance I have been asked to play!'

A slight pause. A slight frown on both brows. His face cleared.

'Then your reluctance is inexcusable,' said D'Annunzio gaily, 'since the doors of the Renaissance will be thrown open to you by Sarah the Magnificent herself.'

She accepted defeat, in part.

'Then write me something,' she begged, 'something in verse, in honour of the occasion!'

'In a *week*?' cried D'Annunzio, startled. 'You're *mad*!'

Beautiful, elated, she said mockingly, 'Then write me the part of a madwoman!'

The union was made whole.

TWENTY

Ten days later, Count Primoli was ravished by a vision of white, hurrying down the stairs of the Hotel Bristol in Rome, brandishing a manuscript bound in antique brocade and garnished with green moiré silk ribbons.

'I've got it!' la Duse cried.

Sogno d'un Mattino di Primavera. 'Dream of a Spring Morning.' A one-act play pressured from D'Annunzio in record time.

The Count congratulated her.

Schürmann was not too sure about it, though Eleonora insisted on calling it a masterpiece.

'Listen, if you do not believe!' she commanded, and began to speak the lines with immense feeling.

'Beautiful, beautiful,' Schürmann murmured, 'but is it a good *play*?'

How could her judgement be faulty?

'We shall rehearse it in the country,' she said, aloof and obstinate, 'in a green meadow under the trees, among the flowers of the Frascati landscape. And, José, find Flavio Andò somehow! He must come back as my leading man, for Paris!'

Schürmann raised his eyebrows and shrugged. At least she would have her other plays, and he was sure of those. As Magda no one could touch her. In *La Femme de Claude*, though it was beginning to sound a bit old-fashioned nowadays, she had always been superb. The moments when she struggled to pull out the stopper of the poison bottle never failed to move even Schürmann. *Cavalleria rusticana* — had Verga not said it was more hers than his? *La Locandiera* had become Duse's own indisputable comic role. No Ibsen? A pity. Her Nora was renowned. And why not *Denise*, which Dumas *fils* had written for her? Why not more Italian plays? *La Moglie Ideale*? — Marco Praga's own work on which Duse had helped and advised, so that the poor boy had hurried back to his hotel, and gone without supper and sleep in order to re-write that act just as she liked it! Why not?

He knew very well why not. These plays did not figure in Sarah's repertoire, and Eleonora intended to show up Sarah, whatever she might protest about art. Moreover, she was opening at the Renaissance in Sarah's pet role, *La Dame aux Camélias*. Well, well, it was all marvellous publicity, and he had persuaded *Figaro* to publish an article on her. Meanwhile, her head was full of this new *folderol*.

'Gabriele has asked Monsieur Hérelle to translate *Sogno* in time for it to appear in the Revue de Paris, before the première!' said Eleonora, commanding more enthusiasm than he was prepared to give.

'Delightful!' said Schürmann, amiably.

After all, one little one-act play. So long as the wretched fellow did not write any more, and insist on Duse producing them, all would be well. For himself, he considered D'Annunzio a doubtful and expensive encumbrance.

The poet's precocious talents and equally precocious sexual appetites had made him an *enfant terrible* at the age of seventeen. In his thirty-fourth year he was considered the greatest hope for Italian literature, and he worked prodigiously hard. But fame and notoriety, glory and infamy do not always pay bills, and D'Annunzio's passion for luxuries exceeded his income. He drew a fixed salary as editor of the Roman *Tribuna*, wrote poems and articles and stories, collected a trickle of royalties from the French publication of his novels, and never kept up with his creditors.

Besides his own expensive tastes he entertained royally, pursued women gallantly, was fretted periodically by his first wife and her three sons, and then by his discarded mistress Princess Maria Gravina and her daughter Renata. It would have been a rich man who lived without debts in this fashion, and the d'Annunzian estate had been lost when Gabriele's father died four years before, so he could look for no parental help or inheritance.

He knew that Duse earned, and spent, great sums of money. He did not ask to live on her charity, but he did hope that his desire to write plays would be harnessed to her acting ability, and make money for both of them. Nor were writing and fornication his only interests. He was fascinated by politics, placing himself on the extreme Right, and was considering the possibility of offering himself as a candidate for the August elections, in Abruzzo — his home ground. He was physically brave, and had fought duels of honour. He took stock of Italy's affairs, both domestic and foreign, and would willingly have died for his country.

But Schürmann watched and judged the affair and shook his head. He had seen too many gigolos to be misled by fine words and an aristocratic exterior.

A small black cloud hovered in Duse's radiant sky. Arrigo, loving and unsuspecting, must be persuaded to persuade her to act in D'Annunzio's play and give his unqualified blessing to their reunion.

Perhaps Tebaldo Checchi, her husband, had glimpsed his future when she mourned Cafiero that afternoon in 1884, and decided then that he could bear only so much participation. Arrigo Boito was not to cut himself away from Eleonora quite so cleanly. She required love and devotion, and if a former lover — discarded by her — could stand by to comfort and advise her on a new lover's idiosyncrasies, she was well content. Her command for Flavio Andò to be summoned back to her company was wholly professional; she felt that Paris would enjoy his dark good looks. But it would not harm D'Annunzio to see how wonderfully well they were partnered on the stage, or to witness Flavio's undiminished devotion.

With regard to Arrigo she nursed a bad conscience, and therefore wrote to him, beseeching. His reply was subdued, and she discerned that he felt stricken. Flurried, guilty, she scrawled three letters in one week, underlining, the ink blobbing as the pen drove across the paper. He replied with dignity that she had hurt him. She knew very well she had hurt him, and the extent to which she had hurt him, and how badly she had behaved.

I hurt you? she scribbled, distraught. *After so much love between us? What could I do without you?* And she must, must, must have his unconditional surrender, his praise and permission, given without stint. *What agony it would be today, at this final stage of a career, if I had to renounce the sublime work! Your consent alone can restore life to my blood.* Desperate with him, with D'Annunzio, with herself, she implored, *I* must have *wings! Give* me *wings!* And signed his pet name for her: *Lenor.*

Of course he would do as she asked, with old age breathing over his shoulder, for the memory of a woman who meant more to him than any other had or would. Maimed, lost and selfless — as Tebaldo Checchi had been — he gave his permission. The long-drawn-out death of their affair was over, and only a corpse remained to be buried. Eleonora placed the final wreath on the coffin at the end of the following year. From the Hotel Hassler in Rome she wrote to Arrigo of the final parting she herself had brought about: *It's like dying, exactly like dying.*

His reply was dredged from some abyss with which, for all her sufferings, she was not yet acquainted: *It is more than death, because it was more than life… this is more than death.*

'Sarah is travelling post-haste back from Brussels for your première!' Schürmann announced, amused and intrigued by both women.

The actress clasped her hands, conveying delight at the honour. Schürmann, taking his cue, said that Bernhardt's gesture was a handsome one. He knew he did not have to translate that dash back to Paris. Sarah intended to be there in order to provoke the duel, and for all those clasped hands and humble smiles Eleonora was aware of Sarah's intentions, too.

'I have the greatest admiration for Madame Bernhardt,' said Eleonora. 'I prize her energy, her noble personality.'

'Tell me, Nella,' said Schürmann comfortably, 'cutting out the frills, just *how* great is your admiration?'

'Oh, very great,' she said wryly, dropping her rapt pose, and sat down on a property basket, hands in lap, head bent. 'She is an artist of genius, in spite of her publicity tricks. She is highly intelligent, and therefore to be feared. She has an innate disposition for tragedy, and the gifts of a fine tragedian — though she gestures more than I do, and is sometimes mechanical in her effects. We do not, she and I, work in the same way. But I know that she, like myself, is capable at times of conveying — conveying the *truth*, José.'

Animated now, clever, intuitive, rational, she confided in him.

'When she is at her best I honour her, José. I am the humblest of her admirers. I would kneel at her feet, as I did all those years ago in Turin. And she said, "Oh, *do* get up!" in that jolly fashion of hers, that woman-to-woman way she has.

'In those supreme moments, José, she and I have cast aside personalities and gone beyond ourselves, even gone beyond the theatre itself. And we meet on some level at which we are unimportant instruments of something infinitely important. *She* says the god is there. I don't know what *I* should call it. Some day, perhaps, I'll find out — if I don't die of work first!'

He sat by her, quiet and respectful, as he had sat by so many of these strange wandering creatures who supplied his bread and butter. But she was away from him, thinking out loud now, musing.

'She must feel it, too,' she said. 'But, you know, she never appears to show it. There's no pain in her recall. She can snap back from the last speech to the first curtain call like a marionette. That's where, in one way, she beats me. And in that one little difference lies the chasm between us. She's faster, harder, cleverer, and more unscrupulous than I am. I could be humble before her, before anyone who spoke to the best in me. Could she, do you think?'

He lifted his shoulders and spread his hands.

'It's all a parade to her,' said Eleonora. 'A side-show in which she wins all the prizes and enjoys all the fun. I would kneel to *her*. Would she kneel to *me*?'

He said dryly, 'If it was good publicity — yes.'

The conversation was finished. She rose and yawned, straightened her shoulders, rubbed her back where it ached.

'To Paris, then, José, eh?'

'And sharpen your knife. She'll be waiting to stick hers between your ribs!'

'The knife,' said Eleonora, grinning, 'is an *Italian* weapon.'

TWENTY-ONE

The Comte de Montesquiou-Fézensac, descendant of one of the noblest families in France, brought the two ladies together in Sarah's studio at the end of May 1897. Polished, witty, with a wicked eye for detail, he recorded the event. And finding his own sex more diverting that the female one, he was in an ideal position to judge dispassionately.

I was, he wrote, *present at the initial encounter of these two women, who fell so violently into each other's arms that it struck me as something in the nature of a collision rather than of affection.*

He stood by, missing no fixed smile, no velvet barb, as they complimented each other: Duse still feeling respect, Bernhardt merely showing it. As an artist, the Count admired Duse, but as a personality she disappointed him. Plain and pale and small, she faded before Sarah's barbaric magnificence. Also, he observed, though the Italian actress was fifteen years Sarah's junior, Sarah's vivacity and paint disguised that hard fact.

With la Duse dismissed, Sarah summoned Schürmann and got down to business.

'How are the sales?' she asked, without preamble.

Bowing, unafraid, Schürmann replied, 'There are no seats left, Madame. We have taken 800,000 francs in less than two days.'

'You don't know,' said Sarah, smoothly, 'how delighted I am!'

'I can guess, madame!' said Schürmann, imperturbable.

The ladies' meeting had whetted the Count's appetite for the contest, and with relish he escorted Eleonora to the Renaissance that evening to watch Sarah play *La Samaritaine*.

Bowing to the edicts of the Parisian public, Eleonora had taken particular care over her clothes and appearance. Nervous, elegant, she awaited the rise of the curtain, in her central box which was exotic with orchids. And as Sarah appeared, to a fusillade of clapping, de Montesquieu saw the little Italian rise and stand in homage. He rose with her, and remained standing. From time to time he glanced at la Duse, but she seemed unaware of his presence, absorbing every word and gesture.

When she rose again at the beginning of the second act, he realised he was in for an exhausting evening. White and composed, trembling a little with fatigue, Eleonora stood throughout the play in her hostess's honour. And the Count, inwardly damning all such gestures, stood too.

The drama of curtain calls had not altered appreciably.

Sarah made her symbolic embrace of the audience, was overcome by the sight of flowers, required the arm of her leading man, was inexorably restored to the multitude, and retired only when the last ounce of energy had been drained from the audience. And she bowed particularly to the central box and that erect little figure, making a mental note that she was due for an evening on her feet at Eleonora's début the following night.

A pinprick awaited Duse: Sarah's personal dressing room had been locked against her. Schürmann, unsurprised, was still annoyed.

'Come,' said Eleonora, determined not to feel the pea beneath the mattresses, 'let's not be troubled by petty things.

Madame Bernhardt has need of luxuries. I have not. This smaller room will be quite good enough. I'm dressing in it — not living in it!'

The house filled with the elite, including Madame Eugénie Doche, now in her old age, who had played the title role in the very first performance forty-five years before. The French actress Gabrielle Réjane was there, in a box in the upper tier, chatting with her husband, pointing out the glories of the Renaissance to her small daughter. Jeanne Julia Bartet, who — with Réjane — was one of the most important actresses on the French stage, after Bernhardt, was there. Francisque Sarcey, master-critic, white-bearded, stout and immaculate, put on his spectacles and glanced through the programme. And when the house was quite full, Sarah appeared, graciously acknowledging the applause.

Escorted by the indefatigable Count, who observed maliciously that she resembled Iphigenia brought to sacrifice, she had outdone her usual splendour. Her henna-ed hair was wreathed in roses. Her fingers were studded, her arms weighed down, with jewels. She wore a multi-coloured gown of taffeta brocade, heavy with fringes, rich in tassels. A gracious movement of the hand indicated that though she appreciated their adoration she begged them to reserve their energies for la Duse. Then she sat down, smiling, rested one elbow on the balustrade, cupped her chin, cleared her throat, and snapped shut her ostrich feather fan.

Her timing was perfect. Three loud knocks on the floor of the stage brought the audience to silence. And into the polite patter of handclaps, as the curtain rose, came Sarah's own vigorous encouragement, loud and prolonged and just a fraction too pronounced.

A long-drawn 'ah' of pleasure greeted the entrance of Eleonora, clad in a gown of Parisian cut. And at once Sarah stood up, followed by the resigned Count, and all faces turned towards her. She frowned slightly at them, and shook her head. Obediently they turned their attentions back to Duse, who showed signs of nervous strain already. Sarah was plainly worried for her protégée, and drew in her breath when Eleonora clutched a chair back for support, or missed or fluffed a line. She padded out the applause when it sounded thin, smiled and nodded when it came spontaneously, and led it at all times. During the intermissions she held quite a reception in her central box, almost a play on its own.

Distracted by Sarah's presence, puzzled by Duse's rendering of a Parisian *poule* as a lady-like creature of great sensibility, the spectators became increasingly restless and disappointed. But Sarah would have none of them, and confusing the issue further she described Duse's perfections in a penetrating voice, particularly as those perfections had been noticeably absent.

Totally lost between the drama on the stage and the drama in the central box, they applauded Flavio Andò in the fourth act. And he, paralysed with embarrassment, realised that he had stolen Duse's big scene without trying or even meaning to do so.

She was in her stride for the last act, far too late, and accepted their well-mannered ovation with a sick heart. The first round had gone to Sarah for a technical display which, whatever it lacked in scruple, was undoubtedly a masterpiece of strategy.

The critics were worse than cruel: they were kind and understanding. They made no comparisons with Bernhardt or Réjane or Bartet. After such a debacle no comparisons were possible.

Eleonora made a better job of *Magda* on the second night — though it was not her usual class of performance — and they were slightly more impressed. But she had called too hard on her nerves, and the rest of that week's performances had to be cancelled.

'Not,' said Schürmann, drumming his fingers, 'an auspicious beginning.'

As Duse struggled with humiliation and physical frailty, Sarah's ruses suffered from the gossip that always rims from mouth to mouth in times of controversy. Sarcey, his claws tucked mercifully away, had been gentle with the Italian actress, giving the impression that he expected better things once she got her first wind. The audience, though enjoying Sarah's own performance in the central box, were not naive enough to attribute her behaviour to disinterested benevolence. Paris whispered about the locked dressing room; hinted that a piece of scenery had fallen dangerously close to the little Italian; murmured that Sarah had manoeuvred la Duse into a draught during one intermission, and kept her there shivering while she paid effusive compliments, though she knew Duse easily caught cold. Sarah was becoming slightly flustered under attack, but had not attained her present eminence without learning a trick or two on the way. Still in the role of hostess and benefactress, she announced a benefit night, the proceeds of which would help to finance a monument to Dumas *fils*, who had died the previous year. And, said Sarah, she would ask la Duse, with her incomparable genius, to take part with her. They could act *La Dame aux Camélias* between them. But here she overplayed her hand. She announced that she herself would undertake the burden of the play and offered Duse the act in which she had failed so conspicuously in her début.

'I should be a fool to do it!' said Eleonora, 'and I am not a fool!'

Crying with rage and disappointment, she offered to play instead the second act from *La Femme de Claude.*

Sarah could not object. So she intensified the campaign. By special request of Sardou himself, she said, she had been forced to open the evening with *L'Aveu*, a poor little one-act play she herself had scribbled. Then Tamagno and Héglon were to sing a duet from *Il Trovatore*, followed by Emma Nevada in an aria from *Lucia di Lammermoor.* Then the vivacious Yvette Guilbert would deliver a monologue. Then Duse could play her act from *La Femme de Claude*, and Sarah would struggle somehow through acts four and five of *La Dame aux Camélias.* After an interval, the audience could enjoy a recital by Coquelin and three more songs by the operatic stars, with *L'Hommage de Marguerite Gautier à Alexandre Dumas* as dessert — in which Sarah was reciting Rostand's verses alone, surrounded by all her colleagues.

On 14 June the curtain rose on a Milky Way of stars, each determined to make their mark upon the evening, if not upon each other. The audience greeted Sarah as a reigning goddess, cheered the singers to the roof, and prepared to relish a witty interlude by their gangling, red-haired Yvette Guilbert. She had, unluckily, fallen into the clown's ever-present pit of wanting to play Hamlet. And chose to appear, elegantly gowned, reading excerpts from Marcel Prévost's *Lettres à Françoise.*

Their gasp of disappointment almost unhinged her, but she began in great style to render the words of the master as they had never before been rendered. They loved her, but the incongruity of her choice tickled their fancy. Perhaps, they thought, she intended to amuse them by playing the *grande dame*. A chuckle from the stalls made her pause. She looked indignant and, comic artist that she was, could not help her indignation looking staged and funny. The house shook in silent amusement. Tears of anger threatened her voice. She attempted to continue, was annihilated by an audible tittering, and swept offstage without finishing.

As the banging door shook the scenery, they sobered down, repentant. She wanted — they saw it all now — to be one of the galaxy; had chosen her well-mannered gown, her erudite monologue, to show them that she too, Yvette of the *Variétés*, was as good as any other actress. They loved her for herself, and it seemed little enough to ask of them. They called, they stamped, they roared, they begged her to come back and do as she pleased. But, dishevelled with grief, rousing even the sympathy of the rivals backstage, Yvette wept upon a property basket, and refused to return.

It was at this point that Eleonora was expected to go on and face a distracted audience in the wrong mood, but she meant to do the best she could with what little she had been allowed. Sympathy might have finished her, but the challenge did not.

Savage, pathetic, seductive, she charmed them into her hand. And watching her through a hole in the set, surrounded by a group of cronies all imitating the Italian's gestures, Sarah ground her teeth at each burst of applause. But, never beaten, she fell into Eleonora's arms as she came off, crying, 'Divine! Ah, my dear, you were simply divine!'

Her transports were cut short by the spectators intimating that they wanted la Duse back. And back she went, four times in all, flushed and ready for anything. In her dressing room,

Sardou himself, and a deputation from the Monument Committee, congratulated her on a superb performance — then rushed off again to watch Sarah, whose mettle was also up, give a marvellous rendering of the last two acts of *Camille*.

There was as much noise and excitement behind the scenes as in the auditorium. All the ladies embraced each other at the appropriate moments, and Eleonora wept with fury and admiration. Finally, on stage, they all gathered round Bernhardt as she began, exquisitely, to recite the homage to Dumas; smiling jealously at her, and at each other, in a frenzy of frayed nerves and professional annoyance.

Then the unexpected happened, though the reason was not clear. Was it fair-mindedness, a flair for publicity, or simply fellow-feeling? But Sarah held out her hand to Eleonora, who had been allotted only one item on the programme, and brought her forward to share the adulation. Certainly she returned her firmly to the back immediately afterwards, but the gesture had been made and the audience loved it.

With la Duse put in her place, Sarah sailed off to dazzle London, and Eleonora began, jewel by jewel, to dismantle Sarah's crown. She had recovered her health, had never lost her courage, and she was very, very angry.

D'Annunzio, arriving for the première of *Sogno*, was amazed at Paris's lack of perception. And Sarcey, who had held his tongue over Duse's failure, did not extend the same courtesy to D'Annunzio. He wrote:

The theme is childish. On the stage the play, if we can call it by such a name, this infantile and pretentious poem is an insufferable bore. Duse was also badly costumed.

D'Annunzio turned on her.

'Had Sarah performed the role,' he said, 'the play would have succeeded. But what can you expect? You were insane even to dream of competing with her! Thank God, at least, that *she* will produce *La Città Morta*. What a fiasco! What a disaster! What a *fool* I've been!'

From London the dulcet voice of Sarah announced that *she* would perform *Sogno*. And at this piece of impertinence Sarcey's beard bristled, and he charged into print.

What fly is biting her? Ah, how ill-advised she is! If she wishes to engage in a duel... she should take refuge rather in those inaccessible regions in which it would seem Duse could never penetrate, and act Phèdre *for us...*

Many flies were biting Sarah. They arrived by every post in the form of press cuttings, describing how the Italian actress had moved Paris with *La Femme de Claude*, with *La Locandiera*, with *Cavalleria rusticana*. They implied that now that the dust had settled, Paris began to see what Duse meant by her meditative silences, by the words coming now rapidly, now slowly, by signs no more emphatic than a tremor of lips or the faintest movement of a hand. In the place of Sarah's string-plucking and tear-jerking, came something more profound, a stirring of soul which made one question what so far had passed for the finest art.

Even the voice of Sarcey, recalling his fellow critics to earth, was gall to Sarah.

There is no one but Duse now, he wrote ironically. *Duse for ever! No more Desclée, no Réjane, no Bartet...*

She re-read the next name, certain he had gone out of his mind.

...no Sarah! La Duse, only la Duse! And recollecting the pendulum-swing from theatre goddess to theatre goddess, he had added, *We are a funny people.*

A funny people indeed. That first night they had applauded Flavio Andò. Then, suddenly, he could not please them.

'It's not so much because of his little moustache...' wrote the feline Sarcey.

Outraged, Andò caught the next train home, and was replaced by Carlo Rosaspina.

Well, thank God in his heaven, Sarah thought, that the woman's trip was at an end. Or who knew what might happen? Ah, Paris must be brought to heel. She would return immediately.

But before she could issue a single order came the final sting. Under the pseudonym of *Sganarelle*, Sarcey wrote an open letter in *Le Temps*, begging Duse to give a special matinée for those actors and artists of Paris who had heard of but never seen her.

You have so many admirers... it is a great disappointment and a real grief to our artists not to have heard you. You have brought a new style: they would be eager to study it and some could benefit by it. No doubt it is enough for them to know that you are one of the great artists of our time. But they would be happy to admire you.

The telegram which asked Sarah to extend her lease of the Renaissance for another week, in order to allow Eleonora to perform on 6 July, was torn into fragments. The Renaissance, said Sarah, had to be closed for repairs on 1 July, so where could the dear creature go?

But this was Schürmann's business, and he was too old a fox to be caught. The Renaissance, he said blandly, would after all be too *small* a theatre to hold the crowds who were demanding to see la Duse. So he had rented the larger Porte Saint-Martin where, alas, they would still overflow into the corridors.

By a curious coincidence the press happened to sniff out this correspondence while it was still warm, and published it, to Sarah's detriment. And at this point, for God knows her patience had been tried long enough, Sarah lost her head as well as her temper and brought an action against Schürmann for inspiring articles which disparaged her. Unperturbed, he called her bluff, stood by smiling while she withdrew the charge, and watched her pay the costs.

Since Duse's evening was a private performance for artists by a fellow-artist no charges were made for the tickets. And only a hundred were sold, to those who could well afford them, in order to cover basic expenses.

Neither Bernhardt nor any other actress had played before such a public, and possibly Eleonora would never again experience a reception of such quality. The tortoise had outrun the hare, and on the hare's course.

Eleonora gave an act from *Cavalleria rusticana*; the last act — Sarah's *chef d'oeuvre* — of *La Dame aux Camélias*, and the second act of *La Femme de Claude*. There were ten curtain calls, a multitude of flowers at her feet, an army of handkerchiefs waved in the air, an ocean of tears, a chorus of *Viva!* from the Italian contingent and *Au Revoir!* from the Parisians.

Jules Huret, of *Figaro*, expressed the feelings of every critic when he wrote: *I am afraid as I take up my pen, yes, afraid of my incompetence to describe, in a few rapid moments, the powerful, profound emotion of these three hours...*

There was electricity in the air, wrote Sarcey. And then, *She must come back! She* will *come back!*

'The old dodderer must have taken leave of his wits!' cried Sarah, surveying the desecration of her private citadel.

The Comte de Montesquiou said, shocked, that la Duse simply left Paris — without so much as a thank you to her hostess. But his was the world of spoken manners. He could not have comprehended that Eleonora never paid lip service to false hospitality; and did not intend to thank Sarah for throwing her to the lions under the guise of friendship.

Only one way remained through which to show her errant public how deeply wounded she had been, and Bernhardt took it. Limping home, she announced to France the instant necessity for minor surgery, long, long postponed because of her duties, and now become a matter of the first importance. About the news hovered an air of life spent in their service, and they responded with telegrams, letters, press interviews, and the tenderest concern. Among them was a message from Duse, taking the illness at face value, wishing her a good and speedy recovery.

Dr Pozzi read it aloud to his famous patient, who kicked with fury beneath the bedclothes.

'Cette rosse!' cried Sarah. 'That old war-horse!'

'I can hardly send the Signora an answer like that!' said Pozzi, smiling. 'What do you suggest I write?'

Sarah meditated.

'Tell her I send her a kiss,' she said charmingly.

To the faithful Count she revealed her undeserved wounds.

'You don't know what petty vileness and infamy I've had to put up with since Duse's arrival,' she said, applying a handkerchief carefully to her eyes. 'You don't know what *moral* agonies I've gone through in the past month.'

He made the right noises, his eyes alight with pleasurable malice, his memory storing away every modulation of the famous voice, every twist of that professional face.

'The whole thing has been so unsavoury,' said Sarah, horrified at this revelation of human vice, raising her eyes to heaven to witness how the pure were slandered. 'And Duse's role has been *cunning*,' she finished, trying to put her finger on whatever had gone wrong, and failing. 'Oh, you don't know *how* cunning!'

TWENTY-TWO

Eleonora's daughter, Enrichetta, was no longer at Dresden, where she had lived for two years as a member of the family, among people who stayed in the same place, ate four good meals a day, and watched over her welfare and education as though she were their daughter. Her mother's profession had long been hidden from her, and even now she was forbidden to attend a single performance — though she collected cuttings and worshipped at second hand. But each day la Duse sent a telegram to her child, and each year they spent a month together in some remote Italian village. Each holiday they said they must never part, until the demands for a new tour came in, and la Duse was restless and guilty at the same time, and they did part: Eleonora to move on again, and Enrichetta to resume her orderly life.

A tall pale serious girl, already devoutly religious, she had inherited her father's quiet undemanding nature and his adoration of her mother — whom she barely resembled. At fourteen years of age she felt tongue-tied and awkward, incapable of competing with or understanding that turbulent personality which swung from modesty to tempestuous rage — though the rage was never directed at Enrichetta. And there were rumours, carefully kept away from Dresden, which nevertheless crept and seeped through cracks of gossip, of men in her mother's life. With one, such as Arrigo Boito, Enrichetta prepared to transfer the affection that could only trickle through letters to her real father. But Boito had gone, and the name of an Italian poet hung on the fringe of conversation, to be checked with smiles and exclamations as soon as the girl appeared.

And now the doctors had told her guardians that she must rest and recuperate in the mountains at Davos, where time moves so oddly that a month there is like a day anywhere else. And her mother, preceded by a flight of telegrams and a distraught letter, was coming as fast as possible, having broken several engagements in order to stay with her for the first few weeks.

Eleonora was not good at hiding her feelings, and between the scored strokes, beneath the underlined phrases of love and hope, Enrichetta read a panic that she herself felt when the doctors tapped her chest and listened, and the waiting faces looked drawn and anxious.

The distinction of being one of the youngest and most illustrious patients at Davos was a torment, since the girl shrank from attention. She felt conscious, as she waited for her mother's coming, that all the others were waiting too. They had been particularly kind, and in her inexperience she could not tell whether they were genuinely interested and compassionate — or merely hoped for an introduction to that famous mother who, despite her gestures, had been no mother at all, except by accident of birth and intensity of affection.

Still, she was a good child, and did as she was bidden: swallowing her glasses of rich milk, lying on her balcony wrapped in two thick rugs, praying that she might not die. *Holy Mary, Mother of God,* Enrichetta prayed, *look down on this poor sinner.*

As usual, la Duse commanded absolute privacy, which made the patients all the more curious. There were faces at every window, walking cases hoping to encounter her by accident, and an air of suppressed jubilation at the prospect of seeing that celebrated, sombre countenance.

The meeting was all that Enrichetta had feared. Eleonora was devastated at the sight of her daughter's bowed shoulders, whose blades started like wings through the expensive dress. She took the thin face in her hands, then held her child at arm's length to scrutinise the gentle eyes and narrow chest. And at once she sensed, as Enrichetta had dreaded she would, the terror beneath the obedience. In the end they were both weeping hysterically. Enrichetta's temperature ran up six points and she was ordered to bed.

The burden of loving and being loved lay heavily upon them both, made heavier by lack of intimacy. The doctors felt, privately, that la Duse's presence did more harm than good. But Enrichetta's temperature went up again when they spoke of parting, and Eleonora became so devastated that they shrugged their shoulders and waited for the world to intervene. It did. A little avalanche of letters and telegrams fell like snow on the sanatorium in Davos. Trains were apparently covering the continent of Europe without la Duse on board. Theatres lay empty for her. Audiences waited. And an entire company, on full pay, idled without employment in her absence.

They walked together, arm in arm, so white and tortured that the one appeared as ill as the other. An evil spirit led them past the cemetery in Davos where the bones of the unhealed had come to rest: some of them girls in their fifteenth year, whom all the care and money in the world could not save. Eleonora was reminded of that other child beneath the earth, remembered now only by her and a dusting of leaves in the locket about her neck. She feared that this one, too, might be taken from her, for death was terrible and undiscriminating.

Like Niobe, she wept for her children and could not be comforted, and Enrichetta wept with her.

The parting promised to prostrate the girl for a week, though the mother would drag herself exhausted to the theatre, and use that personal tragedy to move her public. She could not help this, being an artist as well as a mother, but Enrichetta had no such comfort. For two long years she would lie on her balcony, resting. She would be drawn, in spite of herself, to read the names and ages on the headstones. She would press her face to the window to watch the snow falling. She would breathe the thin pure air, and drink her milk and eat the excellent food, and take her temperature twice a day. And every time the doctor tapped her narrow chest and round back she would watch him — though he was too experienced to register any expression but that of professional interest — and beg him to let her go home. For two long years.

At the moment no end was in sight, whether two years or twenty, and her solitude was a nightmare from which no one would let her awaken. Until the last minute Enrichetta could not believe that her mother really proposed to leave her there by herself, in the atmosphere of the feverish sick, among the moribund who would shortly be taken from their beds to lie in that cemetery. Then as Eleonora, wrapped in sables against the cold, prepared to go, Enrichetta begged her in a small voice, in the French that was more natural to her than Italian, '*Maman*, take me with you. I want to die near *you*!'

'You are not going to die,' said Eleonora, her mouth quite colourless. 'You are going to get well here.'

She would not listen, not to her mother, not to the doctors, not to anyone. The staff hurried Eleonora away, assuring her that all was for the best and she must on no account worry. But of course she would worry. The words rang in her head as

Enrichetta lost control and passed from obedience to shrieking panic. And the train rattling down the mountain seemed to tune its wheels to that cry, and rattled it over and over again through Duse's head. She would hear it in the theatre, in the privacy of her room, in the void of hotels, and in the early hours when she woke with the *smara* upon her.

'Maman, maman, emporte-moi! Je veux mourir près de toi!'
'Maman, maman!'
'Emporte-moi!'
'Je veux mourir près de toi!'
Près de toi, près de toi, près de toi, près de toi, près de toi.

TWENTY-THREE

I can at last see my way, Eleonora wrote to D'Annunzio, after the conquest of Paris, forgiving his trickery, forging fresh links between them. *The final fine way that leads to an end, so beautifully, so differently from any other way, a way I have searched for so arduously, so painfully.*

And knowing the trouble that must always lie in wait, with a man of his proclivities, she consoled herself with the phrase, *The heart must either harden or break.*

In 1897 she and D'Annunzio made a pilgrimage to Assisi, and received the story of St Francis in their different ways. He watched her expressive face as she listened to the tale of rake-turned-saint; to the philosophy that possessions are man's encumbrances, and humility and selflessness the only way to God. He watched her examine the frescoes, and pale — whether with pain or pleasure he could not tell — at the sight of the patched cassock, the camel hair and needle waist cord, the rough sandals.

'But did St Francis *really* develop the five wounds of Christ?' she asked, incredulous.

'Assuredly, my daughter. The nail marks upon His hands and feet, the spear thrust in His side. The Stigmata. They are the supernatural tokens of favour, given only to a few of His blessed.'

'And he was happy — was he?'

The monk nodded assent.

They saw the body, blackened with seven hundred years of preservation, in the crypt. And bent their heads at the barred window of the Church of St Claire, to catch the gentle tones asking them in which language they chose to hear the history of the crucifix. As the nun spoke, Eleonora strained to see her, scarcely visible in the shadows, her face veiled, and only a white collar and two serene white hands gleaming in the half light.

She was visibly moved as they went out into the sunshine.

'Is *she* happy, do you think?' she asked, and then answered herself, 'I think she is, Gabriele, because she has forgotten herself. Fasting and self-denying, imprisoned in that place.'

He was cheerful, his walking stick over one shoulder, white-gloved, foppishly dressed.

'She's not a woman,' he observed.

'No, she's spared herself *that* infliction!' said Eleonora, waspish. 'Oh — leave me alone, do. I must be alone for a while. I'm sick of myself.'

He waited at a distance, whistling softly, lending himself to the enchantment of the Umbrian landscape; while she sat on the grass and struggled to integrate one side of herself with the other. He had no such problem, obsessed only by beauty, his work and himself. Soon she joined him, accepted his arm, begged him pitifully to endure her. Smiling, he asked if they should continue the pilgrimage? She complied, anxious to be no more trouble, afraid of displeasing him.

They visited the sunny monastery of San Damiano. Saw below the town the chapel where St Francis died, La Porziuncola, and the garden where the saint scarred himself on the rose thorns to resist temptation.

'And since then,' said the guide, in a hushed voice, 'the rose bushes have grown no more thorns.'

They inspected them with interest, and D'Annunzio was relieved to see that Eleonora's mood had passed, and she was busy over some fresh scheme.

'I'm tired of being a nomad,' she said as they strolled away. 'I must find a home for myself again.'

Her pen scratched feverishly across the paper, the ink blobbing a little as she crossed her ts.

I have rented an old house among the olives. It is simple without being poor, hidden without being remote. You reach it down a lane that looks like a convent walk, and the door is concealed among mulberries. There are swallows in the roof, vines and wisteria on the walls, and a large piece of land, some of it crops, some cypresses, rising and falling over a lovely hill. Behind the house are all the hills of Florence and Fiesole... roses everywhere, and a tub of orange flowers before the window of my room.

D'Annunzio gave her new home the name of La Porziuncola, after St Francis's chapel: clever and perceptive at understanding her whims and soothing her nerves, when it pleased him.

She had the house decorated in dark reds and greens, filled it with books and flowers, and installed a bell whose hushed tone echoed the cloister. Through the cedars on the opposite hill gleamed the city of Florence. For a while she tasted peace and tranquillity, then was off on the road again — Milan, Turin, Genoa, Rome, Naples.

D'Annunzio's attitude towards money was a romantic one, and when he possessed it briefly he declined to put it into a bank. He also revelled in surprising himself. He stuffed notes in his pockets, stuck them under cushions and pillows, crammed them into drawers, tucked them into flower pots and bookcases. He never knew how much or how little he possessed, only that it was not enough — either for his present expenses or to satisfy his creditors.

Short of cash, he wrote little notes to himself, in which humour and melodrama mingled, left them lying about the house. Eleonora picked them up and read them, amused and maternal.

I am in the soup!
Misery has moved in on me!
Make room for me, beggars!
Poverty is my name!

A cry of joy interrupted her reading. He had found 500 lire in the toe of an old sock thrown to the floor of his wardrobe.

And that wardrobe was a prince's daydream: possessing eight violet umbrellas and ten green parasols, having one hundred and fifty gorgeous cravats and ten equally exotic waistcoats, boasting six dozen pairs of gloves for all occasions and a similar number of plain shirts. He had walking shoes and crocodile shoes and velvet slippers for the house. His hats and suits were legion. His socks, both silk and ordinary, delicately tinted, were beyond count. He was at once the dandy who selects clothes of exquisite quality and appearance, and the small boy who asks only for a great deal of everything.

Now he, too, wanted a house. And he wanted it to be near Eleonora, who spoke of his work and her art as though they were one lovely child with the virtues of both parents. But a Porziuncola did not fit in with his public and private image. He demanded a palace.

He proposed to rent La Capponcina from the Marchese Giacinto Viviani della Robbia, to remodel it completely and fill it with luxuries. He owed 70,000 lire, but his faith in his future, plus an unshakeable belief that he deserved only the best things in life, enabled him to approach this project blithely.

He had a passion for red: flaming roses, crimson hangings, scarlet cushions. He had a taste for rich and theatrical furnishings: chose damask couches, a Renaissance bed, a medieval desk — at which he would sit dressed in his fur-collared robe, writing in a soundproofed room with goose quills, on sheets of special paper made by Miliano di Fabriano. But all this was yet to come, and not until the spring of 1898 could he enter La Capponcina as its master.

So he dreamed imperial dreams, and ordered a thousand rose bushes to be planted round his mistress's house. And the roses grew thorns as sharp and stout as any saint could desire.

TWENTY-FOUR

On 11 January 1898, Eleonora Duse appeared at the Teatro Valle, Rome, in the Italian première of *Sogno dun Mattino di Primavera*, with *La Locandiera* as light refreshment. Queen Margherita sat smiling in the royal box; the author sat smiling in the stalls; and backstage, Eleonora, unsmiling, remembered the première in Paris and what D'Annunzio had said to her afterwards.

The title of the play, promising lyrical and youthful transports, somewhat belied the plot. It revolved round the intense Isabella, who unknowingly holds her murdered lover in her arms all night, and goes mad when she discovers his death in the morning.

All la Duse's art and emotion could not transform this ghoulish little piece. The audience, puzzled and sophisticated, received it in complete silence. The curtain rose and fell, hopefully, but not a sound came forth to persuade it to rise again. And Duse, for the first time in her career, raised her arms and threw back her head to a hush as deadly as it was insulting. Fortunately Queen Margherita's presence in the royal box presented a more forcible discontent.

Eleonora walked straight to her dressing room with a frown that scattered the cast, and prepared to change into her Goldonian costume.

D'Annunzio sat coolly enough, a flower in his buttonhole, smoothing his whiskers. Then as the curtain revealed a Venetian scene, and Duse appeared hand on hips, grinning impudently from her ribbons and flounces, the entire theatre gave a great shout. She belonged to them, they meant to say, and they loved her. They had not cared for *Sogno*, but all was forgiven.

So they cried, 'Viva! Viva la Duse! Viva Goldoni!' and waved their handkerchiefs and went mildly mad.

In his seat, smoothing his whiskers, D'Annunzio smiled and smiled.

Now had Sarah decided from the fullness of her heart, and a genuine interest in the future of the theatre, to produce *La Città Morta*? Or was she, perhaps, still smarting from that Parisian encounter? A flurry of correspondence in the August previously, had assured D'Annunzio that Sarah proposed to begin rehearsals, and just a fortnight after his failure in Rome he travelled alone to Paris for the world première.

Eleonora's enemies gathered round to view the kill. Count Primoli held a small friendly party for her in his Roman mansion, and arranged for news of *La Città*'s reception to be telegraphed from Paris, act by act, throughout the evening.

She arrived elegantly dressed and incredibly pale, clasped her hands together, seeing the circle of concerned smiles, and said something inaudible about friendship. Soon afterwards she lay down on a divan, complaining of a vague pain. Someone brought her a hot water bottle, which she held to her stomach. And then they all stood around, making polite conversation in quiet voices.

'The curtain is going up!' said Eleonora, watching the clock.

They sat with her, chatting constrainedly, while she retreated into a dark world of her own, her eyes fixed on the Count's handsome timepiece, her lips moving slightly as she recited the lines she had learned, though the play had not been given to her.

The first message brought her to her feet, hot water bottle tumbling on the floor.

'The news seems good,' said the Count. 'The first act has been quite well received.'

'I am glad,' said Eleonora, clutching her hot water bottle and lying down again, watching the clock. 'The curtain is going up,' she said, almost inaudibly.

Someone began, wittily, to comment on Sarah's weaknesses, but was hushed by Duse's instant defence of the actress. They could not, for obvious reasons, make fun of the play, so hung about, paralysed by inactivity. The Count moved hospitably among his guests, starting up spurts of conversation, but as soon as he had left they were sucked back towards that melancholy divan.

'Come now, Eleonora,' said the Count, very polished, very urbane, 'you must admit that the woman is a mechanical performer.'

A flicker in her eyes encouraged him. He sat down beside her, courteous and clever.

'She dominates,' said Eleonora at length, 'because she is mistress of herself.'

'So is an organ grinder,' said Primoli. They all laughed, and Duse smiled.

'And he grinds the organ in exactly the same way for every tune!' Primoli added.

Throwing away her hot water bottle, and her championship of Sarah, Duse sprang up. Exhilarated, feverish, she paced the room.

'Yes, you are right. She is always the same. The same tones, the same gestures, the same movements. Precise, oh so precise. You must admire her precision. I have watched her play Marguerite several times. Do you remember the scene where she tells Armando to go back to his father? She walks the same number of steps to a writing desk. She sits down in front of it, and nervously — nervously, mark you — turns the key in the lock of a little chest that stands on it. Now does the key ever get stuck, or does she fumble with it, as one would if one were so upset? Does it ever strike her afresh, that so-called nervousness, so that a new piece of management is created? Certainly not. She turns that key in the lock the same number of times, each performance. I can see her face as she does it — all that paint! One, two, three, four, five times — I know, I have counted them.'

The second message, predicting success, took away her colour and vivacity. She ran her hands through her hair, stared about her distractedly, accepted a glass of wine which she immediately put down untasted.

'I have heard,' said the Count smoothly, 'that Sarah's company call the play not *The Dead City* but *The City to Die in*!'

Eleonora laughed twice as long as everyone else, savouring the title. Then, regaining a sense of charity, sat down and began to recite some of D'Annunzio's most lyrical stanzas. Her voice and his poetry moved them all to silence. A great vase of flowers stood near her and, as she spoke, her fingers betrayed her. She reached for a flower and pulled it to shreds, still reciting with tremendous feeling and beauty. And another, and another.

The last message spoke of a glowing victory. Wordless, dishevelled, exhausted, she sat head in hands among the torn flowers.

'Is there anything we can do for you, Eleonora?' the Count asked gently.

She shook her head, and was ready to go.

As the cloak was placed about her shoulders she said composedly, 'I must congratulate Madame Bernhardt. I must send her a telegram as soon as possible. What shall I tell her?'

She looked round at the circle of helpless faces, and drew herself up.

Speaking high and clear, she said, 'I shall tell her that I am happy at her triumph, and that — speaking as an *Italian* – I am grateful to her.'

The critics were unenthusiastic, finding *La Città Morta*, with its undertones of incest, too long, too morbid and too slow, though Sarah and Paris feted D'Annunzio royally, and Eleonora joined the party.

The play ran for thirteen nights, to smaller and smaller audiences, and was taken off. But Bernhardt, determined to make Duse offer the other cheek, said it must be shown everywhere. Prettily, she begged the honour of producing *La Città Morta* in Italy.

Coldly la Duse replied that an Italian première was her prerogative. She was not, as she had said in Paris, a fool. Her knight might temporarily have defaulted, but she did not propose to lose her queen as well.

TWENTY-FIVE

Paris had been too much a city of bright lights, late hours and brilliant conversation, and she was tired. Between engagements she retreated to La Porziuncola. In March, D'Annunzio entered his mansion, almost at her gate.

No cell-like bedroom for him, with a portrait of Keats over the bed and an air of austere beauty. His carpets were hushed and thick, his draperies rich and heavy. Antique armour and fine statues vied for attention with illuminated murals. Plaster masks of Beethoven and Wagner frowned at a copy of Verocchio's 'Lady with a Posy' — whose graceful hands reminded him of Eleonora. Gardens and vineyards and olive plantations were his: no mere tub of orange flowers and a trail of wisteria. And the view of Florence was superlative.

His puckish sense of humour led him to have a motto carved over his high-backed chair, making a play on his heraldic name. *The Angel of the Lord is with us*, it read. As a personal emblem he adopted the laurel wreath, crown of poets, and took as his personal motto *Per non dormire* — as if to say *Don't Rest on Your Oars*. He adored mottoes. They were everywhere.

He engaged a veterinary surgeon, Dr Benigno Palmerio, primarily to look after his pack of hounds and his stableful of horses, but also as a general manager of the estate. He placed a statue of Minerva in his olive grove. He bought an old lamp and draped it with the gown Eleonora had worn as Isabella in *Sogno*. With his mistress at his door, his work to hand, and ostentatious luxury all about him, he prepared to celebrate life in style: a literary country gentleman.

At seven in the morning he bathed, fenced, and took a gallop on his favourite horse. His physical health and fitness being as important to him as his writing and his love affairs, he worked hard at all three pursuits. Then he inspected and petted his dogs: the Scotch deerhound with its rough thick iron-grey coat; the red Irish wolf-hound, whose brown eyes gleamed white when he ran; the black and yellow spotted Tartary hound; the Spanish galgo and the Arabian slonghi; and his small pale silky Persian with its feathered tail. Kneeling to examine them he would stroke their backs and ears, lay his face against their muzzles, feel their warm breath on his cheek, the lithe muscles beneath his hands, watch their proud gait, taste their names in his mouth. Crissa, Nerissa, Altair, Sirius, Pinchabella, Helion.

At ten he was ready to begin the day's writing, covering sheets of hand-made paper with his slanting elegant script: polishing, sharpening, re-writing the pages of sonorous verse and prose. Cold and self-contained, he worked on new versions of old themes for his plays. And turned back at intervals, again and again, to Eleonora's novel *Il Fuoco*, which grew in proportion to the minute personal notes he made on their intimate relationship.

She had worked so hard, found life so difficult, and still hoped love might mean happiness and protection in spite of past experience — in spite of destroying it when it did offer those two gifts. She had said, feeling herself atrophy with age and success, that it was better to burn than mummify. So now she burned merrily and found love a torturous business, tied to a man who seemed fire-proof. In art she could accept her years; in life they frightened her, and she made the mistake of fretting him. Sometimes his response would be gay and kind, sometimes he drowned her worries in violent love-making, sometimes he just watched her with those glacial eyes that missed no shiver of flesh or spirit.

She felt ashamed of her abandonment to him, conscious that an ageing woman in the throes of physical passion can be an ugly or a comic sight. In times of clarity she longed for the peace of Arrigo Boito's relationship, or the peace of solitude; but could no more resist D'Annunzio's courtship than she could resist courting him. Many times in the past she had denied the body to enrich the spirit. Now, in a final flare of panic, the body exacted payment. Her endeavour was to become his inspiration, because she then combined the best of herself and him, and he was gentle with her. Or in an excess of tenderness, finding him afraid of the phantoms loosed by his imagination, she turned them into mother and son. And that, too, seemed good.

So she crossed the short distance between the houses, treading soft-footed beneath the vibrant chandeliers, her shadow slanting strangely across the brocade hangings, and stood at the door of his study. Only the rustle of her dress betrayed her as she stooped to listen at the keyhole, but he did hear — perhaps listening for her, too — and laid down his pen and called her to come in.

'You have been twelve hours here,' she said. 'Isn't that enough for you, Gabriele?'

He nodded, her presence soothing him. Motioned her to approach and hold him.

'Like a beautiful thought,' he murmured into her shoulder. 'You enter my room as a beautiful thought enters the mind. Did you know that?'

She stroked his neat head, his bearded cheek, gauged the pile of written sheets, felt him trembling with fatigue.

'You have been *flying*, my son,' she said serenely. 'Are you coming back to me, now? How pale you are!'

'I saw the warrior again,' he cried at random, 'in his bronze helm and black plumes.'

'You have seen him before when you were tired. He won't hurt you, my son.'

'I heard the hooves of his charger, and they were also forged of bronze.'

He clenched his teeth to stop their chattering. And she rocked and cradled his head, talking as one talks a child out of a nightmare.

'Who has told me of this warrior before?' she began, making it a tale of long ago, to invest the phantom with a degree of safety. 'Who told me of his bronze helm, and black plumes stirring, and the hooves striking sparks from the stony ground?'

He listened to her, eyes closed, at rest.

'And another time,' she went on, noting that he grew quieter, 'did not some poet, whose name I forget, have a vision of Persephone and the Lord of Hades, and ask if this had happened in order to inspire him? Who was that, I wonder — and who told me of these things?'

He was smiling into her shoulder. She put her hands on either side of his head, shook him gently, and repeated softly, in mischief, 'Who has told me all these things?'

Angelica shone from her now: patient and loving-kind. And he kissed her hands and eyes with reverence and called her *Consolazione*.

In the autumn they gripped each other's hands as though night were upon them. Chestnut leaves smouldered crimson beneath their feet. Behind the Tuscan hills the day burned splendidly to its close.

'I carry the autumn within me wherever I go,' said Eleonora.

She had conveyed it to him, too, reminding him that love and the body die: that the poet's work may be immortal but the poet is not. So he clasped her hand.

A black velvet ribbon was about her throat. Her gown, simply designed in dark soft heavy stuff, fell in folds at her feet. Even as he had, in his poet's eye, seen the woman of his play so he now saw her, and the images impinged one upon the other. Lifting a hand that shook with fear and tenderness, D'Annunzio commanded her to halt.

'I have created you,' he said slowly, his tongue slurring with tiredness. 'I have *created* you. Stay a moment. Don't even move your eyelids. Keep your eyes as still as stones!'

She was motionless in the shadows: a nocturne of a woman in noble black.

'You see all that others do not see,' said D'Annunzio. 'Hear what they cannot hear. See things that to them are invisible.'

She nodded slightly, moving into the role.

'Here in this room the man you love has revealed his love to another — who is still trembling at the revelation…'

She trembled too, following him into the dark.

'They are still here,' said D'Annunzio. 'The air is warm with their love. Their hands have not long parted. But you love too, and nothing is unknown to you.'

She nodded again, and he picked up his pen.

'What will you say?' he asked, beseeching. 'Tell me what you will say!'

Writing the words down as she brought them forth, like children broken on a wheel.

The logs fell in the grate. The rain beat at the window. The garden darkened.

She was reclining, head on hand, musing bitterly. He stood apart from her, philosophically dabbing a bitten lip.

'I fill myself with revulsion,' she said. 'I must fill you with revulsion, too. Do I? Do I?'

He replied coldly, being already weary of the scene. The longing to be alone with his beautiful blank sheets of paper and a score of goose quills was a sharp as hunger: as sharp as his desire for her an hour ago.

'I have told you I love you. That you alone please me. That everything in you pleases me.'

'You are a damnable liar, then. You talk of love as though it were hate. Sometimes I think it is.'

He did not answer, wanting to escape to his desk.

She said, holding out her hands to the flaring logs, 'This is not what I want!'

He did not ask her what she wanted, since she did not know herself.

'It is like hatred,' she said, nodding. 'You make love to me as though you would kill me.'

'And don't you?' he cried, goaded out of his chill composure.

She looked at him proudly.

'I am not a whore.'

He drummed his fingers on the pane. How long before he could go without an avalanche of reproaches and questions? Why must he stand idle while she scourged herself and him with her jealousy?

She began to cry that she would die before he hated her. That this was the only thing she could do — to go away and leave him with his freedom. Again and again she asked him if there was another woman, and would not accept his denials. He stared at her, graceful even as she sprawled across the divan, weeping and running her hands through her heavy hair. She started up rapidly.

'What are you looking at?' she demanded savagely. 'A white hair?'

Useless to deny anything, though he was guiltless of this last offence at least. Her face expressed fear, fury and then suspicion. She pointed to the door and ordered him out.

'Go on!' she cried. 'Or do I have to take you to her? Shall I call her for you? Hurry — she will be waiting! Run! She will be waiting!'

And as he moved towards the door, released by a situation that had become unbearable, she rushed after him and gripped his wrist so that he carried the marks of her nails.

'Run!' she cried, her voice rough with jealousy. 'Hurry! She must be waiting!'

Then she let him go, flung herself down, and wept. He sighed, turned back, soothed her, stroked her hair. She became quiet again, begging his forgiveness, saying she would rest. For half an hour he sat by her, holding her hands in his, placing them gently across her breast as she drifted into sleep. Then he hurried home to set her down in writing.

In the austerity of night and silence he chiselled out his wealth of images, and the expression in his eyes was akin to love.

TWENTY-SIX

Eleonora toured France, a wretched round of little theatres on the Cote d'Azur and in the provinces. She toured Spain and Portugal, where the ladies made a path with their lace mantillas in her honour. She went wherever they would pay for the privilege of seeing her, because she must raise money for D'Annunzio's new play. Groaning, Schürmann helped her in a project for which he had no relish. He also secured the services of Ermete Zacconi, one of Italy's finest tragedians, for three months. And, void of hope, watched the rehearsals at Messina and thanked God and the Blessed Virgin that several old favourites on the bills would preserve them from ruin.

Who listens to the morning bells at dawn? Eleonora wrote to a friend. And answered herself, *The one who doesn't sleep. Here we are, each on his own road. During the night, with my eyes open, when dawn never comes to relieve me from my obsessions, I alone know that being a prima donna is poison to me — and being an apostle is futility...*

The transience of her art weighed heavily upon her. All the odds seemed to be in D'Annunzio's favour.

Within five, within ten years, his work will reach the masses, she wrote. *But you, poor Duse, rest assured you'll be a blade of grass! If only I could break with everything and go away in peace.*

The old dream: sitting on a stone step in the sun, eating her bread with contentment.

To D'Annunzio, Eleonora aching for a line of love, for a little kindness, scrawled pitifully:

It's cold. During the journey we had hail and wind against the windows. And tonight I have a cough and can't sleep. Here I am — now — here — alone as always, alone and responsible for every one of my actions.

They opened at Palermo on 15 April, 1899 at the Teatro Bellini, to an audience who had come to see Duse and found her new play a heavy vehicle. The beauty of the lines was overshadowed by a horror made still more horrible by D'Annunzio's evident power; clumsy as yet, in this new art form, but strong and magnetic. Nor did they care for the recognisable thread of autobiography that ran through the four-act tragedy.

La Gioconda was the story of a sculptor, dedicated to art and beauty, married to Silvia of the beautiful hands, and in love with his model Gioconda. Silvia first prevented the sculptor from committing suicide over the love affair, and then attempted to dismiss the model by saying he no longer needed her. La Gioconda tried to break an unfinished statue for which she had posed, and Silvia saved it at the cost of her own hands. Alone by the sea, maimed and deserted, she was tormented by the demands of her child to be lifted into her arms.

The audience did not care for the taste left in their mouths. They disliked D'Annunzio's dedication of the play — *To Eleonora Duse of the beautiful hands* — set beside those tragic bandaged stumps. His reputation as a philanderer, his love affair with Duse, were well-known. Consideration and affection, let alone good manners, they thought, might have prevented his advertising the fact that he was already looking at shop girls while his lady tried to make a name for him. And *that* punishment! No. The whole thing stuck in their throats, stank in their nostrils: foul and cruel, without compassion or common humanity.

As they grasped the trend of the play they became increasingly restless and displeased. Duse exerted her powers, but their dissent was audible, not only in the theatre and throughout the whole performance, but in the streets afterwards until the early hours.

'I was afraid,' said Eleonora, bending her pride and loyalty sufficiently to discuss the reception with Schürmann, 'that they were not yet ready for his work.'

'In another few years, perhaps?' suggested Schürmann hopefully.

She withdrew from the hint with disdain.

'I shall fight for his success as I have fought for mine!'

He threw up his arms in despair.

They toured the Italian cities, drawing audiences who flocked to see her and went away disappointed and highly critical. They were not squeamish — they had survived a revolution, they knew life — but something about *La Gioconda* sickened them. They smelled corruption in the beauty: a stench of decay in the lilies. They wondered at *her*, too, stooping to connive at rottenness disguised as poetry.

She took the failure upon herself and soldiered on until Venice, where the Teatro Rossini was crammed, enthusiastic, and kindly disposed.

But the strain called upon reserves of physical strength she no longer possessed. She was almost forty-one, frail of constitution, struggling in the toils of a love affair which demanded more than it gave. In December 1899 she and D'Annunzio went to Egypt to recuperate: she from her wretched tour, he from a new creation of blood and lust called *La Gloria*. They visited the Cheops monument and the tomb of Tell-el-Amarna. One sepulchral chamber, recently opened, contained a jar of honey buried to solace its owner beyond the grave two thousand years before. A faint scent seemed to fill the tomb, and the honey glistened in the dim light. D'Annunzio was enchanted. Later that day a bee blundered into their carriage and threatened him in a frenzy of buzzing and swooping, until Duse attempted to save him and the insect by capturing it in her hands — and was stung for her trouble.

In his mind he connected the entombed jar and the errant bee, and wove them into a story round Eleonora's fluttering hands. And, as so often happened with him, the writer's fantasy became the man's belief.

'The bee was in the tomb,' he said, recounting the tale.

'The bee was in the *carriage*!' Duse protested, amused.

But he could never separate fact from fiction, particularly when the fiction was so much more artistic.

But in the garden of the Khedive she provided material for his novel by losing herself in a maze. At first he joked with her through the myrtle hedge as she called and protested, half-laughing, half-afraid. And then as her concern became panic, and his teasing cruelty, he prolonged her release. Enthralled, his cat-like eyes cold, he pictured her blundering like the bee in a labyrinth that seemed like eternity. Saw her running, running, running like a mad woman from alley to blind alley, tearing her hands on the imprisoning hedges. Heard her calling, sobbing, and finally screaming for him. Imagined her as she was eventually brought out, in terror and dishevelment.

She lay on the floor of the carriage and he comforted her; listening to the broken phrases of fear and reproach, observing the stained eye sockets, the stained cheeks; hastening to his notebooks as soon as he returned, to write her down without compassion or restraint. The suffering one, the lost one, the wandering woman.

Yet she drove away his own ghosts, sent his hallucinations scurrying back into the shadows. She consoled him, as he begged her not to let them take him away, thinking him mad.

'Why, how rich you are, *mio figlietto*,' she would say. 'Madness itself is not so rich, my son.'

He called her *Consolazione*, and clung to her.

TWENTY-SEVEN

The prospect of producing *La Gloria*, after *La Gioconda*'s reception, stung Schürmann.

'All her life,' he cried, 'on the stage as in reality, la Duse has been the victim of love!'

The liaison, now entering its fifth year, showed signs of wear but few signs of flagging. Schürmann bore no affection for D'Annunzio, and had a healthy respect for the rascal's tenacity. He foresaw years of these long-winded unpopular tragedies, with la Duse trailing her lover's cloak before the public until at last they stayed away entirely.

'Love is very well,' said Schürmann, 'but business is something again!'

Romain Rolland and his wife had met them at Zurich the previous year, and were embroiled in a matter of hours. Hoping for a few pleasant days at the Hotel Baur au Lac they discovered themselves instantly cast as supporting members of a gruelling vivisection. *Il Fuoco* was almost ready for publication, and Duse had not yet decided whether to say she opposed it and let him publish in spite of her; or declare it a work of art and say she had urged him into print. For publication he intended, whether she gave him permission or not, and he knew she would never take the matter to court.

With an egoism which was part-temperament and part-despair, she and D'Annunzio divided the Rollands between them, changing confidantes as the tale was told. And speaking rapidly in French, Duse turned the full force of her obsession on Madame Rolland, bewildering her with multiple confession and contradictions.

'I thought the book was true art and I wanted to defend it!' she cried. 'But it's dreadful, dreadful!'

'Often he would arrive home in the morning, exhausted. Throw out his disgust at the night he had spent, his disgust of those women — oh, he told me *everything*!'

'When we met in Paris, that year, he gave himself to pleasure like a madman!'

'Listen to me, Madame, I am no longer the captain of my soul. A wild despair possesses me. I abandon myself to a chagrin which would be pitiful even to encounter. I abandon myself to a terrible, painful rage. To an anguish that sings in the blood. To a misery I have not the voice to express. To a sadness that is mute.'

Spent, she laid her head upon her arms, speaking now more to herself than to the kindness of the woman beside her.

'The suffering is permanent,' she said, touching unconsciously on the root of the matter.

She raised her head and looked into the distance at something beyond the human eye.

'It has the nature of infinity,' she said.

Romain Rolland found D'Annunzio more companionable and much more natural without his mistress.

Rueful, sensible, lucid, D'Annunzio said, 'I have touched fire and burned myself.'

But he frightened Eleonora by threatening to commit suicide, not from any desire to immolate himself on the altar of love but, paradoxically, out of self-preservation. Unable to keep pace with her private theatre he deflected it with a personal drama.

She hammered on the Rollands' door in the early hours of one morning, begging the writer to come at once and play the piano to D'Annunzio, to wean him away from black thoughts. Rolland put on his dressing-gown, left Duse in the arms of his wife, and found D'Annunzio shaken and apologetic, but relieved to see another face.

'One wakes up at night in such a terror in these hotels!' said D'Annunzio, pacing up and down. 'One should surround oneself with music — shut the doors on the world.'

The suicide was temporarily postponed, and Duse swung from fright to bitter calumny.

'His life is like an inn!' she cried. 'Everyone goes through it!'

And back to herself:

'I have such a fear of closed spaces, both physical and emotional. I am living with that fear day and night — and yet I must work. I can neither endure him nor leave him. I am losing all my friends.

'A letter, a telegram, brings terror with it: terror lest I must go somewhere without him, terror lest I am too ill with his presence to fulfil my engagements. Hotels terrify me. But when I go home the familiar becomes unfamiliar — and just as dreadful.'

She said, 'I was lost, you know, in the garden of the Khedive, and heard him mocking me from the other side of the hedge.'

Exhausted, the Rollands moved from one to the other, consoling, nursing, listening, mediating. The crux of this latest crisis, the proposed publication of *Il Fuoco*, was known to them only by hearsay. They could not judge how much responsibility lay with each protagonist. But Rolland himself was inclined to sympathise with D'Annunzio, finding Duse exquisite and impossible.

'She leaves that sadness of hers behind like a taste of ashes in the mouth,' he told his wife. 'And I could have done without her casting me as the David to D'Annunzio's Saul! But he is pleasant enough by himself. I know he seems a cruel little beast with her, but the man is simple and sincere enough. She sees him as a debauched god, but he's human, has troubles of his own. Only, he should not insult my intelligence by saying that prostitutes disgust him. The world knows better than that! And something in his work is morbid. Too much blood and death at the bottom of it, too little feeling and awareness of life. And *now* look at them both!'

She was hurrying through the lobby of the hotel, though the hour was well past midnight, dressed all in black. Her sadness affected the very air about her, the space in which she moved. Behind her hurried D'Annunzio, placating, hen-pecked, harassed.

'*Something* drives her!' said Rolland. 'Something infinitely more powerful than Gabriele D'Annunzio.'

Schürmann found her sitting up in bed, an old shawl flung over her plain nightgown, her spectacles sliding to the end of her nose; and he thought how much she had aged in the last three years. Waves of grey hair sprang from her temples and flowed into the black, carelessly pinned to the top of her head. Face and hands seemed almost transparent. She was white and weary even after a night's sleep. Her eyes burned with tiredness, and her movements as she turned the pages of the morning papers were languid.

'Well, José?' she asked, eyebrows lifting.

She saw the proof pages under his arm, and her lips compressed into a line.

'My dear Eleonora,' said Schürmann gently, because one could never browbeat nor cross her, and stern reason resulted in hysterics. 'My dear girl, you cannot — you must not — allow him to publish this book.'

She took off her horn-rimmed glasses, silent, and motioned him to sit.

'You can't!' Schürmann repeated. 'Eleonora, I'm not talking as your manager now — because God and the Blessed Virgin know that every theatre in the world will want you even in his plays when this muck is raked over. I'm talking as your friend, as an old and true friend who has your welfare at heart, and as a great and very humble admirer.'

Still she did not answer, playing with the spectacles, pushing away the newspapers restlessly.

'I'm a man of the world,' said Schürmann, 'I'm no moralist. But this stuff is disgusting. You've read it, of course?'

She said, with difficulty, that her art was transient, and D'Annunzio's eternal.

'Does the story of a love affair between a famous actress and a famous poet bring nothing to your mind?' he asked. 'The actress, La Foscarina, is no younger than she used to be.'

Eleonora pushed both hands through her hair, and flinched.

'She is afraid of losing him, as she is losing her beauty,' Schürmann continued inexorably. 'She is a jealous and passionate woman. He is a sensual and cruel man. Isn't that enough autobiography for you, or for anyone?'

She pressed her hands to her head as though it would break, and watched him with frightened eyes.

'But that's not enough for our fine gentleman,' cried Schürmann, growing angry. 'He must take us to bed with La Foscarina. Page upon page we read as they make love and quarrel, as he betrays her with a younger woman — who sounds to me the spitting image of that Gordigiani lass you had so much trouble over! — page upon page of downright pornography. He doesn't even respect your feelings. Whole conversations written down, word for word. I can hear you in every sentence — so will everybody else. And descriptions of grey hairs and wrinkles and white lips — and God alone knows what else besides.'

Eleonora said stiffly, 'I have read the book, José.'

'Then tell him to stop publication or you'll sue him. No,' he said, seeing her expression, 'you'd never do that — though I would. But you mustn't let him make a prostitute of you, Eleonora. You are a great actress, not a street tart. You can't risk your reputation like this. There's a difference between fame and notoriety!' He could not resist adding, 'You've risked quite enough already, in my opinion.'

She said, 'Please go away now, José. I'll let you know what I decide.'

A note followed him, heavily underlined, the *t* strokes almost penetrating the paper.

I did not tell you the truth a while back. I know all about it and have agreed to publication. My sufferings, great though they be, count for nothing when it is a question of adding one more masterpiece to Italian literature. You are probably right, but I must choose between the head and the heart. I choose the heart. And then — I am forty, and in love.

'Women!' said Schürmann wretchedly. And to her who was present only in the frantic scrawl, 'And you above all women — to sacrifice everything of value for the embraces of a fifth-rate mountebank. May God help you, since nobody else can!'

The furore when *Il Fuoco* was published on 5 March 1900 frightened even D'Annunzio. He had ridden for so many years on a wave of public debauchery that he underestimated the public sensibilities. Sarah, electing herself general of the Parisian faction, openly denounced the book and declined to produce any more of his plays. Her reaction was a mirror in which France saw its own face.

Panicking, D'Annunzio wrote to Romain Rolland, begging him to convince the French public that *Il Fuoco* in no way represented his love affair with Eleonora. She had known, he insisted, all about the book from beginning to end, and loved every word of it.

For many weeks, he wrote, in easy lyrical d'Annunzian prose, *my companion of the beautiful hands lived beside my work. Sitting in a choir stall...* — he did not see the funny side of this image, totally humourless in the grip of his muse — ... *she read the still-warm pages, one by one.*

Rolland, unmoved by this picture, refused to become involved.

Yet, despite the furore, Schürmann had been correct in surmising that the world would want to see D'Annunzio's mistress in D'Annunzio's plays. Her art and her reputation held their ground, but the binoculars were now trained in curiosity as well as reverence. The men in the audience knew pretty well, these days, after *Il Fuoco*, what it was like to go to bed with la Duse.

In a tumult of publicity Eleonora was invited by the Emperor Franz Joseph to play *La Gioconda* before him, on 11 April at the Imperial Burgtheater in Vienna, and was awarded the highest decoration an actress could receive: the Golden Cross of Merit.

At the Mercadante in Naples the audience rioted over *La Gloria*. The author, wearing a jaunty carnation in his buttonhole, took hoots and taunts with composure. But he could not have been pleased at the cries of 'Down with Rapagnetta! Death to Rapagnetta!' His own fantastic name, reminiscent of the Archangel Gabriel, would never have existed but for his father's adoption by Don Antonio D'Annunzio; and though his grandfather's money had long since been squandered the name remained, and D'Annunzio relished its heraldic overtones. Still, it pleased his enemies to think that he might have been a Rapagnetta, and from time to time they reminded him of his origins and savaged his vanity.

So he suffered, and Eleonora made him suffer more. From Venice, at the end of May, he wrote to Angelo Conti:

For me and my friend there is no happiness. After the performance — he meant *La Gioconda* in Vienna — *I went through some of the saddest and most tragic hours of my life. She is possessed by a kind of wicked demon that gives her no peace. The deepest tenderness, the purest devotion, is of no avail. Everywhere, all about her, she sees lies and deceit. The gentle creature becomes unjust and cruel — with herself, with me, and nothing can be done about it.*

Il Fuoco had been a hammer to break the ice, and now the torrent was evident to all their friends. Before, Eleonora had knocked at their doors and begged admittance after some quarrel — only to sit in troubled, loyal silence. Now she hurried from one to the other of them: confiding, abusing, weeping, asking for advice and help. D'Annunzio preserved a far better surface, but as she smote down his facade he began to emerge as the arch tormentor.

He had not foreseen the reactions to the book, though he would have published it anyway. And up to a certain point he accepted public denigration and private hysteria with some philosophy. But as she clung obsessively and became less maternal, he hardened. He sought consolation of a different kind. He looked up all his old friends, detaching her grip, finger by finger, in a legion of little ways. But still he returned, afterwards, as netted as she was in this awful toil of wills and weaknesses: needing her inspiration and support, needing her professional reputation while he established himself in his own right. And as their relationship waned he chose to keep it as peaceful as possible, listening for false notes in his voice that so easily offended her, abandoning compliments in favour of courtesy or silence.

She was losing him, and in an effort to hold his attention she now submitted her art — that last stronghold — to his direction. He had never allowed the alteration or deletion of a single line or stage direction in his plays, insisting that the words she dredged from her very being should be *his* words alone. In the past she had taken liberties with most authors. With him she was allowed none. And now he criticised even her renderings of his plays, changing rhythms and cadences as she worked. Doggedly, she tried to live with his tyranny and to cherish the tyrant. And her company stood about her, in mute astonishment, as D'Annunzio began to make her over in his image, until the actress was as much his property as the play.

He allowed her to give *La Città Morta* at a disastrous opening in Milan, in the spring of 1901. And he had written yet another play, *Francesca da Rimini*, which she determined should make his name. The public outcry and D'Annunzio's increasing lack of humanity only spurred her on. Feverishly she led the crusade, spending a little fortune on fine materials, genuine antiques, elaborate properties, calling in experts on historical costume and background to advise her. She was working, she explained, not only to place D'Annunzio on his rightful throne, but to earn money for that dream of an open-air theatre — where the noblest of dramas should be performed by the noblest of players. Since the beginning of their relationship that vision had been in the air, and stayed in the air. Only a few years ago D'Annunzio had announced the opening as arranged for the March of 1899, with the play *Persephone* — though not a stone had been laid nor a word written.

Vainly, seeing her lost, Schürmann thrust out the old money-making planks for her to cling to, trying to save her from the d'Annunzian shipwreck.

'*Either* you produce his plays *or* you make money for your theatre,' said Schürmann. 'You can't do *both*!'

'No change in repertoire!' she repeated, obsessed. 'I will play to empty houses if I must!'

Francesca da Rimini opened to an audience worthy of its sadistic tendencies, and proceeded to enrage them further by an unfortunate accident. The staged bombardment of the city walls actually damaged a wall of the theatre, and simulated gun smoke reduced actors and spectators to choking, stinging, streaming, voiceless confusion.

Out of the riot that ensued, Pirandello raised a still small voice. *The art of the great actress seemed constrained, distorted and even shattered by D'Annunzio's overdrawn heroine,* he wrote.

This fresh and disturbing criticism was echoed by others. Hermann Bahr wrote:

She had been the greatest actress in the world before D'Annunzio appeared; she did not need him; as an artist she would have been what she is if he had never met her.

In an interview with the London *Sketch* a year later, Adelaide Ristori said, 'Let us not speak of *La Gioconda*, a wound to good sense. I do not deny D'Annunzio's talent, but he must stop writing for the theatre. Duse has great talent, but she is ill, neurotic, like our century.'

And now Enrichetta was back from Davos, tall and thin and gentle, old enough to feel stones thrown and to assess hard facts. To her, in Berlin, Eleonora trailed for the final and the worst judgement of all. They had never understood each other in the best times. Now they were bound only by their relationship.

The girl looked at the whitening hair, the compressed lips, and was sick at the notion of that publicised intimacy. But Eleonora, stripped to the heart, had nothing to lose but the truth. Art had long since become part of her, so the beauty of those extended arms sought no theatrical effect. They rose from her sides in supplication of mercy.

She simply said, 'Enrichetta, I have two arms to live by: one of them is called Enrichetta and the other is called Gabriele D'Annunzio.'

The girl's stiff face did not alter. She had felt the humiliation.

'Am I to cut off one and sacrifice it to the other?' Eleonora asked, trembling.

No answer. The arms fell, and Eleonora turned away.

'If I cut it off I shall die,' she said to herself, 'and I *can't* choose. I *can* only die.'

She had appealed from her weakness to Enrichetta's strength, and the girl had too much of her father's generosity to refuse the appeal.

They cried together: graceless and touching in their grief, calling each other by old pet names, attempting to comfort one another. Eleonora had achieved for her daughter all she had ever lacked: shelter, education and respectability. She had achieved it by willpower and hard work. Now she placed the roof on that achievement with this final ill-advised affair. Because, looking at her mother, Enrichetta determined that her life should be as ordered and serene as her mother's was chaotic and wilful. From the mother's emotional travail came the daughter's happy marriage to Edward Bullough, a Cambridge don. From the mother's lost and unsatisfactory motherhood rose healthy children, brought up in an English home. From her mother's haphazard and agonised searches for divine truth rose a good Catholic family with sound principles. Out of the mother's restlessness grew the daughter's roots. So Enrichetta loved and pitied her mother, and comforted her, and stood apart lest she too be lost.

The public gorge could swallow no more D'Annunzios, but la Duse forced her medicine upon them.

Four Giocondas or nothing! she telegraphed to Berlin.

'Are you intent on suicide?' growled Schürmann.

Her temper, controlled overlong by fear and apprehension, caught them both up in a spiral of denunciation and accusation. Both said exactly what they thought, and what other people had said about them. They opened up old wounds, raised forgotten issues, brought grievances back from the shades. And when eight years' trust and affection lay dying, they went their different ways.

TWENTY-EIGHT

As D'Annunzio became more cruelly courteous, more hurtfully withdrawn, Duse demanded love of him, any love: loving lies, loving phrases: physical love, emotional love, spiritual love. She, who had been the least vain of women, now consulted her glass sorrowfully and at length. She feared women younger than herself, time no longer on her side. Helplessly, friends read her dumb letters, her beseeching telegrams.

In her sleep she fled from hedge to hedge in the garden of the Khedive, lost in a labyrinth of her own making and his.

Awake, seeing D'Annunzio mount his horse she would catch at the bridle, brows drawn together, crying, 'Where are you going to? Where are you going?'

Fresh and immaculate, concealing annoyance which nevertheless struck at her with every syllable, he would reply lightly, 'At random — as usual.'

The fingers on the bridle, clutching and shaking. The demanding voice.

'But which way? Which way?'

He had found his latest diversion: two sisters versed in the lute, the virginals and the erotic arts. For three hours or so they would run the gamut of music and perversity, from which he would return in excellent humour. And seeing her closed door, sensing behind it the huddle of despair, he would call her by one of the pet names he had given her.

'Ghisola! Ghisolabella! I love *you, only* you, *always*!'

She no longer, these days, kept him waiting, created scenes of her own, opposed his ideas and desires. She ran to him, as all the others except the little Gordigiani had done. And if common sense or pride tried to dissuade her she had one feverish, hopeless answer.

'A little while longer I shall please him. A little while longer.'

She did not cry, now, 'There is only one thing I can do — go away and leave you with your freedom!' — lest he agree with her.

She never asked whether he was looking at a white hair, nor suggested in jealousy that she should go to his mistress, nor said she must die before he hated her. She was finished, and they both knew it.

One good friend found her another house, just as pretty as La Porziuncola but away from D'Annunzio, and took her there on a pretext. She clasped her hands at the poppies flaring in the field, at the dark peace of the olive grove.

'You must live here, Eleonora,' he dared say, 'and find yourself again.'

Yes, of course she must, and at once, at once. She was so grateful to him, and he was so right, so kind, so good to think of her. She would take it for a year.

Weeks later, hearing that the house had indeed been rented, but that the Signora never came near it, he climbed the steps of La Porziuncola and rang the bell. She was sitting listlessly at her window, knew why he had come, and answered the unspoken question without looking at him.

'It would be just the same there as here,' she said, 'for, you see, *I* would be present.'

She lived much in the d'Annunzian past, becoming animated over lost glory.

'Do you remember Bologna?' she would cry, 'where my poor mother died — God rest her soul. Do you remember when they dedicated their theatre to me? Gabriele came to the hotel to double my pleasure. They had decorated it with white roses in my honour. White roses everywhere — in the passages, against the walls, on every table in my suite — smelling so delicious. But in *his* honour I had the stairs hung with scarlet. I stood at the head of that staircase and he kissed my hands, running up to greet me, calling me *Dolcezza*.

'Do you remember Venice? The poppies on fire by the water edge. The sky on fire with sunset. And the silence. I still hear the splash of oars, the cry of a gull.

'Do you remember?'

In the autumn of 1902 Romain Rolland visited Florence and presided for the last time over the dying relationship. Eleonora's championship of D'Annunzio had cost her money, and a third tour of the United States was being arranged to make up her losses and found their vanishing ideal of a theatre. She admitted that the tour was necessary, but her terror of dying abroad, plus her terror of losing the last hold on her lover, had lashed her into a hysteria no one could subdue.

Rolland sat with them at a meal where D'Annunzio ate fastidiously and well, and Eleonora played with a bit of bread and a glass of water. Her hair was quite grey in front, her lines deeper, her eyes weary. Small vertical wrinkles came and went in her cheeks, near the nose, as D'Annunzio talked. She tossed her head, smiled aggressively, then lapsed into her hopeless sadness. Her bitterness disturbed Rolland, but he helped to keep up a stream of conversation. The only time Eleonora showed animation was in personal comment on D'Annunzio. which embarrassed Rolland and banished D'Annunzio to dignified silence. But when she had said what she must say, he smiled, as one might smile at the interruption of an ill-mannered child, and continued to speak of other happier matters. Once he said, light and emphatic as a cat's leap on a draggled bird, that a woman's nature was obedience and a man's was tenacity.

Seeing that she wanted to confide in him, and did not know how to make the approach, Rolland suggested that she show him round her own small garden.

As soon as they were alone she clasped Rolland's arm and poured out her troubles.

'I am ruined, you know, Romain,' she said in a low rapid tone. 'Ruined physically, emotionally, morally, financially. I must go to America, and I am afraid that when I return he won't be here. He will leave me soon. I know that. And I cannot keep him.

'I can live neither with nor without him,' she cried. 'What shall I do? No, no. Don't say anything. There is no answer, no help, no hope for me. I know that, too. The whole affair has been fatal from the beginning. I knew it years ago, when I first met him. That meeting haunts me. I should have listened to my first voice.'

She tore a late rose from a bush and shredded it, petal by petal, as she talked.

'I am not a whore,' she said, trembling. 'I have had love affairs — many love affairs — though not perhaps as many as people think. But each time I have loved that particular man and no other, with all my being. This creature *plays* with love. He finds girls for himself, girls who know all the tricks of the trade. I sicken at the sight of him, coming back from them. I would escape if I could. But where is the place that would keep me safe from him? Fatal, all of it, fatal. He has drained me of life, and faith, and hope, and even courage. And *look* at him! He has fed on me. Fed on me.'

Her thoughts hurried ahead distractedly, and encountered another phantom.

'I lie awake at nights, fearful of dreaming, and am afraid whether I wake or sleep. I see that great journey ahead of me, Romain, across the bitter sea. America. How I was tormented by that first voyage, alone in a hostile climate, troubled by people who did not understand me. You know how women suffer, Romain. You are a writer. Imagine my solitude and my terror.

'There are fifteen days before I go. Oh, he is a genius and a monster. And I — since I read that terrible book — I have felt naked, Romain. Naked, and so ashamed. Wherever I turn there are eyes watching me, thinking of that book. He made me a public whore, and I loved him. More fool me, eh? Poor Duse! I should have known better by this time. He has bewitched me!'

D'Annunzio, strolling about his estate, fondling his hounds, was the wounded knight.

'She has always tormented herself with imaginary terrors,' he said coolly. 'She is a lost and wandering woman, full of fear and torment. Even in our happiest moments she has turned to jealousy and violence. She accuses me of unmentionable excesses, though I have a horror of pleasure for the sake of pleasure. I seek, and will seek, and have only ever sought true passion and beauty.'

Rolland did not answer, sensing the strength of D'Annunzio's defences. Indeed the man seemed to be both armed and armoured, and an army in himself. Reason, pity and understanding would be cloven by the steel of that egoism. And Duse's mortal struggles filled him only with annoyance. How can you tell a man that his mistress is his victim?

'*You* seem in excellent health,' said Rolland at length.

'I have always taken care of myself,' said D'Annunzio, smiling. 'I sleep well, I eat well. My only impatience in life is when meals are late!'

Supper was a quieter affair. D'Annunzio chatted amiably. Rolland listened. Duse sat, spent, in her chair, looking from one man to the other. Once, D'Annunzio patted her hand, rather as he would pat a dog's head. She flinched, flushed, and submitted. There was nothing to be done, and Rolland prepared to return to Milan.

His departure was delayed only an instant by Eleonora, who ran after him and kissed his hands, tears running down her cheeks.

'Pardon me,' she whispered rapidly, for soon D'Annunzio would join them. 'I feel I have given you pain. *Mi scusi*. It is the sadness of parting that made me talk so.'

He endeavoured to calm her, but the hoarse broken phrases tumbled one upon the other.

'I know I must go,' she whispered, 'but what I ask myself is this — is the danger so great that I must go *altogether*? *Mi scusi, mi scusi*. I will collect myself. I wished to hope, my friend. I wanted to chase away my sadness. I thank you for listening to me — I hope I shall meet you again some day.'

The American tour had been arranged through George Tyler at the end of the previous year; and Eleonora, coerced by D'Annunzio, had attempted to smuggle him in on the wings of her reputation to give a lecture tour. Tyler's reply forecast the American reception. He wrote to Duse's representative, Joseph Smith:

I regret very much that Signor D'Annunzio has such a high estimate of his drawing power. Frankly, between you and I, I believe a lecture tour by this gentleman would be anything but a success... It really seems outrageous that Signora Duse, who could come to America and do perhaps the biggest business ever done by a foreign artist, has to be hampered by this proposition.

Tyler did not trouble to wrap up public opinion:

Signor D'Annunzio's actions towards the lady are very well known in America... with the result that he has gained the contempt of every woman in the land... He would not only be a failure himself, but he would absolutely ruin her position in America... My offer to Madame Duse still holds good. She does not need a new play... Let her come to us and play her old repertoire... I can assure her the largest season she has ever enjoyed.

Eleonora made a show of rebellion, though her financial position would leave her no choice in the end. But Tyler was adamant. He wrote:

If I am forced to lose Madame Duse, I shall regret it very much indeed, but I don't propose to lose a whole lot of money on D'Annunzio with the full knowledge that his coming is a hindrance instead of a help. She will be a success whether he comes or not, and oh, so much greater success if he stays at home.

The general disgust at D'Annunzio's treatment of Duse trickled through Tyler's frank pen. *I wonder if it ever occurs to D'Annunzio that he would be doing the lady inestimable harm by this arrangement?* he wrote.

Eleonora embarked at Cherbourg on 8 October 1902. From the ruins of the love affair her obstinacy dictated one last, lost decree. The proposed repertoire of Goldoni, Sardou and Dumas *fils* was cancelled, and since they would not receive D'Annunzio she commanded them to receive his works. *La Gioconda*, *La Città Morta* and *Francesca da Rimini* were to be stuffed down the American throat. But she had relied too much upon her own dramatic genius. The audiences thronged to see her, once — and then stayed away.

Boston, Philadelphia, New York and Chicago taught her one of the bitterest lessons of her life: they could do without her.

Odiferous! said the *Tribune*, of her repertoire.

The critics were unanimous in their praise of her art and their condemnation of D'Annunzio's. Another thorn rankled. Had they said the plays were over-daring, too shocking, she could have borne with that. But slighting remarks on their length, boredom, and poverty of thought and feeling damaged her.

Perhaps for her audience's sake, perhaps for her own, Duse gave one performance of *Magda* on 14 January 1903, and heard the old acclaim. For one evening she had experienced again the proud modesty of a daughter breaking her father's tyranny. She had blushed — that blush Shaw so professionally pondered and admired — at her lover's entrance. She had come from gentleness to flaring anger, from indignation to sorrow. One critic had said of her, long ago, 'It seemed as if one could hear the beating of her heart in the broken whisper of her voice.'

But the *Tribune* summed up her third American tour in less than two dozen words:

The distinguished Italian actress has had a season of variable fortune, making known some of the worst plays that have ever been seen.

Still she protected D'Annunzio: cabling him every day; marking down his royalties as though the theatres were filled to capacity instead of three-quarters empty; losing money, losing confidence, losing self-respect.

Only once did she admit the emptiness that had become her life. In Washington, on a cold December day, she enclosed a flower in a sheet of paper and sent it to Arrigo Boito.

TWENTY-NINE

Impoverished, Eleonora crept back to Italy in the spring of 1903, and found D'Annunzio ready for the only intimacy she could now offer him: that of companionable silence while he created a new play.

She was incapable of work, and having no money accepted a loan from Robert von Mendelssohn the banker. He offered her a million lire. She took 300,000, and meticulously planned its repayment within the next twelve months. Then she retreated with D'Annunzio to the Villa Borghese in Nettuno, some miles south of Rome. D'Annunzio's daughter, Renata, went with them, giving a curious air of respectability to that tired union.

Rumour had spread strange and exotic tales of the Duse-D'Annunzio affair when last they took a seaside cure. Rumour said that the poet rode daily into the sea, naked upon a white stallion; and that the actress waited for him, holding out a cloak of purple velvet. Rumour now noted that D'Annunzio left both mistress and daughter to enjoy the sea air alone, and was visiting a beautiful Roman widow in her early twenties.

Eleonora shut her ears to everything but the sound of the sea on the shore, and the sight of her dramatist writing another play. For this time, he said, eyeing the pages of blank paper, he would create something unsurpassable. Joyful, monk-like in his silence, he wrote *La Figlia di Iorio* in a fever of concentration.

Once more she rustled to his door to listen. And once more she experienced the rapture of his attention, and read the pages he handed to her as he wrote.

She recognised, with a pain undulled by habit, that the role was written for a much younger woman. But the play itself was better constructed, more in touch with reality. The disciple in Eleonora had never uttered one doubt or complaint. But the professional actress, while recognising that the other dramas might be difficult for the public to accept, saw that this one would not.

He finished his pastoral tragedy in twenty-eight days, and announced that he would like Duse to join the young Talli-Gramatica-Calabresi Company for its production. Their leading lady was the charming Irma Gramatica, already forecast as a future rival in the theatre. But Irma was quite prepared to step aside for the première, and then take over Duse's role when the company went on tour.

Eleonora made no enquiries into the nature of the lady's relationship with D'Annunzio: she was too tired to begin or sustain a scene, too bruised to cope with possibly unpleasant truths. Instead she concentrated on her part, in a play which she was sure would place him in the front rank of Italian dramatists: the play which was to be the answer to six years of crusading on her money and genius.

In the January of 1904, during rehearsal at Genoa, she fell ill; but, sustained by desperation, pushed herself back into rehearsal — and fell ill again.

'Really, we cannot wait for her, I am afraid,' said D'Annunzio, and sent her a messenger with instructions to turn over her costumes to Irma Gramatica.

She read the note, and let it fall to the floor. Désirée, her companion of many years, picked it up, and waited for whatever storm might come: imperial commands, berserk rage, hysterical tears, wild protestations. There were none. Eleonora pulled herself up from the divan and crossed to the clothes cupboard.

'I will pack the costumes, *illustrissima*,' said Maria, her dresser, divining what Eleonora wanted.

Duse motioned her to be quiet. And one by one took down the costumes. One by one folded them. One by one she handed them to the waiting messenger, without a word.

Her calm was ominous, and broke on 3 February when she scrawled to D'Annunzio:

And so I say to you, goodbye. You have done for me. We are two, *but I am* dead.

Rumour was truth. Though D'Annunzio might play with a girl or two on the side, he needed as an artist that ecstasy he had experienced with Duse eight years before. He needed another space of halcyon days. And now his muse blazed again in the form of the Marchese Alessandra Carlotti di Rudini, the young Roman widow he had been meeting in secret. Tall and splendid, with her coronet of gold hair, her classical features and white skin and dark blue eyes, she provided an element Duse had always lacked — though lacking elements that Duse alone could provide — she possessed great physical prowess. An excellent horsewoman, she revelled in youth, beauty and daring.

Dazzled, D'Annunzio renamed her Nike, the Greek word for victory. He introduced her to all his private little ways of written communication, such as beginning and ending a letter with the hail-and-farewell invocation of *Elabani*; using the single word *Adel* to convey the ten-word phrase *The great fire of your soul and mine is impenetrable*; writing the subtle *Alis, Do you not feel my hand upon your hand?* — and so on.

For the moment Eleonora had enough trouble with her health and his play. She would face the complication of Nike later. Immured in her hotel suite at Genoa, her lungs burning, her voice hoarse, her temperature wayward, she sent a cry for help to Matilde Serao. And together they waited for Irma Gramatica to appear in the première.

They had known each other for twenty-six years, so sat in sad and companionable silence on the evening of 3 March, with Duse watching the clock and describing the scene at the theatre in Milan.

'Now Ristori is sitting in her box,' said Eleonora. 'Eighty-two years old, Mati, think of that! Why, you and I must seem like girls to her. I love Ristori. She likes me, too, she always said so. What nobility, Mati, what dignity. What an ornament and inspiration she has been to the Italian theatre.'

She stopped for a moment and drank water. Saw the hands of the clock. Started off again.

'Now the curtain is going up, Mati. Oh, that theatre, how well I remember it. Wait a moment, Mati, and I will show you the opening scene.'

In spite of Matilde's coaxing and protestations, she pictured the set, and the positions of the players, in detail: becoming more and more flushed and excited. There were two premières that night: one in the Teatro Lirico, Milan, the other in that hotel bedroom in Genoa. Exhausted, feverish, she played the entire role of Mila di Codra and sketched in the supporting cast: pausing to drink water during the intermissions, noting the clock, remarking on the rise and fall of curtain: until she reached the climax of '*La flamma e bella!* The flame is beautiful!' and fell back upon her pillows, finished.

News of the play's reception came through as she slept, and Matilde noted with irony that D'Annunzio had at last found his place in the theatre, but without the woman who had worked so fanatically for that success.

Some flicker of conscience, some speck of humanity, or some wave washed from Eleonora's sad shore, must have moved him. Surrounded by praise, called to the stage for the first time in his career to receive acclamation, D'Annunzio was oddly out of sorts with his triumph.

'How do you feel?' someone asked him, jubilantly.

He stood there quietly. A small dapper man in a long overcoat.

'I feel a great melancholy,' he replied.

Well enough to make a fool of herself, Eleonora scratched a pathetic, over-written, underlined note to Nike, suggesting that they should share D'Annunzio's affections. Nike was not interested.

'Rest yourself, Nella,' her friends persuaded her, anxious to help her preserve some remnant of dignity since health, reputation, happiness and money were gone.

It was May, an important month in her life. She had spent a glorious May with Cafiero in 1879, had married Tebaldo in May 1881, had met Arrigo Boito in May 1884, had triumphed in Vienna in May 1892, had undertaken her first Parisian appearance in May 1897. In this miserable May of 1904, not entirely sane, she retired to La Porziuncola, and could not resist taking one look at D'Annunzio's bazaar next door. She told herself she was merely evoking his presence, and knew she was hunting for evidence. The servants let her in with misgiving, seeing the white face and burning eyes, and she went straight to the main bedroom. There, stooping to the floor, she seized a small gold hairpin, and let out that long dark sweet wail that had petrified the Prince in *La Femme de Claude*.

The servants stood frozen to their separate places. Then one of them brought Dr Palmerio, D'Annunzio's estate manager.

She was rushing here and there in the house, gasping out inarticulate phrases. They heard her say something about the garden of the Khedive, and from time to time she would batter at a wall and cry that she could not find her way out. She demanded that they bring her fire, at once. Fire. Then she threw herself on the ground, as she had done in her early Sardou days, when one critic said with awe that she had no regard for propriety.

She howls, he had written. *She just lies on the floor and howls.*

Dr Palmerio caught her arms as kindly as he could, and tried to restrain her. There was no beauty left in that driven face, no dignity in the struggling body, no grace in the striking, tearing fingers.

Over and over again, recognising nobody, she cried, 'You must burn this house at once. At once. The temple has been profaned.'

They half-assisted, half-carried her back to La Porziuncola. She was crying, 'Fire alone can purify. Fire alone can purify. Fire alone can purify.'

Désirée and Maria put her to bed and sat with her until she grew quieter. She asked for water, for solitude. An hour or so later Désirée opened the door noiselessly to make sure she was all right, and saw that the demon had left her.

She was lying against her pillows, looking at the hands stretched out, palms upward, before her. She had accepted that it was finished. Désirée closed the door again just as quietly, and listened to the words Eleonora was saying into the cloister of her room.

'Cenere, cenere, cenere. Davanti ogli occhi, su le labbra, nel caro delle mani...'

Ashes, ashes, ashes. Before my eyes, on my lips, in my empty hands...

Death passed over me a few days ago, she wrote to a friend. *Leave me alone for a few more days and I shall be on my feet.*

Burned out, she lay in the shell of herself and listened to an old river running. She knew that sorrow must return, that peace lay a long way off. But she had been freed, since she could not free herself, and little moments of joy from a former freedom crept back again. Perfect silence and solitude had been strangers to her for years, spoiled by fears of what might happen when she left D'Annunzio alone, by remembrances of injury and wretchedness. But now the silence was hers alone, the solitude hers to be enjoyed.

She read a play by Maurice Maeterlinck, *Monna Vanna*, in the original French, and scribbled a note to Adolfo de Bosis asking if he would kindly translate it into Italian for her:

I don't want to be killed like this. I want work... and so I beg you to help me. Pay heed to the music, like a faraway music one hears again, but also close, close inside. And added, *There's a beautiful phrase — 'plus de courage en face de l'amour.'*

To his American wife Lilian she wrote:
What I need today (and the days pass, everything passes!) is tenderness and faith.

She had slept all the afternoon, and woken to that particular golden haze that ends a summer day. Light poured into her room, and she was young again, lying on the carpet reading some book she had bought because she liked the cover. Ideas flocked and jostled, and some important answer trembled on her lips. Meaning and strength and promise came in through the slats in the blind.

'But I am too old,' she said aloud, a little reproachfully.

She lay on her pillows peacefully, trying to fit the significance of light into the only work of which she was capable, that of professional actress.

A train whistle in the night drove her on. To where, then? To Paris. To whom? She did not know but, remembering the kindness of Romain Rolland and his wife, dropped them a note from her hotel.

Perhaps you have forgotten my name. Therefore I recall myself to your memory. I want very much to see you.

Slowly, she picked up old friends she had flung down for the sake of D'Annunzio. Her old audiences had gone. Schürmann had gone.

How much has he cost me? she wondered.

But de Bosis sent her the translation of *Monna Vanna*. She read it through, suddenly seeing her way ahead. And wrote to him in affectionate gratitude.

Do understand *that I asked you for help — and that you held out your hand to me*. Do understand *that* no *vital force has been destroyed in my soul — on the contrary*. Do understand *that 'Life is one' — and that that comprises and enfolds* all that dies *and* all that lives. It is all one *— but it's no use writing — or talking. Eleonora.*

From the Tyrol she asked him to translate *John Gabriel Borkman*.

I must work, I want to work. Monna Vanna *is not enough. I need a play whose pulse beats firmly... I have found one I have loved for a long time, but towards which I lacked the necessary courage. Today — just today, in this* first peace *I have found in the mountains, I have re-read it, and feel that I might try it ... What I need is the word, the living word, the lived word, like a sword, but always true.*

A flower-seller held out violets from her basket.

'I shall give *myself* a bunch,' said Eleonora, reaching for the flowers, paying far too much.

She stood in the winter sunlight and saw each of them separate and illuminated. Each small and dark and perfect, and different. She looked around the street and saw it as yet another separate and illuminated thing. And she knew that the break with D'Annunzio was no accident, not a leading away to another affair, not a falling away into suicide, but a perfect bit of jigsaw fitted into a larger pattern.

'Why,' she said to herself, suddenly radiant, 'I am *meant* to be alone. Meant to reach some goal successfully. Meant to live through and among other people. And yet, curious though it seems, I am *not* alone. Separate, and myself, and not alone. I am not alone.'

She had received — as, five years ago, D'Annunzio had written of La Foscarina — 'the order to go away'.

PILGRIMAGE

I alone am my own friend or enemy: the rest is legend.
Eleonora Duse

THIRTY

She watched the rehearsals of Maxim Gorky's *Lower Depths*, knowing that the Théâtre de l'Oeuvre in Paris was fighting for his life; and offered the young manager, Aurélien Lugné-Poë, her own services in the part of Vasilissa for one evening to draw the crowds. Lugné-Poë, not so dazzled that he lost sight of the financial obstacle, asked her hesitantly what her fee would be.

'What do you pay the boy who is so good as the lunatic?' she asked, naming a minor role.

'Ten francs, Signora.'

'Then pay me that.'

The audience came to see la Duse, but with the exquisite tact she could always exercise when she had a mind to do so, she kept herself in the background and gave Lugné-Poë's wife, Suzanne Despres, the chance to shine. And the young couple were drawn, both willingly and unwillingly, into Eleonora's orbit.

In 1905, therefore, came a new manager in the shape of Lugné-Poë, modern, enthusiastic, far-sighted; a new eminence in the return of an actress legendary in her own lifetime; a new repertoire in Maeterlinck, Ibsen and the young Russian Gorky. And, while Paris waited to welcome Duse back again, there was the prospect of a new and highly enjoyable clash with Bernhardt.

Lugné-Poë suggested that they skirt Sarah's patch of ground entirely and book the Nouveau Théâtre: a move noted with interest by everyone, including Sarah herself — who wrote a letter of sweet reproach to her dear sister-at-arms offering the magnificent Théâtre Sarah Bernhardt.

Had Sarah forgotten the Parisian Campaign of 1897, or her published memoirs which damned Eleonora with some praise?

Eleonora Duse is a great actress rather than a great artist: she takes roads which have already been laid down by others. It is true she does not ape other actresses: she plants flowers where they planted trees, and trees where they planted flowers; but she has never created by means of her art a character which is inseparable from her name, she has never given form to a vision or a figure which makes one think of her and her alone. She has done nothing but put on other actresses' gloves; only she has put them on inside out. And she has done it all with infinite grace and imperturbable unconsciousness. Eleonora is a great actress, even a very great actress, but she is not an artist.

This assessment, this bucket of cold water, thrown at a time when she was in the last throes of her love affair with D'Annunzio, had brought Eleonora to the surface, fighting. Her reply augured future battle.

'Tell Madame Bernhardt I am not writing my memoirs,' she said, 'nor have I any intention of writing them — but she had better pray *God* that I never change my mind!'

The memoirs were old history now, but Eleonora — like Sarah — never forgot a grudge until it had been properly paid off. Now, with Sarah's offer of her theatre on the desk, la Duse took up her ready pen with considerable relish, and expressed her feelings in fluent French.

Pas d'oubli dans mon coeur. *This is, Madame, my first thought for you, which I set down in these few words — out of gratitude — in the* first hour *of my arrival in Paris. I have never forgotten your hospitality, and I never shall.*

The other time I was here you were everything great and good to me. You offered me a close friendship which filled me with a deep respect.

Alas! Why is it that today my heart does not find its way to yours?

I cannot ignore the judgement that you expressed for my art. I cannot ignore it, admit it, nor forget it… but the memory of your judgement must not allow me to forget past kindnesses, for in life every hour has its value, *and I like to remember the time you were perfect and good to me.*

So what must I do?

I repeat to you, Madame, these affectionate words: Not forgotten in my heart. *The memory of the one, and the remembrance of the other, is preserved. I pray you also, Madame, in your turn, to recall my boundless admiration and my unlimited gratitude.*

Eleonora Duse

That salvo fired, she prepared to enjoy Paris, with the added knowledge that her repertoire was avant-garde and Sarah's somewhat old-fashioned. But Sarah, not to be outdone in knife-edge politeness, wrote back.

Yes. Every hour has its value in life, and the one in which you write me such a noble and beautiful letter has infinite charm. I wanted to love you. I approached you. Obviously I was unable to show you this because you did not see it. Can the tiresome proximity of those who love us too much have kept us apart? I don't know! Would you tell me at what time I might find you at home tomorrow? I shall be very happy to thank you then for your sweet thought.

Sarah Bernhardt

Both ladies satisfied, both ladies established in the eyes of the theatre world, and both ladies now past the hectic years of love affairs — Sarah over sixty, Duse within sight of fifty — they let each other be.

The new life constituted a new approach in all matters. Duse made greater efforts to meet the writers and artists, both aspiring and established, who wished to know her. She became a guest of honour at receptions, dressed once more in the ensembles designed by her good friend Jean Philippe Worth. Inevitably his name was linked with hers, and gossip spoke of a love affair, but she had consumed herself in D'Annunzio and was content with friendship. And she steeped herself in Ibsen, whom she called her deliverer.

If I can work as I wish, she wrote, *I am saved. To work is the only remedy. It is necessary to go on, to go on until one can go no further — and after...*

After? To sit in the sun and eat her bread in peace.

Meanwhile she studied her new scripts by the hour, feet propped on another chair; underlining, making notes, or staring out of the window absorbed by some inner vision. Her reading intensified. She studied philosophy, religion, history in a new endeavour to find meaning in life, even in those events and sufferings which seemed without meaning. Restlessness still beset her, would always beset her. Worth had said, 'A nomad she was born, and a nomad she will die!' But she accepted her restlessness, and used it.

She studied people even more deeply, drawing away from the vain and the affected, drawing near to the sorrowful and the gentle. And behind all masks she discovered a common human loneliness, and sought something beyond this loneliness that could sustain and explain it.

But outwardly she retained the entourage and mystique of a great artist, for her own protection. While people gossiped of her pride and arrogance, they were not intruding on the workings of her heart and mind. She let them talk, less concerned than she had ever been over public opinion.

She kept her rooms overheated, coddling her capricious lungs and throat. She set Désirée as a watchdog over her privacy, and used Maria as a sounding board. Impatient, fastidious, she not only checked every item on the set before each performance but forbade any stranger to cross that magic line between the house front and backstage. She inaugurated a 1000-lire fine to be exacted from any member of the company who permitted a visitor behind the scenes. But occasionally the importunate did manage to penetrate the mystery, with results sometimes amusing, sometimes sad. One wretched man blundered into her and was received with the clarion cry of 'How did *you* get here?'

Stunned by the remark and the august presence, he attempted to introduce himself.

'Signora, I am —' he began hopefully.

She fixed him with a devilish eye.

'Very good!' she said crisply. '*Continue* to be that!'

And turned away before he could collect his wits.

On to her sacred set wandered the Italian comedian Ferruccio Benini, who had been so successful in his own plays and those of Goldoni and Gallina, who possessed his own company and a fine reputation. Possibly he felt, in the humblest way, a little akin to la Duse since he was a master of the Venetian dialect, and a descendant of Luigi Duse's own line of theatre. So he poked his ugly, funny, rubbery face round her stage, and raised his expressive hands in wonder at the perfection. Whereupon a human tempest collided with him and gave voice.

He recognised the famous sombre eyes, the angle of the whitened head, the regal supple carriage, and the magnificent tones now lifted for his benefit in a belligerent *arpeggio*.

'Who has *dared* to come here and disturb me during my working hours?' demanded la Duse.

He was grateful even for her rage, bowed low with his comical clown's obeisance, and said very softly, 'I am Benini — please excuse me.'

A flick of recognition came into the black eyes. One hand went to her mouth. Then she turned and swept away, slamming a door behind her.

Discomfited, he began to find his way out.

The door opened. A graceful little woman, whose eyes glittered with tears, whose mouth trembled, whose hands stretched out beseechingly, hurried to detain him.

'Forgive me,' said Eleonora. 'Forgive me, Signor Benini. *Mi scusi! Mi scusi!*'

She had made his evening and delayed her own, for she was far too upset to go on stage, and the curtain rose several minutes late. But la Duse being a legend, her subjects were pleased to endure the wait, and sat entranced and expectant as long as she cared to keep them.

Able to strip any player to the bone, she sometimes used her tongue on them with disastrous effect. To work with Duse was to enjoy an incomparable honour, to suffer incomparable outrage, and to see — if one could bear to see so little — the exact value of oneself in comparison with her.

'Bring me, *at once*, this very minute, a giant copper vase! Don't ask me where from! How should *I* know where from? Why should I *care*? Just find it — and *quickly*!'

'I *detest*... strong scents, artificial flowers, anything less than perfection.'

'I *will* have... the moon if necessary — and at once.'

From the moment she woke, generally at seven in the morning, until the moment she slept, which might be any time at all, she devoured the time and energy of all about her. Should some technical or business point trouble her she would summon her manager, young Lugné-Poë, and his wife, Suzanne Despres, in the early hours. And Spinelli, her secretary, was required to bring in the daily papers at seven in the morning, clad in full evening dress.

As a letter-writer Duse was prolific. As a sender of telegrams she was obsessive. The theatre gossip read in several papers, the day's telegrams dictated, she received her maid. Hot baths, long days in bed, valerian for her nerves, champagne for her vitality, cognac for her strength, oxygen for her lungs, and attention at all times.

Then she would indulge in one of her sporadic bursts of solitude, and retreat into the country, leaving the company to hang about on full pay until she chose to return.

She could be stupidly capricious, summoning a friend from Florence at a few hours' notice, in order to have her company on the train *back* to Florence. A telegram saying *Come. I am at the end of my strength* would bring the recipient across a continent, ready to give all of himself or herself for a few hours at her side. Her terrifying magnetism, her incessant demands, her wilful vagaries, held those who interested her in thrall. Not everyone enjoyed subjection, and in retrospect Lugné-Poë wrote bitterly about her.

She could be stupidly generous, touched by any begging story, however unconvincing. The poor, the unfortunate, the sick and the fallen were sacred to her. She never forgot an old friend, and when Cesare Rossi was in debt she offered him a benefit night in Rome — with a tact so delicate as to assume he did not really need the money, but that the gesture would please her.

She could be stupidly self-pitying: loving to draw and shed tears, to hear condolences and cries of compassion. And when the pity was not forthcoming, or did not come fast enough, she would whip it up herself.

'You don't *know* misfortune!' she cried to Ciro Galvani at a rehearsal of *Hedda Gabler*. 'And if you don't know it you must *find* it. Tell yourself you are unfortunate and you will see how your acting improves — I do it well, because I carry bitterness within me.'

She still hated rehearsals, but held what few she must in the drawing-room of her hotel suite, and was punctual to the minute. Some of Angelica's genteel upbringing — against all odds — must have dictated the wearing of a hat and gloves indoors. Eleonora said she dressed in this formal way, while rehearsing, to make her company behave. But by this time everyone was past caring what she did, provided they could keep from under her feet and reasonably out of her clutches. Directing, explaining, placing, shaping, ordering, she forced her players into a pre-cast mould she herself would never have endured in her youth.

She still cancelled performances as personal health or personal omens or personal whims dictated. Rarely did she play more than one night a week, never the same play twice running. And yet she could travel spontaneously from Florence to London to join in the celebrations of the Ellen Terry Jubilee in 1906. And she gave her 'Nora' costumes to Suzanne Despres — saying that Suzanne was truly Nora, and she herself would never act the part again.

She was capable of the finest and shabbiest emotions, of the noblest and meanest actions. Only, in this great range of feeling, the middle section was totally lacking. Whatever else Duse was, she was never mediocre — though she did once remark that mediocrity was the true gift of the gods.

Worth dressed her in the colours of autumn for *Rosmersholm*, inspired by a vision of copper leaves in the Tuileries Garden. Her hair was now silver-grey, her bones beautifully prominent in the pale face. Every movement was meaningful, every gesture pared down to its core. They flocked to see her because she was a great actress at her peak and because they loved her. Her wanderings took her to Belgium, Switzerland, Russia, Austria, Germany, Hungary, Holland, France, England and Scandinavia.

In Norway, home of Ibsen, she longed to meet and thank the man whose own work had helped both the theatre and herself, and she travelled to Christiania. But Ibsen had been struck by the paralysis from which he would die in a few months. She accepted that a meeting was impossible, but hoped she might at least glimpse his shadow on the blind. Dressed in her sables, and a pair of Norwegian boots, she stood in the winter cold and snow outside his window for over an hour; then turned away, saddened, to enthral his countrymen with her Ellida, her Hedda, her Rebecca.

She rode the crest of the theatre wave, alive to the importance of new plays and the little theatres which struggled to breathe fresh life into an old body. She asked Gordon Craig, son of Ellen Terry and E. W. Godwin, to design and produce *Rosmersholm* for her in Florence in 1906, at the Teatro della Pergola. A couple of years later he settled there, and influenced Europe and America with his prodigious gifts of invention.

The critic Giuseppe Antonio Borgese wrote of her performance in this production.

Her pauses and silences were even more significant than the outpouring of words... nothing, down to the minutest fold, appeared casual about the fluttering curtain behind which Rebecca was spying: the play of light and shade across her smooth face made fleeting masks, that moment by moment seemed to become permanent pieces of sculpture.

And writing to a friend with that ready, restless, volatile pen, Eleonora said, *Without* Rosmersholm *I should have been dead some time ago.*

But the trip to Florence had saddened her, and she decided to cut the remaining ties with La Porziuncola. To her friend, Emma Garzes, from the Grand Hotel in Florence, she sent one flower and a few words: *To thee alone I send this rose of La Porziuncola.*

Hermann Bahr wrote of her performances in these last years:

She often seems to shudder away from the text, seeking words in her own dumb and frozen soul, and while the crowd frantically applaud her she walks away with the weary tread of a captive, so that one seems to hear the faint clanking of heavy chains.

Not every critic succumbed to her spell. Jarro remarked that, whereas at first she had inclined towards a too-rapid diction, she now broke up her phrases to an intolerable extent. He said that some of her low tones sounded forced and guttural.

These pauses are commonly used by her so as to hash up all her periods. It is a very defective method of phrasing, which comes either from an exaggerated attention to the art of speaking or from some defect in breathing which she has contracted.

And Max Beerbohm, succeeding Shaw on the *Saturday Review*, said she was so remote that he could not imagine anyone calling her by her Christian name, and wrote:

True I see power and nobility in her face... I admire, too, her movements, full of grace and strength. But my prevailing emotion is hostile to her. My prevailing impression is of a great egotistic force, of a woman over-riding, with sombre unconcern, plays, mimes, critics and public.

And Pirandello said she never found the right author. Adding, with mischievous sarcasm ... *or found the* wrong *one!*

Resting on the Riviera, she met Guy de Maupassant's mother, who spent her days at her son's graveside. They talked together a great deal, finding a mutual ground of grief, giving each other comfort.

Before they parted, the old woman said kindly, 'What can I wish *you*, Signora, who are in the full splendour of your fame?'

Eleonora said, 'Peace, madame.'

She toured South America and returned to Europe. At Turin, in those few quiet moments between the final adjustment and the rise of curtain, she was seized by a small cold wind. She had had a premonition, in the city where she had enjoyed an early triumph as Lionette, that this evening was to be one of her last triumphs. In body and mind she had reached some end, and demanded another beginning. That zenith of radiance and wisdom and art flickered, guttered, and finally went out at Berlin in 1909.

Her retirement, at fifty-one, was headline news. Different explanations were given, all of them to some degree true. She was exhausted, she was ill, she needed rest and solitude, she was weary of travelling and the demands of theatre life, she was suddenly sick of the whole business.

Her final performance on 31 January 1909 was a poignant one: all the more poignant for being the gay *La Locandiera*. The audience laughed as she courted one man, and burned the hand of another with her smoothing iron, and accepted presents from all three suitors. And the laughter hurt. They could not let her go. Call after call she took, head thrown back, eyes sombre, mouth sad, an air of melancholy on her face. Then she extended her arms to them one last time, and made her way through the press of people to the dressing room.

THIRTY-ONE

Robert von Mendelssohn had invested Eleonora's money wisely, and she was able to indulge her desire for a settled residence, as well as a nomadic existence. But her house in the small hill-town of Asolo near Venice was ten years away. Meanwhile she rented apartments and hotel rooms, even in the same city and at the same time, with prodigal extravagance. She shuttled herself and her furniture between one flat and the next, took the train to Paris when she heard that haunting whistle in the night, appeared suddenly before her friends, and then retreated back to her books. The need to leave the theatre was strong enough to keep her out of it. Her desire to attain some state of grace drove her to extensive reading and meditation. But the stage had a lifetime's grip, and drew her to the brink of return many times.

In the shadows of a Ravenna theatre box in 1911, hearing the ripple of recognition turn to standing acclaim, acknowledging the cries of 'Viva! Viva la Duse!', she wavered. The following year she and Yvette Guilbert, in light-hearted fellowship, planned a joint recital tour of university towns in the States. But Eleonora changed her mind. She had always, quite apart from her need to retreat, been superstitious about America.

But her capacity for eating men alive had not diminished with the years. Rainer Maria Rilke, the writer and poet, provided a tasty and sensitive morsel in the summer of 1912. He was magnetised into persuading her, naturally without success, to return to the stage. The effort cost him a great deal of time and a river of tears, but being a writer he managed to survive the experience and translate it into words.

Her talent for suffering was phenomenal, but genuine, and because she had suffered she knew how to comfort. When Isadora Duncan's children were drowned in the Seine in 1913, Isadora sought Duse — who embraced her, and wept with her, knowing that words held no solace.

She had been born in a year of revolution in Italy, and still revolution elsewhere was not at an end. News of Mrs Pankhurst's suffragettes in England, fighting for the vote, lobbing soot and flour and leaflets at Members of Parliament, chaining themselves to railings, setting fire to a church, smashing shop windows, trickled in to the Continent from the beginning of their campaign in 1906. Their cries for greater freedom and equality, the stories of their rough handling by police and crowd, of prison sentences, forcible feeding and domestic upheaval, penetrated even the patriarchal stronghold of Italy. A Women's International Congress was held in Rome, and Duse attended it, though she was not wholly in sympathy with their aims and demands. She had always said it was a pity to fight against a man instead of with him and for him. Also, in truth, she had enjoyed freedom and more than equality — but this last point possibly escaped her.

Hands buried in her thick silvery hair, spectacles tipping slightly, she studied and pondered, striving to discover what she must do with the rest of her life. She resolved, at last, to be useful to those girls who reminded her of her youth: ardent, dedicated, and with no place of retreat. She had a vision of herself when young, multiplied: avid for books and fine conversation, longing for beauty, bedevilled by lack of privacy. And for these many Eleonoras, creatures fashioned out of her memory and imagination, she decided to found an Actresses'

Home. Her friends wasted much time trying to dissuade her. She knew, she said, what was needed: rooms full of light and air and flowers, easy chairs, excellent books, the opportunity for young minds to rest and expand.

That fantasy cost her 10,000 lire. The Casa delle Attrici, a pleasant house situated on the Via Nomentana in Rome, opened in May 1914, with an august list of patrons and friends. Unfortunately there were few young actresses with Eleonora's single-minded determination for self-improvement. The average girl hoped for a rich husband, and made do with a susceptible manager. The old concept of actresses as travelling whores still contained a pinch of truth. Eleonora offered them peace, meditation, education. They were blithe and silly and immature. They preferred a noisy party, a handsome escort, a new dress. But the home did not, as other dreams had done, crumble slowly before her eyes and display the poverty of its foundations. It was despatched naturally, almost painlessly, by a great cataclysm. A month after the opening ceremony, the Archduke Ferdinand of Austria and his wife Sophia were assassinated in Sarajevo, and war became imminent.

Italy entered the arena in May 1915, and Duse entered with it in spirit, realising that now no one was alone any more, and no one any longer could count themselves separate.

Bernhardt, campaigning against the twilight of her career, increasing age, uraemia and the loss of a leg, took on the entertainment of the French troops with gusto. She travelled, minus her usual flummery and comforts, over roads that were ruts. She performed on makeshift platforms, in barns and tents and hospitals. And she brought the men to their feet, louse-ridden, ragged, muddy and unwashed, with her cry of *'Aux armes!'* Then she journeyed on to the next rough stage.

Duse was less conspicuous, though no less useful. The war eclipsed her own interior battles, driving her out of herself and into the lives of those less fortunate. She stayed for long intervals in Udine, eighty miles from Venice, where the Italian Army had their headquarters until they were defeated at Caporetto. She walked between the beds of sick and dying, wrote letters for and about them, brought them small gifts and helped their families. She sold her library, sold her costumes, and spent the money on them. She kept in touch with her friends, and their sons at the Front.

For one soldier she carried a message to the poor quarter of Milan, and, seeing the poverty of his mother and his two motherless babies, added lire to it. She then took the next train back, triumphant, and reported with Duse-like accuracy every detail of appearance and conversation. When the soldier was posted missing, she returned to Milan with more money. When he was found dead, she kept his mother until the pension came through.

She did not advertise herself, and few recognised la Duse in the pale little woman who sat by a wounded man's bed, and scrawled diligently, with a pen that tended to blob as she filled the paper with exhortations and exclamations and underlined important words and phrases.

A new art — flickering, jumping, badly focused, silent, and accompanied by a tinny piano — had joined the theatre world: the cinematograph. The queens of the stage were asked to transfer their genius from the boards to an oblong screen and a reel of celluloid. Ellen Terry did. Bernhardt did. Finally, Duse consented, having turned down many offers. Grazia Deledda's novel *Cenere* had been made into a script in 1916. Drawn by the challenge, spurred by the prospect of work, Eleonora woke at four every morning and humbly adapted herself to this new medium, rehearsing and chiselling the more flowery parts of the script, even though she would not be heard.

Deprived of sound, she concentrated on form, movement and expression. But she flinched when the cameras came in for a close-up, afraid of hollows and wrinkles taking precedence over performance.

'Film me in the shadows, if you please,' she begged. 'People should see an old woman — not old age itself!'

The story of the peasant Rosalia, who gives her illegitimate son the chance of a good life by relinquishing him, was dear to Eleonora's heart. And later she would choose a play by Gallarati Scotti with a similar theme: *Così Sia*. Her own son had been in his grave for thirty-five years, and was still remembered.

This is something that fascinates me, she wrote, *and I am doing it with passionate interest.* And then, loving the return, *How can I have lost my soul like that, for seven years?*

At fifty-eight she looked seventy on the screen, and played the early scenes with her back to the cameras, acting the movements of the young woman. The film was not well received, but she accepted its limitations and hers with philosophy.

'If I were twenty years younger,' she said, visualising what the cinema might become, 'I would begin all over again. But I'm too old for it — isn't it a pity?'

With a genuine twilight of the gods on his doorstep, D'Annunzio came into his own and reaped new laurels. At fifty-four he was a national hero, and Eleonora — following his exploits in the press — ventured to send him good wishes by letter and telegram. More than a decade of separation and regrowth lay between them. She asked no more than a maternal friendship, and D'Annunzio — who probably needed a mother more than a mistress — was grateful. Finding herself a small standpoint on the fringe of his life, she drew upon her experience and intuition to help him. Scraps of advice and comfort travelled from her hands to his, signed *Consolazione* as in the old days of their alliance. But she did not attempt to meet him, preferring to hide behind her vigorous pen. Once, in 1917, waiting at Udine station for the train to Florence, she heard the sound of cheering, and cries of 'D'Annunzio!' and he was hurried past her in a group of soldiers. She stood upon a bench to catch sight of him, and when eyes and ears convinced her he had gone she sat down again, and was cold and shaken for an hour afterwards. But she soothed herself by concentrating on his coming dangers, and endeavoured to look ahead for him. Having a superstitious regard for her inner sight, D'Annunzio heeded her prophecies like a child, though their accuracy varied. And between them passed the message which now applied to both of them — *mutar d'ale*, 'changing wings'.

Arrigo Boito died in 1918, and took something of her with him. For three days she lay in her bedroom at the Hotel Cavour in Milan, the blinds drawn down, mourning him. She was sixty, unable to afford the loss of an old friend and lover.

'What loneliness!' she said. 'Life rushes on, rushes on like a river that wreaks havoc and cannot find the sea.'

The image troubled her, as she visualised the flooded land, and she returned to her books for an answer.

Heed not the written word but what lies behind it, wrote St Catherine of Siena.

'You must simply *pray*,' said her friend Paul Claudel, the poet.

'*Pray?*' said Duse, 'It must be a profound faith that can say "You must simply pray" to *me*!'

Nevertheless she tried, though when ecclesiastical dogma entered one door of her mind Duse promptly left by another. She subdued herself in one direction, only to find herself breaking out at another point.

'How well I understand the struggle in you between the artist and the woman,' another friend observed.

'*The* woman?' said Duse. '*The* woman? Don't you know that there are a *thousand* women in me, and that I am tormented by each in turn?'

Then, coming to a spiritual cul-de-sac in her solitude, she attempted action. Futile action, such as taking the next train to somewhere simply because it was a different place.

'Work! That's the only remedy!' she cried. 'One must go on, go on until one can go no further — and even beyond *that*!'

But there had been no work, apart from the Great War and that one short film she described as being 'only a sketch'. She practised for hours with her beautifully-made marionettes bought in Berlin, striving to express emotions by the minutest movements of their limbs. And back to her books.

'I know nothing, *nothing*! I have *everything* to learn!'

And then she found the house in Asolo overlooking the Venetian plain. A house so high that it seemed to float in the blue. Streets clambered up the hill and down again, wound gracefully round gabled houses, came suddenly upon narrow lanes in which every door and window was shuttered. And at the top of one precipitous climb rose the home from which she could view the summit of Monte Grappa.

She wrote to Matilde:

I have an altar at my window. When I open the shutters and place two candles on the sill, framing the view of Grappa, I feel I am in church!

To Marco Praga she scrawled:

This is where I should like to spend my last years, and this is where I should like to be buried. Remember that, when the time comes, let it be known.

In 1919 the Deutschmark crashed, and took her investments with it. Shaken, she reckoned her losses.

'I shall have to go back to work,' she said, and was temporarily elated. But her age, her frailty, her long retirement from a precarious and changeable profession frightened her. 'I must think. I must have time. I must know what I am meant to do.'

In a last loving gesture Tebaldo returned to her from the dead, by dying. He left his savings to his wife and daughter.

'Poor Tebaldo — would you believe it, Matilde? He left a legacy for Enrichetta and me. He left it to us. Think of that. He had laid by a few savings, a few thousand lire, and they came to us when we needed them. Always the same Tebaldo!'

'Always the same,' said Matilde, 'in life and in death.'

'Yes,' said Eleonora, looking at her hands, remorseful. 'That is true.'

His money gave her a brief respite, and then she faced her new poverty with courage and fatalism.

'For twelve years,' she said, 'I have done as I was bidden, and kept in retreat. Now circumstances require me to work once more.'

She could no longer order somebody to get her an agent, nor drum up old resources with a roll of telegrams. Knowing the obstacles, she sounded out her friends and found Marco Praga eager to assist. Penniless, she was unable to form a company, and then Ermete Zacconi the Italian tragedian met her before she thought of approaching him and asked her to join his own.

The January issue of *Theatre Magazine* in 1921 heralded her return to the stage in an article by Alice Nielsen, who had worked with her many years ago. But Duse was afraid.

'Write me an article yourself!' she begged Marco Praga. 'Tell them that *you* persuaded me!'

Her thoughts flew elsewhere, in her fear and excitement. She clutched her handbag.

'I have my passport in here,' she said hopefully. 'Always ready!'

She said much, to many of her friends: swooping here and there in excuse, in explanation, in uncertainty, in exultation. Her mirror had only been a cause of sorrow while D'Annunzio existed to note every wrinkle; now she reviewed her face with something of the old cavalier attitude. Could she still be beautiful when she wanted to?

'At any rate,' she said resolutely, 'I shall wear neither paint nor wigs. I shall appear before the audience with my weary, aged, wrinkled face and my white hair, and I shall give them my soul!'

Win or lose, this was the last hand of cards.

'If they want me as I am,' she said, 'I shall be proud — if not, I shall return to my silence.'

But to her friend Olga Signorelli she confided another and a deeper truth.

'Believe me, Olga, it isn't to earn my bread that I'm acting! No pain is worse than that of being dead *before* death!'

Her love for children was great, though nature and circumstances prevented her from becoming truly maternal. But a child could bring out her affection and, on one occasion at least, her genius as well.

The couple were young, their baby demanding, and Duse friendly.

'Out!' cried Eleonora. 'Out by your two dear selves for a long and lovely evening together. I shall babysit!'

They protested sufficiently to fulfil their notions of politeness, and hurried to get ready.

'You are quite *sure*, Signora?'

'I am positive!' said Duse, embracing the child before she was tucked up in her cot. 'I have a natural feeling for small creatures,' she assured them. 'We shall enjoy each other.'

Their home was wrapped in hallowed silence when they returned, but Duse was not to be found in the sitting room — head on hand, spectacles awry, reading some book picked at random from their shelves. They tiptoed to the nursery, and heard a light, emphatic, regular snore.

Should they? Could they? Might they walk in upon a famous actress, obviously asleep?

They pushed open the door noiselessly, and discovered a tired tragedienne snoring in an armchair, and their daughter in a hushed and scarlet sleep. And as they hesitated Duse opened her eyes, put one finger to her lips, and ushered them out. She became animated, jubilant: eyes glowing, hair in white disarray.

'Your daughter,' she cried, 'requires a private theatre to herself! What *tribulations* I have suffered to get her to sleep! First she cried, so I nursed her. Still she cried. I put her in her cot and she demanded entertainment. I danced, I sang. She wept. I acted the whole of *Paolo and Francesca* for her — and do you know, it was not a *bad* performance, not bad at all! — and still she wept. She howled the place down. I gave a deep sigh — something like a snore — and... she... *paused*. I snored again, lightly. She was enchanted. Finally I sat down in that chair and closed my eyes and simply snored. She stood and watched and listened, and chattered quietly to herself. Then she sat. Then she lay. Then she closed her eyes and put her thumb in her mouth. Still snoring like a madwoman, I tucked her up. Still snoring, and peeping from time to time, I lulled her to sleep. And now look at her...'

She waved away their apologies and laughter, delighted by some inner fancy, some irony too delicate to pass by. She put on her regal hat and speared it with a couple of pins. She drew on her long gloves, unconscious art in every smoothing of the fingers.

'Tell her, when she is older,' she said, 'that she was quite the *worst* audience I ever had — though at least, she did not throw things and whistle, or boo me off the stage!'

She said, bright and eager as a girl, 'I remembered all the lines — even after that number of years!'

'But what can I do to please them these days?' Eleonora cried, beset by yet another problem. 'The new audiences need new heroines, and I am very old-fashioned, you know. Something classical, perhaps?' She was struck by a remarkable notion. 'What about *King Lear*? I could cut off my hair for the part, and when one is ancient and past love affairs it really doesn't matter whether one is an old man or an old woman!' She had forgotten her criticism of Bernhardt in masculine roles. 'And I could *play* Lear,' she added, 'for Lear is a soul in pain, and I know pain like an old friend.'

Paul Kalish, the singer, could have told them that her Lear would be stupendous. For he had once come across her in the years of her retirement before the war, seeking the peace of an isolated Franciscan convent. He had recognised her supple carriage and the sombre head wrapped in a fluttering violet veil, and had watched her, unobserved, walking to and fro among the cypresses as a storm came up from the sea. And she had reached out her arms, veil and hair blown back, and answered the tempest out of her own trouble and that of the aged king: 'Blow, winds, and crack your cheeks...' He had walked quietly away, rather than intrude upon so elemental a sorrow.

Zacconi said gently, 'No, Eleonora, not Lear. Give them Ellida in *The Lady from the Sea.*'

'Yes, of course,' she cried. Off on a fresh tack, 'For I am a daughter of the sea, Ermete, and I love it better than anything!'

No one pointed out that each voyage had been preceded by tears and fears of gargantuan proportions, nor that she was usually sick before the ship was a mile out to sea. They agreed, naturally, that she was descended from the Duses of Chioggia — and what could be more perfect?

Italy awaited her return in the words created by D'Annunzio: *I think that if I were to hear again, in the silence of the theatre, that divine voice ... my heart would stop beating.*

Nevertheless, with one foot on the train headed for Turin and the other on the platform at Rome, she suffered violent panic. 'No, no! I *cannot*. Tell them I will not come. It is too late!'

But Olga Signorelli pushed her firmly on board.

'*Not* too late!' said Olga, for once as obstinate as Duse herself.

THIRTY-TWO

5 May 1921. D'Annunzio had filled her dressing rooms with wine-red roses. Désirée was still opening and reading telegrams. Maria had wept for joy as she made the costumes ready — and been sent out summarily by la Duse for some impossible thing ten minutes before the curtain rose. In front, the audience suddenly hushed.

And she was quite alone, gathering together all she had learned, and all she had become, into one sheaf to lay at their feet.

A respectful distance away from her, cast and stage hands saw her bow her head and move her lips silently. Then she straightened. Her arms fell to her sides, and the woman blended into the mask as she lifted her chin and spoke her first lines offstage. Then, still frightened and a little tremulous, she walked on. And as she advanced, and the players turned towards her, the house stood in tumultuous applause. She attempted to speak, and could not be heard.

'Give me your arm, Ermete,' she whispered. 'I mustn't cry or I'll never stop.'

She clung to him, afraid to look about her, while the Teatro Balba went mad. They were all clapping, out in front, on the stage, and behind the scenes. She saw a multitude of faces with little holes for mouth and eyes; ranks upon ranks of palm striking palm; the smiles and the tears; and strove to hold herself and her role in readiness.

All action but that of uproarious acclaim was stopped for a full ten minutes.

I am too old for all this, she thought, clinging to Zacconi's arm, hearing his quiet encouragement.

'They are ready now, Eleonora,' he said, as the noise abated.

She waited for the silence before the speech, which Ristori had said was the actor's most moving moment. And proceeded to give them *The Lady from the Sea.*

They brought her back for call after call. They heaped the stage with flowers. And when at last, outside the theatre — as in the past — they unyoked her horses to draw her carriage, she observed with delight that the young also were paying her homage. She was gloriously, incredibly back on the road again, after twelve years: a legend come to life.

Afterwards, alone with Matilde, she drank a glass of champagne, stretched out her fingers to clasp those of her friend, and smiled at Matilde's answering smile.

'How strange, Mati,' she said, 'that we are both old, don't you think? I feel extremely young myself. I'm sure you do, too. Mati, I must tell you something.' She settled herself more comfortably in the easy chair. 'Tonight, everyone was moved — except me. I mean — *I* cried as well, *I* loved it — but the applause was not for *me*, it was for something much greater than myself. It was recognition of some power of which I am the *vehicle* — but which is not myself.'

She sipped reflectively.

'Being a writer,' she said, always ready to pay tribute to the other arts, 'you can express it better than I can. But what happened tonight was some truth I've sought *through* the theatre, which is *beyond* the theatre. I have found it in many things and many people and many places. I've seen it in sunlight, in the red sails of Venice, and in the night sky. I've found it in books, and heard it from the inarticulate, and seen it in faces too humble to have known what it meant. *Something,*

Mati — old fingers breaking bread or folded in prayer, children's eyes.

'And outside, when they've all gone away and Turin is sound asleep, it will be up there with the stars. And I shall go on to the balcony — after Maria and Désirée have finished fussing — and I'll look at those stars as I looked at them when I was a child. And I shall know something infinitely right and peaceful, Mati — though what it is I can't say.'

They sat in companionable silence.

'Do you remember those photographs of us, taken in Vallombrosa? One by ourselves, and one taken arm-in-arm with Tosti?'

Matilde giggled. Two elderly ladies in flowered hats, smiling into the sun, a little stout and short, a little old-fashioned.

'I'll tell you something,' said Eleonora. 'I don't feel half as old as I looked then, or now. Do you?'

'Certainly not!' said Matilde, drinking champagne.

'Then let's sit up all night,' said Eleonora, with sudden relish at the prospect, 'and talk. I just wish we were either at your home or mine, and then we could go down to the kitchen — that's always the best place. You can eat and chat at the same time!'

Milan, Genoa, Rome. Everywhere she was given the same acclaim, the same tribute from old admirers who had known her before, and young admirers who saw her for the first time. And on the heels of her new triumph followed a familiar demon: ill-health, now accentuated by age.

One lung had ceased to function properly. She suffered bouts of asthma which kept her up in a chair, gasping for breath. Spasms of coughing racked her, roughened her voice, burned her chest. Neuralgia tormented her. She could no longer stand the emotional demands of adulation. The endless curtain calls, the banks of flowers, the crowds waiting outside the theatres and the hotels, asked more than she was able to give.

Any setback, from a warning from Zacconi that the new manager she proposed to employ was unreliable, to her four-leaved clovers drooping in their little pot, despatched her to bed. The return had made it possible for her to form a fresh company of her own, with further responsibilities. In the October of 1921 she asked young Tullio Carminati to take the burden of directorship on his shoulders. But no one could relieve her of her burden of frailty and decay, and the pattern of a lifetime once more took shape.

In January 1922, with her company fully paid and standing by, she gave only ten performances out of a promised thirty-three. There were deficits of 100,000 lire. She disbanded the company in the spring and retreated to Asolo, temporarily defeated, but with a new play clutched to her heart to keep her warm. The Lombard poet, Tommaso Gallarati Scotti, had written a tragedy of motherhood called *Così Sia* — 'So let it be'. She rested in her garden, as on an island, stared out over the Venetian plain and on to the white rock of Grappa, began to make notes in the margins, to visualise the words and walk and gestures, to build up the woman who sacrifices herself for her son.

Well enough to be on the road again, she planned changes in her repertoire, balancing plays and parts and her inner self one against the other. *The Lady from the Sea* — a study in longing; *La Porta Chiusa* — a study in loneliness; *Ghosts* and *Così Sia* — studies in tragic motherhood. And finally, why not? *La Città Morta* — if D'Annunzio would let her make certain modifications. *La Città Morta* — the study of Anna, the blind seer.

On 21 July she sent a telegram to D'Annunzio from Paris.

'I beg immediate consolation and consent,' she dictated, with hidden emphasis on the *consolazione*.

They met in the Hotel Cavour, Milan. She, very fine-drawn, very white, tremulously in possession of herself. He, fired as ever by any situation that might be inwardly digested and translated into words. Their meeting, as legendary as themselves, gave rise to wild reports of what was said. Of how he told her she would never know how much he had loved her. Of how she had said he would never realise how much she had forgotten him. And other fantasies. Their interview was their own, and private. But Eleonora said afterwards that they had both knelt, on seeing each other again.

The Roman première of *Così Sia*, that autumn, was a further accolade for Duse but a failure for the author, Tommaso Gallarati Scotti. Bitterly disappointed for him, she took the play to Milan, to Turin, to Trieste. They did not boo as the Romans had done, but their applause was reserved. An old wound ached, reminding Eleonora of those wretched years hawking D'Annunzio's bloody melodramas over the face of the earth. She was hurt but she was resolute. She kept *Così Sia* in her repertoire.

Winter came with bitter rain and cold. In Verona the heating failed, and Eleonora, confronting another old enemy, caught bronchial pneumonia. The illness would not let her be, but returned to plague her just as she thought herself cured, and then returned again.

Performance and cancellation. Performance and two cancellations. Nights in an armchair as she gasped for breath. Fits of coughing between the acts, held by Maria and Désirée, and on again. A week between performances. Four performances given out of a promised twelve.

The company hung about, waiting, and were paid regularly. Caught now, on the tiger's back, as it were, she could neither get down nor keep up; and her debts reached such astronomic proportions that she faced possible bankruptcy.

D'Annunzio galloped to his lady's rescue and flourished a magnificent sword in the press, calling upon his country to aid its greatest dramatic artist. And he did not send so much as a solitary lira to help her. Half-laughing, half-crying, Eleonora weighed him in the balance and found him wonderfully wanting.

'He summed up all I had done,' she told Édouard Schneider, 'all my past work, even the things I had forgotten. It was very nice of him to remember them and say them... The letter was lovely, very touching, but that was all... He thinks of a thing, he speaks it, he writes it. And, no sooner has he given form to his thought...' — herself and *Il Fuoco*, for instance — 'than it is finished!'

A loan from an admirer shored up her crumbling finances, and the new Prime Minister, thick-set, heavy-jawed, came to pay homage and offer assistance.

'Tell me, tell me,' said Mussolini, good-humoured, anxious to use her as an ambassadress of the new Italy he was forging, 'what can we do for the Italian theatre?'

She wanted, as she had always wanted, a theatre of her own which would be a national theatre. And she told him, quite taken by his friendly manner, though not particularly caring for his politics.

'Present a project!' he said magnanimously. 'And I shall, in any case, instruct the government to give you a pension in return for your great service to the theatre!'

The project hung heavily upon her, since she was no administrator and knew nothing about presentation. But the pension she proudly comprehended and rejected.

Quickly she said, 'As long as I can drag about, as long as I can stand, I must work, for it is right that I should live by my work alone. No money, no.'

Her aims must have been as incomprehensible to him as his were to her, but her steadfastness caught his fancy. He recognised her quality, even though the subtle ties of her art and beliefs were beyond him.

'I shall never forget this interview,' he said, bowing over her hand in farewell.

Then he recollected something else, which led to three farewells instead of one, and delighted her.

Delight was brief, her difficulties long and bitter.

'Where are the offers for my services?' she cried, distracted. 'Why won't they give me work?'

An offer arrived from L'Empire Music Hall. Would Madame Duse deign to appear in some short sketch of her own choice? She cast her eyes down the suggested programme, outraged.

'What?' she cried. 'Perform between a group of dancing dogs and a hypnotist? Even Bernhardt never asked *that* of me! These *miserable* people!'

But she was quite unable to be sensible about the smallest need when the theatre was in question. Chiselling her role of Ellida yet and yet again, she remembered that somewhere among the legion of books and manuscripts in Asolo lay a single annotated edition of the play, which was exactly what she required. Spinelli was sent on the next train to Asolo to unearth this treasure, but had to telegraph his inability to find it. By return, Eleonora wired him to crate and ship every book in the house. At once. Fourteen crates arrived, and she sat on the floor, swooping here and there, unpacking, reading a little, until she pounced on one small volume with glee.

'Here it is!' she cried.

She did not enquire, nor would she have cared to hear, the financial cost of this particular whim. And Zacconi reasoned with her, unheeded and unheard.

'I must tour. That's all there is to it!' she said, on reflection.

A wasteland of travel stretched before her as she struggled to surmount influenza, and then to live through its post-depression.

'What you should have is a permanent Italian theatre!' said Bacchelli, the young playwright.

She replied, looking from her eyrie across the plain, 'I am preparing one for myself — in Asolo cemetery!' And with macabre humour, 'In *that* theatre we shall all of us act!'

Courage, Nella, wrote Matilde. *God has never abandoned you, and He never will.*

His messenger came in the form of Miss Catherine Onslow, who presented herself as an admirer with news of assistance, at Milan in the December of 1922.

'What do you think of doing, Signora?' asked Miss Onslow, polite and composed.

'What do I think of doing, Signorina?' Duse said severely, for her chest and throat hurt, her eyes stung, her head ached, and she was exhausted by the evening's performance. 'I am waiting for *death* to come!'

Miss Onslow, faintly troubled by the extravagance of the reply, administered a dose of the British stiff upper lip.

'But you must make an effort,' she chided gently. 'Money can be got — I'll get it for you! I have some influence.'

Later, describing the interview with distrait gestures, Eleonora cried, 'I must tell you what this foreign lady did for me. It was so beautiful. She spoke very simply, but from the *heart*. And at a time when nobody in my own country could be found to come to my aid. Nobody, nobody, nobody!' With great vehemence. '*They* all said, "Seeing she can't act any longer, it isn't worthwhile!"'

Miss Onslow's influence being Charles Cochran, and Miss Onslow's capacity for effort supreme, she raised the money to settle Duse's more pressing debts, and did not rest until Duse was booked for a short season at the New Oxford Theatre the following June. Eleonora was at once grateful and terrified.

'And now I am going to London to give six matinées,' she cried, 'and I ask myself, how can I give these matinées? Every morning, when I wake, I tremble with fear!'

Sarah was playing in Genoa, very close to her final curtain: balancing on one leg and helping herself unobtrusively about the stage by means of chair backs and table tops, playing — in her late seventies — the part of a thirty-year-old man. The red dye was streaking on her hair, her teeth were rotten, her face was ravaged. Colette took coffee with Bernhardt, and recorded *that indestructible desire to charm, to charm still, to charm right up to the gates of death itself*. The gates were very close, but Sarah said to Queen Mary of Great Britain, 'Your Majesty, I shall *die* on the stage; 'tis my battlefield!'

Sarah and Duse were now so old and frail and supreme that rivalry had died, and only a sense of kinship remained. Eleonora was devastated to think that she could not see Sarah — still wringing hearts and drawing tears with her old panache — hop gamely through an evening at the theatre. So she arranged that an actress from her company should go to Genoa in her stead, with a message of goodwill and two hundred *roses de France*.

'You must arrange to see her at her hotel,' said Duse, imagining the scene she herself would play so well, with Bernhardt acting at her side. 'And the roses must be scattered at her feet!'

The girl was anxious to oblige Duse, but unfortunately Sarah had left her hotel and received the cascade of roses in her dressing room. And Sarah was so overcome, and talked at such length, that Duse's message was never delivered.

Only, Sarah did say, 'Where *is* la Duse?' and wished she could see her once again, both professionally and personally, and preferably both.

Sarah had been naughty in the past, and wondered — on mention of Duse's name — 'Whatever became of *that* old lady?' But in old age one forgets both slights and slighter. So she touched the roses and shook her head and wept, and said, 'Where *is* la Duse?' and wished to see her just once again.

The young actress carried back every detail, faithfully noted, in order to re-enact the scene at Genoa.

'No,' said Eleonora, 'it is better that we should not meet. She is vivacious, amazingly so for her age.'

Then Duse put on Bernhardt's mask and swaggered a little as she spoke of her.

'She would say to me, "I'm short of a leg — what are *you* short of?" And I would say, "A lung!", and despite our courage that would have been *sad*!'

Sarah was struck down on the night of the dress rehearsal for Sacha Guitry's play *Un Sujet de Roman* in 1922. The lipstick rolled from her fingers and she stared at it, astonished, falling away in her turn. She recovered a little, gliding out of coma as one comes from a cat nap, and asked when she was to go on. But she never went on stage again, though the following year she had a last dab at filming in *La Voyante*. There she was, captured on celluloid, pondering the Tarot cards, foretelling the future, probably wondering — in the seventy-ninth year of her life — when her next tour would be.

It was, she realised in bed, on the first day of spring 1923, to be the longest tour of all. She knew all about her destination, lingering on for five days more, asking if the reporters were outside, joking with her last breath that she would make them cool their heels.

'*Messieurs,* Madame Sarah Bernhardt is dead.'

The British public paid nobly for the privilege of seeing la Duse again. The British press heralded her with trumpets of welcome. The pens of the British critics flowered into lyric prose.

With Duse, speech is silver and silence is golden… It is not so much that she acts when she is silent, as that your mind hastens on to take in the accumulated wealth of all that has been said with voice and face and hands, wrote James Agate.

A chalice for the wine of the imagination, wrote Arthur Symons.

Time had whitened her hair, hollowed her cheeks, added mystery to the depth of her eyes; enlarged and enriched the tone and range of her voice… one no longer cared whether she was young or old, she was right, she held you in the hollow of her hand, wrote Maurice Baring.

It was not necessary to understand what she was saying because we understood what she was feeling, wrote St John Ervine.

Not an artist, a religious spirit… she never interprets, she reveals pulsations of the soul and works through those, said Arthur Livingston.

But Duse wrote from London, *So as not to die one must live.*

And on again. Germany, Austria, Switzerland. Coughing, aching, resting.

'I can still work, so I must work. My people were poor people, and died poor and working to the last. It is only right that I should end my life like them.'

In her dressing room cylinders of oxygen were kept in readiness, lest she suddenly collapse.

Morris Gest, having netted the Moscow Art Theatre Company and Max Reinhardt's players for an autumn season in the States, drew in Duse also — with promise of such money as she could not refuse. American triumphs and disasters, and her superstitious fear that once across the Atlantic she was done for, caused her to accept with foreboding. But she must go, therefore she would, and as she might not come back she made certain that without her the company would not be stranded. She approached Benito Mussolini and exacted a promise that, should she die, the Italian Ambassador would be responsible for their return home. Mussolini promised, and gave her 30,000 lire. And Morris Gest insured the tour with Lloyd's of London.

Having been very sensible and practical, Duse's mood swung due north on her personal weathervane and became ridiculous. Matilde found her huddled over some obscure malaise.

'I shall travel everywhere, every minute of the tour, with my *trombones*,' said Eleonora, referring to the rest of the company by a pet name. 'I shall not be parted from them for an instant!'

Matilde doubted this, knowing Duse's demands for solitude, but asked why.

'I shall be safe with them now that they are insured!' said Eleonora darkly.

Apprehension mingled with superstition, followed by fatalism and then acceptance. She arranged all her affairs and said goodbye meticulously to all her friends.

'Pray to God,' she said to Olga Signorelli in Vienna, 'that I can give the first ten performances. I have a debt of honour, and I promised to pay it off at the rate of 5,000 lire per performance!'

To Romain Rolland she wrote, *I hope to see you again... One has suffered much over the last years... we must see each other again.*

Lastly, and with great tenderness, she visited D'Annunzio at Vittoriale degli Italiani, his princely villa on the shores of Lake Garda. One of life's natural actors, he had now played almost every role. He had been the lover, the writer, the politician, the dilettante, and when war came he was ready to be a hero for his country. He had flown his flimsy hydroplane to improbable targets and over incredible obstacles. He had courted death as he had courted his ladies. He inspired courage and confidence.

He had lost an eye, and gained six medals and the English Military Cross. Italy loved and lauded him, and he worshipped her with poetic-military ardour. So when the city of Fiume was given over to the Allied Administration after the war, D'Annunzio saw this as a stain on Italy's honour.

He was fifty-six when he collected a private army, en route from Venice, took Fiume by storm and occupied it for nearly eighteen months. 'The city of life,' as he called it, brought out a quality that had seemed absent. He felt compassion for the poor and wretched of Fiume, and no one was forbidden the presence of the Commandante. He helped them and cared about them because they were his people. He set up a free state and framed a constitution; and a young politician called Benito Mussolini came to see him in 1919, to hear one of his passionate orations, and to read his dream of poetic freedom. It was not D'Annunzio's fault that Mussolini's interpretation of his ideals was different.

Embarrassed by this latter-day Garibaldi, isolated and besieged in his little stronghold, the Italian government finally persuaded him out on 18 January 1921. So passed the soldier.

His latest role was that of the retired mystic, and Eleonora viewed it with amused affection. D'Annunzio had adopted a monk's habit, but fashioned from brown velvet and set off by a lustrous gold scarf. He referred to his villa as his grotto, to his luxurious leisure as meditation, and to his affluence as poverty. Thirty-five watchdogs guarded his privacy. Seven servants looked after his comforts. He had been many men, and now, he told her, he was a Franciscan hermit. As she was about to leave he indicated the Franciscan begging bowl, and beneath the small bald man she saw a boy dressing up, and would not for a moment have hurt his feelings. So, hiding a smile, she dropped a coin delicately into the bowl, and he invoked a blessing on her.

Resting before the voyage, she wrote him a last letter from the Savoy Hotel in Lausanne: *Greetings and good wishes, my son. Living is as hard as dying...*

The blinds were drawn in the house at Asolo. Newspapers lay protectively on the bookshelves, and covers over the furniture. She picked out a few familiar books to take with her: dog-eared, annotated, underlined. She collected her treasures together. Then she stood in her garden overlooking the plain to the white rock of Grappa, and remembered the dead: her mother and father, Martino Cafiero and their son, Arrigo Boito, Tebaldo Checchi, and Sarah — buried like an empress.

At some appointed hour, she reflected, she was bound to take her leave of life. She was born, after all, on the way to somewhere else, and would die on the way to another place. It was required of her graciously to accept and obey life and death, for some purpose which none was wise enough to know.

The Venetian sun warmed her bones, and Asolo became an island of gold floating above the plain. Her own prayers had never seemed adequate, so in her need she borrowed one from St Thomas Aquinas, who surely would not mind, and said it quietly to herself, looking out towards the mountain in the evening light.

'Give me, O Lord, a vigilant heart that no curious thought can distract from Thee; a noble heart that no unworthy affection can debase; an upright heart that no dubious intention can lead astray; a strong heart that no adversity can break.'

CURTAIN FALL

L'artista passa e non lascia traccia.
('The actress passes, and leaves no trace.')
Eleonora Duse

THIRTY-THREE

At Cherbourg a surprise awaited her. Enrichetta and her husband, Edward Bullough, had come to see her off. Eleonora produced enough demonstrative love and tears for them all. Nor did she immediately vanish to her cabin and shut herself in before the ship embarked, but stood waving at the rail until neither she nor Enrichetta could distinguish each other in the distance. Then she went below to use the voyage as an intermission between one act and the next.

America was thirty years older and mellower than when she first arrived. Morris Gest, her impresario, and Otto H Kahn, his financial backer, had treated her reverently. And the public had booked all seats that could be reserved, and were preparing to stand for twelve hours in a brisk October wind to snatch up the general-admission tickets. New York stopped the traffic to allow her to drive past with her escort of mounted policemen. Telephone calls jammed the switchboard of the Hotel Majestic. Flowers stood in the corridors outside her suite. The telegrams could have papered the walls. And the vast cavern of the Metropolitan Opera House swallowed her up.

Slightly feverish, Eleonora saw herself detached and as through the wrong end of a telescope: a minute figure transmitting her art to a vaulting theatre of eyes and ears, a face at the window of a train no bigger than a caterpillar, traversing a continent. Returning to her own body she found it frailer and more demanding than ever. An entourage revolved about it, catering to its needs. Oxygen cylinders stood in its dressing room. A portable invalid kitchen, manned by Maria and

Désirée, concocted nourishing soups, boiled chicken, fruit jellies for it. Champagne started it off, and cognac kept it going. It sank on to strange beds in strange rooms, in strange hotels in strange places. Maria brushed its thick white hair, massaged its aches, dressed it for sleeping, waking, acting. Désirée read telegrams to it, kept visitors away from it. Nursed carefully for five days of the week it could be wound up to act on the other two, when it was transcended by the spirit.

Ten performances in New York City brought in massive takings, and the first night made financial history with a revenue of more than 30,000 dollars. Another ten performances were spread over Baltimore, Philadelphia, Washington and Boston.

And still she could not make enough money to cover more than old debts, present expenses, and the American cost of living. She had fulfilled her commitments to the letter, and must somehow find more work still, must somehow pack up and move on. From the depths of a Washington December she sent a one-word telegram to D'Annunzio: *Auguri*.

Auguries. In order to move on she must have somewhere to move to, something to move for. Fortuno Gallo offered her a contract on even more generous terms than that of Morris Gest. She accepted, and set her face towards the south.

New Orleans. Havana. Ill in Havana. Los Angeles. San Francisco.

'One feels well here,' she said in the warmth of the Pacific, enjoying the sun on hands and face. 'Higher up,' nodding her head at the northern cities of the midwest, 'it must be cold.'

Nevertheless, the tour lay before her: an obstacle race between herself and home. Detroit, Indianapolis, Pittsburgh, Cleveland.

Trains rattled across the continent, speeding her from exile to exile. Dust seeped through the windows, dried her throat, irritated her lungs. Closed cars, their blinds drawn against curious onlookers, bore her from hotel to hotel. The 'trombones', as she called them, rattled along with her, their arms weighed down by their Italian suitcases, their young faces and bodies weathering the journey, looking to her for bread and inspiration.

'Hurry, hurry, children!' she cried, tapping her foot with a vestige of impatience. 'Hurry, children!'

Urging them aboard trains, watching clocks, seeing that all was right before each performance, scribbling little notes of instruction and encouragement. Sitting in her portable dressing room, drawing strength for her entrance. Two hours of magic: thousands of eyes and ears and applauding palms: the theatres retreating and diminishing, enlarging and coming forward, at odd angles. Watching the curtains go up and down, up and down, up and down. Accepting the support of Memo Benassi's strong arm: the stage son in place of the real son. And back to bed where the spirit became separate from the body, and floated to the ceiling, leaving the other to lie weightless and blurred beneath the hotel sheets. Trunks packed, reservations made, and on again into the bitter April of 1924.

Pittsburgh welcomed them with rain, sleet and cold.

Huddled in her furs, Eleonora looked about her at the city imagined by D'Annunzio, as a hunted creature looks about a cul-de-sac. Her final scene had been set in the steel metropolis of the world.

Blind-eyed buildings reared up to blot a heavy sky. Fog mingled with smoke. Machinery throbbed in her head.

'Come, Signora, the car is here.'

To her terrified eyes it resembled a hearse, but she had nowhere else to go, so crept inside and closed her lids.

Désirée held smelling salts beneath her nose, and the acrid tang tugged her back to consciousness. Passively she stared through the window and saw the posters run faster and faster into a blur. On hoardings, on bridges, on the doors of vehicles, ran her legend: Eleonora Duse in *La Porta Chiusa* by Marco Praga.

'The Signora must rest as soon as we arrive.'

She lay in bed for three days, watching the rain drive against the windows, wrapped in her own foreboding. In Italy, thousands of miles away, the wind would smell of violets, filling the sails of the small boats on the waters of Chioggia. And to reach home, to see Italy again, she must somehow crawl over these final obstacles.

Late in the morning of 5 April she pulled herself slowly from her bed and walked to the window. From the fifth floor of the Schenley Hotel, Pittsburgh closed in upon her. Iron, steel and concrete. She turned away from it, summoned Maria, and allowed herself to be dressed for the matinée. From her viewpoint she had seen the Syria Mosque waiting for her to illuminate its vast auditorium.

'I can walk that far,' she said.

They pointed out that it was raining heavily, and she had not been well.

'I can walk,' she said obstinately, and as they begged her to change her mind she said, 'I *will* walk!'

Cocooned in wraps, topped by an opossum coat, she made her way out into the street. Wind buffeted her hair and clothes. Driving rain made her cheeks wet. Breathless, resolute, she battled forward, two hours ahead of schedule. Désirée, close beside her, strove to give protection against the impossible, seeing her small store of strength needlessly exhausted, and drew her into the front entrance of the theatre with relief.

'It's no use trying to get in *that* way!' said Eleonora peremptorily. 'They'll be shut for at least another hour. Come, we must go round the back.'

The Syria Mosque appeared to have cornered all the draughts in Pittsburgh; they crept round corners, whistled from unexpected directions, darted at the two women as they toiled along endless stretches of wall in search of shelter.

'Here we are!' said Eleonora.

She was very white, shaking with cold.

'This door is locked, too, I'm afraid,' said Désirée, worried. 'Stay here and I'll find someone with a key. I'll be back as soon as I can.' Looking with concern at the wet furs and wild white hair.

'Don't leave me!' Eleonora called, as Désirée broke into a run. 'Don't leave me.'

She turned on the door and shook it, afraid. Its resistance menaced her. She stood in terror, hands over mouth. *La Porta Chiusa.* The closed door. Auguries.

And fouler and more cruel than the Pittsburgh wind, the *smara* enveloped her.

She saw the door suddenly mighty, towering up into the sky, dwarfing the buildings, infinitely threatening. She saw it as the end of life, saw the city as an open grave, and flung herself upon it — sobbing, beating the wood with the flat of her hands, a wild old woman at the mercy of the weather.

'*La porta e chiusa! La porta e chiusa!*'

They helped her into a mausoleum of a theatre, where her portable dressing room stood beside the yawning stage like a little tent. Désirée poured brandy down her throat, removed the wet clothes, rubbed her body with alcohol, wrapped her in her blue wool robe and sat her near a small electric heater. One by one the 'trombones' dared to peep at the Signora, and tiptoe away to wonder if the performance would be cancelled. Far less than this unlucky accident had sent kings away disappointed.

'No,' said Duse, breathing with difficulty, 'I shall have to sit most of the time, but I go on. Just give me a minute, a few minutes. That is all.'

Four thousand five hundred expectant faces. Nine thousand applauding hands. The few steps from dressing room to stage had seemed a league. Her feet were numb, her head light, her body heavy. The auditorium changed shape, receded, ran away into curious perspectives, was suffocatingly large and close. But from the maelstrom she heard her own voice, as though disembodied, taking up Praga's words one by one like jewels to be admired. Whenever possible she sat down. When not, she found young hands supporting her unobtrusively, young eyes signalling courage. The 'trombones' were with her and for her, acting for their lives now that she was too sick to quell them with a glint. And after all, she reflected drowsily; sitting like some old boxer between the rounds, gathering heart and muscle; after all, the body is a terrible nuisance and the spirit everything. The role was carrying her with it, and she followed in obedience, sensing that this performance was never to be repeated.

The audience stirred, a sixth sense telling them that this was more than a passing farewell. The body, a frail ghost, seemed almost consumed. The voice sought its way, now light, now dark, in an anguished underworld. The sombre eyes brooded over some inner vision. The arms lifted, bearing witness to a universal sorrow.

'*Sola!*' she cried, clear and high and lonely. '*Sola!*'

And then — so old that she seemed to have been present at the beginning of time, to remember all that was long forgotten in the world — a final '*Sola.*'

She took the curtain calls. She acknowledged the applause. Trembling, reaching out with her arms as if to bring them to her for the last time. White head thrown back, white face all bones and hollows, and the eyes dark and bright, flickering out, until they supported her from the stage. The enormous distance between wings and dressing room sloped for miles ahead, and tilted as she negotiated it.

Heavy in their arms, she dropped her head, whispering, 'Enough, enough. I can do no more.'

She sat at her dressing table, one weary hand supporting her cheek. The other hand moved; touching a brush, a comb, picking up a hairpin. She took in every detail of the room, and of the image in the glass; tracing the mark of years, comparing it in her mind to that eager girl on the verge of success. Then she spread out both hands and examined them minutely: the famous hands, long-fingered, supple and allusive.

Maria's concerned face bobbed behind her in the mirror. Désirée's voice asked a question, a great way off. '

'Yes,' said Duse, 'I am ready to go now.'

Eleonora Duse died at the Schenley Hotel, Pittsburgh, Pennsylvania, on Easter Monday, 21 April 1924.

A NOTE TO THE READER

Dear Reader,

If you have enjoyed *The Passing Star* enough to leave a review on **Amazon** and **Goodreads**, then we would be truly grateful.

SAPERE BOOKS

Sapere Books is an exciting new publisher of brilliant fiction and popular history.

To find out more about our latest releases and our monthly bargain books visit our website: **saperebooks.com**

Printed in Great Britain
by Amazon